Helen Stevenson grew up in South Yorkshire, studied Modern Languages at Somerville College, Oxford, and lives in the south of France, between the Mediterranean and the Pyrenees. *Pierrot Lunaire* is her first novel.

SCEPTRE

Pierrot Lunaire

HELEN STEVENSON

Copyright © 1995 Helen Stevenson

First published in Great Britain in 1995 by Hodder and Stoughton
First published in paperback in 1995 by Hodder and Stoughton
A division of Hodder Headline PLC
A Sceptre paperback

The right of Helen Stevenson to be identified as the Author of
the Work has been asserted by her in accordance with the
Copyright, Designs and Patents Act 1988.

10 9 8 7 6 5 4 3 2 1

All rights reserved. No part of this publication may be
reproduced, stored in a retrieval system or transmitted,
in any form or by any means, without the prior written
permission of the publisher, nor be otherwise circulated
in any form of binding or cover other than that in which
it is published and without a similar condition being
imposed on the subsequent purchaser.

All characters in this publication are fictitious and any
resemblance to real persons, living or dead, is purely coincidental.

British Library Cataloguing in Publication Data

A CIP catalogue record for this book is
available from the British Library

ISBN 0 340 61823 X

Printed and bound in Great Britain by
Cox and Wyman Ltd, Reading, Berkshire

Hodder and Stoughton
A division of Hodder Headline PLC
338 Euston Road
London NW1 3BH

Au clair de la lune,
Mon ami Pierrot,
Prête-moi ta plume
Pour écrire un mot.
Ma chandelle est morte,
Je n'ai plus de feu.
Ouvre-moi ta porte
Pour l'amour de Dieu.

1

At seventy-eight Ludmilla Pike was no longer exactly obese. Somehow it seemed, though, that each bit of body was rather too big for the next one. Her nose was too big for her face; her head too big for her neck; her shoulders were broad as a man's; but her bosom, ah her bosom, biggest of all, brooded huge and matriarchal, untapped and unmistakably female. With the onset of cold old age, the whole vast edifice had contracted a good deal, and cracks had appeared in the veneer. But despite a certain reduction in surface area, she was still one of those rather masculine women who are forever condemned to carry their womanhood all before them. In the case of Ludmilla Pike this condition was so acute that she might often be spotted coming round a corner long before her body's centre of gravity had even contemplated such a move. She would have made a poor private detective. Stealth did not come easily to a woman who, for at least the first fifty years of her life, had been accustomed to being so very large in build – and it seemed as though she had indeed been built, quite possibly on some sort of site, or in a shipyard. But despite the flagrance of her physical presence, she possessed a manipulative art which was so contorted and folded in upon itself that it must have occupied no more than the space of a walnut in what once had been the vast universe of her frame. Imaginatively cast she might have sold antiques.

Instead she taught people to play the piano, a vocation, certainly, but not one in which she had much opportunity to exercise her special gift. Except perhaps when, on occasions, she stood behind her little pupils, and pulled their arms and fingers about, dancing with them up and down on the keyboard. It was

• Helen Stevenson

difficult to tell whether it was her fingers which were too big for her hands or vice versa. Her fingers had been crushed at one point in her childhood by the descent of a loose sash window. For six sickening hours she had sat there like a dummy at a keyboard, hands outstretched in mock five-finger exercises, pinned to the woodwork, fingernails blackening out of sight. For six terrible hours Ludmilla waited in silence until a window cleaner turned up and released her. His first encounter with the dark side of his work. Years later, he recognised Miss Pike in the street by the shape of her fingers. She offered him six free piano lessons. An hour each. It was her way of saying thank you.

It was difficult to imagine a time when Ludmilla's fingers had not been mangled and misshapen like distorted sausage off-cuts. Even as a young girl (never a little one), when exhorted to display her clever, piano-playing hands, as baby ballerinas show off their exquisite little feet, the horror of their deformity must have seemed to lend a sinister aspect to her talent. It was as though her gift had been acquired through some ghastly Faustian pact. With the passing years the deformity had matured, and, like the branches of an ancient, deviant oak, her fingers had taken on an almost old-world charm. They felt soft now, and towards the end of life the bones had found a comfortable position to lie in. The accident had never been an impediment to her performing even the trickiest Bach with complete dexterity.

She lived alone in an Edwardian house in the middle of England. There was no room for a companion in her life. Her outward face was stately, open to the public for seven hours a day, weekends excepted, but her private life was kept upstairs, above board, in a tight-fitting drawing room with bedroom attached.

It was her habit to go to the piano each morning once the kettle was on, before her first cup of tea. In her man-size dressing gown, with its slack-mouthed pockets and twizzled cord, she would solemnly crack her fingers, a bad but ineradicable habit, and shoot the rapids of some treacherous cadenza. In the case of concertos she would sing along a version of the orchestral part, but her voice could only hope to hit the notes by approaching each one with a hectic glissando, like some kind of vocal long jump. This brought a rather baleful quality to her singing, which began to sound more like some kind of protest or lament. At the moment, however, she was working on the cadenza to Rachmaninov III, and the orchestra was sitting quietly in the pit eating polo mints. After the final chord she rose from the piano, which she referred to in front of her pupils as the piano*forte*, pronounced with a distinct *marcato* over the word, pulled together the front of her dressing-gown and lowered the lid. The kettle would be well boiled.

She collected her little tray from the kitchen and paused on her way back upstairs to pick up the post. A weekly magazine by means of which, she said, she kept abreast of the world (men blushed and children giggled to hear her use of the idiom) was dangling through the letter box like a fish hook. She settled herself upstairs with her feet comfortably propped on a bar underneath her dining room table. 'If women spent more time looking after their feet,' she had read in a magazine at the dentist's, 'we beauticians would spend less time looking after their faces.' Ludmilla had pondered that one for some time, and having dismissed it as twaddle, now took pleasure in spending as much time as possible with her feet up, simply in order to disprove the theory empirically through the evidence of her catastrophic face.

She always read the classified advertisements first. The print was very fine, and she found it difficult not to cast shadows. The headings were relatively easy. SITUATIONS WANTED. No interest there. ACCOMMODATION WANTED. No *thank* you. She needed all the square footage she inhabited, and it was tight at that. SERVICES. The memorial service of a long lost friend? A new hat? No, services to the living, as always, to writers baffled by their home computers, to speakerless dining clubs, to city cottagers whose thatch was falling in tufts about their investment. Your needs supplied. She skimmed without interest. Life had supplied her with quite enough needs at the outset. It was too late to start fostering new ones, even with twenty-eight days only for delivery.

She poured her tea, three fluid ounces, a drop in the ocean. Ludmilla carried well over the standard seven pints within. The tiny Japanese cup with its detail of chintzy flowers was brimming over. An escapee leaf of jasmine clung to the spout of the pot.

• Helen Stevenson

Ludmilla pinched the end of her nose with a pigmy handkerchief. Nothing there. But at her age you had to be vigilant in the face of unsuspected seepage. In such respects caution had become a habit with her. She turned the page, wetting finger and thumb with a tongue hot from the tea. And there it was, tucked into a left hand column, cornered by an article about Gibraltar. WANTED.

Wanted. Each week she fondly fancied to read of million dollar rewards for the recapture of violent criminals, perhaps with a shoddily reproduced illustration, disturbingly reminiscent of the man next door. But people's wants were predictably meagre. Anyone wanting anything important would bill it under SITUATIONS or ACCOMMODATION, or PARTNERS. What more *could* you want. Ludmilla had always wanted fame, but third-rate notoriety had put paid to that. At her London solo debut in 1940, an occasion when a freshly broken heart should have lifted her performance nicely into something more than merely competent, she had been just distraught enough to make sure no one ever engaged her to work again. Since then, she sometimes said, it had been strictly children and animals.

But what was wanted here was information. Information was wanting. WRITER SEEKS INFORMATION CONCERNING CHÂTEAU MONVANITÉ, SOUTH WEST FRANCE, 1930s, PIERROT LUNAIRE. CONTACT TALBOT HARDY, CHÂTEAU MONVANITÉ. She was struck by the phrasing and immediately doubted 'writer'. 'Seeks', 'concerning'? What about 'wants', 'about'? The sparsity of the code words. There was no doubting it. Little pieces of festering bait. *Monvanité*. *Pierrot Lunaire*. The cartilage in Ludmilla's formidable nose clicked in her head. A treacherous eighteenth-century mirror, clustered about with gold-spray laurel leaves, caught her in a profile at once beaky and bulbous, the dressing-gown grizzling about her neck where it concertina-ed into chest. She caught it full face with a grimace, stopped short of shouting boo and turned regretfully away. Then with her thousand year old hands, brown stains flecked like tea leaves on the upper side, riddled palms a cartographer's life work on the lower, she reached towards her destiny and the spotless mobile phone.

2

Talbot Hardy was separated from his amiable but middle-aging wife, Posy, who, rather beyond the call of amiability, had arranged for him to spend a year away from it all in a magnificent French property she had recently inherited from her Aunt Isa.

Isa Fontaine, before English respectability and, later, a title had hit her, had seen herself as a rather clever amateur impresario. A slight woman of many accomplishments, taught to dance by Isadora Duncan, with Rodin limbs and an accent of unfamiliarity in all her many languages, she had held court for those three pre-war summers in a house in South West France bequeathed to her by a distant relative, short of ideas on his death bed. Monvanité's proximity to the Spanish border and the langorous look in Isa's opium eyes had spiced the allure of the place for a generation of dancers, writers and artists. In the summers of pre-war Europe, though, the heat was intense, weighing down the dancers' feet, bleaching the artists' colours, dragging back each allegro to andante. Few works of great merit could still be traced back to that particular cradle. Full marks then, to Talbot Hardy, who was sitting on the original manuscript of *Pierrot Lunaire*, a novel by Thomas Hanley Flynn.

Pierrot Lunaire had not found favour with Isa Gresham. Shortly after her marriage, she became editor-in-chief of Gresham's publishing house. When the manuscript arrived on her desk in June 1939 with an accompanying note describing the circumstances of its discovery amongst the effects of Thomas Hanley Flynn, one of her own former guests, killed in action at Salamanca in 1938, she simply cursed once more the proximity of Château Monvanité to the Spanish border and deleted a name from her address book.

• Helen Stevenson

On Isa's death the parcel passed to Posy, along with the deeds of Monvanité, to which Isa had never returned after her marriage. The book was typed on fine onion-skin paper, the pages so delicate that as you turned each one it refused to sink down quietly and seemed to hover slightly under your fingers.

Posy was used to reading manuscripts. It was part of her job. She called the time she spent, as consultant editor for Gresham Publishers, her Marigold hours, after the rubber gloves which stop you getting your hands dirty. She worked as little or as often as she chose, and attended some of the more interesting parties.

Pierrot Lunaire was different. Her Aunt Isa had written her a letter, describing how it had been recovered from the effects of T.H. Flynn, who had died fighting in Spain. He had spent the summer months before his death at Monvanité, where the three-year-long *fête galante* had drawn to a mournful close.

Uncle John and I were married early that summer, Isa wrote, and had honeymooned sensibly in Paris. We didn't bother with chantilly-topped extravaganzas in remote corners of the empire in those days. They tended to come after the honeymoon. Most of the artists had left by then. The party spirit had died. Or perhaps it just went to live somewhere more dangerous. The men seemed to favour Berlin. The musicians all went back to London, but they are always the most sober. Flynn rather missed out, I think. It must have been late spring when I was introduced to him. He'd had a couple of poems published in *Horizon* which showed promise. (It was quite possible to be thought promising in your mid-thirties in those days.) He'd met Ludmilla Pike at a concert in Dublin. She and I were living in London in the winter, but otherwise spent as much time as we could in Monvanité planning and running the house parties. She introduced him to me in London and we invited him out. As far as I remember he looked a bit like Orwell, but perhaps I only think that because of him dying like that. As I say, that was the last summer and by late June I'd had enough, so I married Uncle John who liked Kipling and drop scones and had a lot of money. Of course we had quite a lot too, but it was always so difficult to find. John's was always in the right place just when you wanted it, and you always knew how much of it there was, at least someone who was paid to, did. I don't think I was actually there when Flynn arrived.

The book, as you will see, is a journal intime, which always sounds like two people kissing behind a newspaper. It's written retrospectively – a recollection from not very tranquil Spain. The entries are daily and, eccentrically, in the third person, though from his own clear point of view. They describe how the place gradually emptied as summer reached its height and people began to think of war. By August, according to his account, Flynn was the only one left. Plus the girl, Chloe, who he's in love with, though we don't learn much about her.

Posy was tickled by the poignancy of this relic. She was collecting a bottom drawer for when she divorced. The manuscript almost went in, next to the single person's passport form and a voucher for a weekend at a health farm. But in the end, distracted by the prospect of a safari in Zimbabwe with an old schoolfriend, and with a hint of mischief in her mind, she passed it to her husband. Talbot was a disenchanted television journalist, whose experience had been largely in the area of fly on the wall documentaries. A year's sabbatical was planned, in which he would write and direct the feature film which would allow his long submerged creative flair to prove and rise. Posy kneaded gently, and off Talbot shot with the book to Château Monvanité. Where better to find inspiration for his script than Château Monvanité itself, the scene both of the drama and the writing of the story. For a wronged husband, Talbot was easily righted. What a year it would be. What a figure he would cut in that feature which would no doubt follow in a Sunday magazine, where separated couples display the generous seams in the weightless garment of their marriage; estrangement makes the heart grow larger, warmer, in every way; celebrities both, he a little wayward, artistic, newly fulfilled, bachelor boy again; she a little preoccupied with her career, perhaps even slightly down at heel these days, but loyally supportive down to the latest introduction to an attractive new friend – just your type I think, darling, and oh – she's vegetarian.

Two months on, work wasn't going well. Sure, the material was perfect. Perfection, Talbot wrote to the backers, whom Posy, a powerful lady, or at least well enough connected to carry a hefty current, had lined up on the touchline of Talbot's territory. In Brussels, in Venice, in London and Barcelona, they waited with impatience for Talbot's script. It would be one of those wistful, thoughtful, utterly ravishing pastoral films which would play and play, from St Martin's Lane to the Grand Spa Deluxe in Scarborough. A classic, a drama in watercolour, poignant, elegant, eternally true, a film to remind you of student days in a private cinema, where you queued each time it came to town, and for once, afterwards, somehow didn't feel like chips and a hamburger. Someone would mention Visconti, but no, they would say, it's this chap Hardy, English believe it or not. Incredible. A love story like that, Englishman, Englishwoman – English *director*. The hero's own story. Before I die (head blown off near Salamanca, 1938), know this . . .

Talbot was not above cultivating a bit of mystique before the event. He was incommunicado, or rather, he was communicating with things a little higher than contractual details. They would have to wait. As time went on he staved them off with postcards of the area, written in apparent haste with an elegant ink pen. The time devoted to the composition of these cunningly effete dispatches was not wasted. A meeting was planned for early July, when all would be revealed. Talbot was holding back on copies of the novel. A masterpiece it was. Airplane reading it wasn't. By the time of the meeting, the script would be well nigh complete. That would be what they wanted to see.

Unlike his wife's wealthy business contacts, whom she had largely chosen in order of pocket, Talbot was a well-educated, widely read man. Appetite and discernment in all things. He had not been embittered when, after a hugely enjoyable and stimulating year at Oxford, he had succumbed to glandular fever and eventually judged best not to return to sit mods but to go straight into the newspaper business. But his active and successful career had only been a deferment. All he had ever really wanted was this – the chance to create something living, real, his own – well, the author was dead, naturally – or rather not so naturally (the mine in Salamanca). France, the château, solitude, food, sun, wine, books, money, he had it all. What bitterness, not in him, but in the taste of things, when somehow it wouldn't come alive.

On the telephone, responding to his rather desperate appeal, Miss Pike had sounded nothing if not alive. Indeed she sounded as though someone, a retired colonel perhaps, might have told her at an impressionable age, and one at which one promises oneself never to change, that she was quite a live wire. She possessed, it was said, a very thick skin, but her curiosity lay surprisingly near its surface, and came out like a rash at the prick of the unexpected.

'I'm sorry, what did you say your name was?'

'Pike. Ludmilla. *Miss*.'

Talbot wrote it out backwards on the blotter, feeling already like a detective.

'You have some information about *Pierrot Lunaire*?' he asked gently. He was quite a pro, still.

'That will depend on what you would like to know.' Ludmilla narrowed her eyes in the glass.

'Let me fill you in,' offered Talbot. (Oh yes, it would be wonderful, just wonderful, to be filled in, she thought, mindful of all those cracks across her surface.) So Talbot filled her in, a little indiscreetly, he later thought. There was no trace of the author's family. Unless, of course . . .

'No,' said Ludmilla firmly. Not family. He needed detail, a hint of period atmosphere. Ludmilla was a positive crematorium of period atmosphere, she told him. Talbot did wonder whether that was necessarily a recommendation.

'I could tell you,' she said breathily, 'what really happened.'

With her head tilted at forty-five degrees to the receiver she sounded as frail as any laced and scented gentlewoman who ever received grace and favour.

'Let's separate fact from fiction here,' Talbot replied with professional ease and, for the record, Ludmilla agreed. She would be with him next week.

Talbot, who liked to think he was a dreamer, had always

dreamed that Chloe might still be living. Of course the biographical aspect of the novel, the existence of the source material, as he called it, in the first place, could not help but slightly compromise his determination to work, for once, in the realm of the imagination. He recalled a phrase of Oscar Wilde: 'The true artist is known by the use he makes of what he annexes, and he annexes everything.' Talbot didn't entirely go along with it, but it legitimised, without allowing for formal recognition of, his lack of talent for invention. Had he been aware in advance of the somewhat monumental character of Ludmilla he would perhaps have thought twice about what he meant by annex. Arrogate. Appropriate. Abduct?

But Talbot, who was careless, and already half in love with his heroine, was faint with anticipation. It was late May in Monvanité. Already the heat was rising, with lilac and blackthorn well passed. He cancelled a dinner party and took some long walks.

3

The car in which Ludmilla had driven from Toulouse to the tiny village of Soubyrète was rather too small for her. Although the sheer fact of her physical size had become markedly less explicit in recent years, her powerful presence and an air of flourishing in the face of discomfort distinguished her movements from those of ordinary travellers. Her very joy in being alive appeared to propel her along the narrow country roads, which twisted and recoiled before her like a rabbit caught in the headlamps of a vehicle. She had not driven for many years. Now, with the steering wheel of the sporty little Peugeot grasped firmly at ten to two, her left elbow propped rakishly on the edge of the rolled down window, she kicked the lever under the seat heftily to one side and shunted herself back a good six inches with a grunt of pleasure. She half believed she might meet the adventurous Mr Toad coming in the opposite direction.

A moment's reflection on this pleasant expectation seemed to remind her of some forgotten aspect of the continental highway code and with the fluid, swinging movement of a skater she steered the car over to the right hand side of the road. Would Mr Toad, she wondered, have acquiesced so reasonably to the demands of foreign regulations? It was a most interesting subject for speculation and she might well bring it up with some of her older pupils when she got home. The younger ones were apt to disapprove of Ludmilla's mania for literature for their own age group. Under questioning, they stoutly pretended to read only hardcore science fiction which they knew she would not poach upon. They detected instinctively that she had no taste at all for that which was not at least faintly picturesque.

It was partly what she had been known to call 'the Ruskin in me' and partly nostalgia which brought her to a halt. On a sharp bend in the road, with a terrific view to the left, she snatched at the hand brake, her preferred method of bringing a moving vehicle to a stand still. As the engine stalled, she coasted serenely into the mud tracks at the side of the road. Silence broke over the bonnet of the car. She opened the door, stuck one sensibly shod foot into the cake of mud, and swung imperceptibly to and fro, working up a formidable momentum, little by little, until with a clenching of her bottom and a mighty heave, she launched herself from the car. It was a surprisingly emphatic movement. This technique of planning her vigorous moments well in advance enabled Ludmilla to give an astonishing impression of agility for her years. People often remarked on it, which she found rather hurtful. It was insulting to have so little expected of one.

It was nearly midday in May, and insects were busy in the long grass at her feet. The heat swayed across the landscape, so that it moved and blurred before her eyes like an image projected on a screen. There on the hill stood Château Monvanité, apparently quite unaltered, as though, in a game of musical statues, it had not flinched for fifty years. Fifty years had passed, but not passed away; it was a memory she had held in the air, a bubble that must not touch the ground, subtly modulating in her mind, embellished, diminished, moulded, fancied freely.

Fifty years ago, Ludmilla reflected, she had been magnificent with the kind of monumental beauty normally associated with neoclassical statues in public places. She had ridden a shivering wet horse between her splendid thighs over the brow of the hill there, and dipped down the other side where the patchy woodland and cornfields fell like a tattered skirt from the château and trailed in the valley below. She had sucked the vigour, every last possible drop, from this rich landscape, and sought to pump it into a man who had no time for the land, no eyes for the trees or the fields or even the distant mountains, who might have been almost without sense of smell or touch or taste, so great was his indifference to the countryside which pleased her so well. Then one day she had left, in despair, in anger, resigned perhaps. Before she left she placed heavy terracotta bowls on the table in the courtyard, filled with fruit busy with colour and succulence, to tempt him from his anxious, ashy cigarette. He ignored them, and ground stub after stub into the hot grass beside his chair, scorching the ground, blackening the yellow stalks. She imagined the fruit turning funny, not dying, but becoming busier still with small forms of life as it mouldered and ran to liquid, and then the insects dropping like a cloth to cover the bowl. How had he spent those last days of his life? Could he in fact have willed his own death, crushed among all that metal and screeching and tearing, the very same sounds that had filled his poetry? He had found beauty, if that was what it was, in the grinding of machines and the strain of the grim buildings of the city. The view of the mountains filled him with a pain and an awful loneliness which had been beyond his expression. *Pierrot Lunaire*, the moonstruck, lovesick clown, with his ecstatic sentimentality and ardent yearning, must have knocked poor Isa down like a feather.

Ludmilla smiled a little at the thought of all that rotting fruit. She had rotted a little herself, around her mid-fifties, and then had decided to allow herself to shrivel up instead. She had taken herself out of the light, and her skin had bunched up over her big bones, and her smells had faded and her colours merged to that implacable brown which renders the six-month-old passion-fruit indistinguishable from a prune. Not entirely pleased with this result, she had taken a fancy to shopping at rather inexpensive department stores for her clothes, picking up yellow and black striped trouser suits and distinctly jaunty neck ties. As she was not one for stripping off in those awful open plan changing rooms and strutting around viewing her flesh from new and unexpected angles, no one had any clue as to the colour and cut of her undergarments, but speculation, if seriously entered upon after due consideration of her visible layers, could surely have taken the breath away. She wore a daring lipstick, which was rarely, if ever, changed to accommodate the demands of her couture. She never looked in a full length mirror, and was consequently never afflicted by the incompatibility of Fuschia Breeze and, say, the yellow and black striped trouser suit. People had noticed on occasions recently that her art in the application of Fuschia Breeze had been a little wearied by the years. It looked rather as though she had decided to drop the habit of applying it with painterly strokes over a mouth stretched wide from corner to corner, perhaps in the fear that such a practice would deepen her wrinkles, and instead scrunched up her diminishing lips into a sort of bud and squashed the colour over the surface thus made available. One small pupil had surprised her once as she lingered over her tea in the late afternoon. She had descended from the upstairs drawing room in a fluster, without applying any colour at all to her lips, and he had burst into tears, thinking she was dead.

On this day, however, Ludmilla had prepared herself for her coming encounter with fastidious attention to what details remained in the rather wild topography of her outward form. It was to be expected that the hairdresser she had visited two days previously should have fixed her up with a pensioner's perm, as she had described it disparagingly to Dédé, the absent minded perpetrator, who had tossed it up with all the concentration of a three star Michelin chef making a vinaigrette for a humble green salad. Still, if she didn't look smart, at least she looked on the narrow verge of respectable. She rubbed the palms of her slightly sweaty hands together and remembered just in time not to wipe the little black bits on her camel trousers. It was a habit which harked back to her student days, her true salad days, when it had been developed as a means of focusing the brain on the fingers immediately before the opening bars. She hummed to herself as she straightened her blouse, abandoning the prelude – too busy – for the discipline of the fugue – too solemn, caught herself humming and grimaced. There are few people in the world who actually get round to making facial expressions in the absence of a witness. It would be like wearing lipstick to confession. Ludmilla tended to make the very most of such occasions and exaggerate them fiercely.

The flight from London in the late afternoon of the previous day had been rather tiring, and she had already begun to question her wisdom in travelling this distance in order to rake up the past. It was the prospect of what Mr Talbot Hardy could do for her, not what she might do for him, that had given her the energy to take on history and geography in one bold leap. Once she had secured his cooperation she could sit back happily and watch the show. She must trust in Talbot's indiscretion and her own ability to fix the cards in the unpredictable hand of fate. She could of course have cheated openly, and only the ghost of her long lost lover would have rapped her ugly fingers in reproach. But she was too old for anything but spectator sports. She would give the pack an honest shuffle, leaving a couple of telling cards on the top to be dealt. She had heard that Talbot was an attractive man. She was well aware that at her age and weight her charm as a stately ruin was more likely to bring results than any pitiable winsomeness affected under the guise of a tarted up restoration job. A teaching manual she often used with her beginners, *Miss Waterfield's Opening Bars*, began with a splendid page showing three pianists, each sitting at his instrument. Under the first, an abject, crouching youth, hunched over what must surely be assumed to be the wrong keys, was written: this is a *poor* pupil. Under the second, a prissy little lad: this is a *good* pupil; under the third, a resplendent student with a mop of excited black hair, dressed in tails with his hands high above the keyboard, weight and shoulders flung backwards: this is a GREAT PIANIST!!! She leaned back in the seat, stuck her right foot down, as though it were the sustaining pedal, and thought, 'Today I will be the GREAT PIANIST; no crouching, no sitting up straight, only a magnificent fling will do!!!!' The car shot forward like a bullet, whinnied like a horse trapped in the pens, and threw itself back on its hind legs, before Ludmilla was able to come to terms with the gearstick. As she had been proceeding happily in second gear since she had resumed the wheel, no great damage was done, except to her posture, which to an observer, particularly one supposes to Miss Waterfield, would have looked disturbingly like that of a *poor* pupil.

Fortunate then, that it was not the indomitable Miss Waterfield but Talbot Hardy, the man himself, who resignedly brought his splendid old Triumph down a couple of gears, changed its tune to a high pitched, slightly truculent whine, and buzzed round Ludmilla's hired car as she struggled to regain possession of her sang-froid and the accelerator. She glimpsed the back of his car as it clipped the edge of her vision, and slowed down to acquire a better view of the back of the only person likely to be driving down that road in a British registered car at that time of day. There was a very good chance it was the first of her cards to be dealt, but as she slowed down to focus her picture, she soon realised that the distance thus created between them was hardly advantageous to her ocular pursuit. Large people know a lot about ocular pursuit, which usually evinces itself in a peering, squinting gesture after a retreating object more mobile than themselves.

Ludmilla decided to give Mr Hardy a chance to park his car and potter about a bit before she swept down upon him, so she dawdled happily for what remained of the drive, picking her way mentally along the path which led back through her memory to this place. 'Careful not to tread on the lines,' she thought, and then wondered where that had come from, and what it might mean. 'Tread on a line, you marry a swine . . .' So what on earth had rhymed with prince? Quince? It puzzled her. Well she hadn't married a swine. She hadn't married anyone at all. Her chances of marrying Flynn if he had lived? Talbot had enquired, though in rather subtler terms. Ha, ha! Play the joker on that one, she had thought to herself. His world had been full of lines, dead straight ones as a rule, allowing for few of the kind of flourishes and squiggles which were more particularly Ludmilla's hallmarks.

She parked the car with a swirl to the right, so that it stood beneath a tall cedar, at least three hundred years old, marking the entrance to the woodland which held the château in a crook on the north west side. Approached from this angle, by the back road, the château was hidden from view until you had walked the length of the *allée*, which was about the length of three cricket pitches strung together, bordered by curious trees, which hung inwards and over, peering towards the great cedar, as though craning to hear its announcement of a visitor. 'Miss Ludmilla Pike, LRAM, ARCM,' pronounced Ludmilla, rasping the morning air with her forthright but aging baritone, and stepped forward, brown envelope in hand, towards the sunlight.

4

Before he agreed to Ludmilla Pike's proposal that he take on an English girl for the summer, Talbot had never, he believed, actually had anyone tell him what to do. It was not that he possessed any spectacular kind of authority, simply that licence to do as he pleased had continually been pressed into his hand, like a coin given to a child, by those who were anxious to please him. Women, in particular, from his mother upwards, had practised a kind of protection racket against him. So long as he paid them off with charm and attention, they continued to protect him against his own weakness by appearing always to concede to him. Since they were largely under the impression that it was they who were mortgaged by desire to him, Talbot suffered no humiliation. It had always been a good arrangement. Ludmilla damaged more than his personal expectations of her.

She arrived an hour early. 'My mistake!' she cried gaily, and handed him her handbag.

It was the first of a series of gestures which somehow reduced him. He was obliged to stand there while she swept her eyes over the wide entrance hall, up the staircase, down the walls with their peeling plaster which he had been going to strip, but sentimentally had left in place until Ludmilla had revisited, all the while clutching an item of, what should he call it – *handware*? – made of cracking brown plastic, snapped shut with a chrome, gold-painted clasp and designed to be held lightly between the fingers of an elderly female hand. She had hooked it over his fingers as he held out his hand for her coat so that, overcome as he was by the sight of her, he was momentarily immobilised in a thespian pose suggestive of an elderly char lady in drag.

Talbot was trying in vain to swallow his shock. It seemed, as Ludmilla could not fail to notice, to remain lodged between the roof of his mouth and the back of his throat, temporarily impeding speech.

'You *have* got your work cut out,' Ludmilla said, as though cheered by the thought, and it was not clear whether she was referring to the badly needed restoration of the interior, or the increase in stature, grace, and general manliness of the person she saw before her which would be required to rectify her impression that he was a poor wee thing.

'Now, if I remember rightly, *this* way, isn't it?' and she led the way into the kitchen. Talbot followed, still holding the bag. He had prepared a table on the lawn outside the french window of the library – coffee, and some light patisserie, with napkins secured in Posy's family silver. It was like the handbag. Incongruous. False-footing. He would be looking for dirt under his fingernails in a minute.

Ludmilla was standing at the sink. There was, actually, rather a lot of washing up to be done. She sighed, looked a little sad for a second and then visibly, theatrically recomposed herself.

'What a lovely room this once was,' she said. 'I used to make bread at that table there, and let it rise on that shelf by the wood burner, or at the window in the summer.'

Talbot could not think that anything substantial had changed in the room. After all, the whole place had been empty since the beginning of the second war, and he had had no time since his arrival to do anything but clean – admittedly not too much of that.

There was an awkward pause.

'I can't let you stand around in the kitchen,' he said in a sudden rush of bluffness. 'Come through and have some coffee.' He found he was already backing out of the room. Ludmilla had quietened down. She was all smiles as she followed him mock-meekly to the library. Talbot was watching closely as she came into the room.

'Ah,' she said, 'yes, one never forgets.' And for a moment they both stood looking at a chaise-longue upholstered in dusky pink silk, where Tom and Chloe first made love. A breeze caught the branches of a laurel tree outside the open windows, which gave onto a lawn. A white linen cloth pleated slightly at the corner of a table set for two.

'Dear Lord,' said Ludmilla, and her voice was her own. Then she made a puckish little noise in the back of her throat and, Talbot could have sworn, clicked her heels.

'Let's go,' she cried, in her *Annie Get Your Gun* voice, and marched out onto the lawn.

While Talbot poured the coffee, cursing the dainty little cups and the breeze, Ludmilla started her deep breathing exercises.

'Do you play?' she asked, in a voice raised over some imaginary background noise, heaving away, chair turned ninety degrees from the table. She didn't look at him while she spoke, as though she were lifting dumb-bells and couldn't spare the effort. Her hands were flat on her kneecaps.

Talbot immediately thought of golf. 'No,' he said, smiling affably, 'not my game. I'm more of a tennis player, if anything.' It must have been the accessibility of the image of Ludmilla in plus fours striding about Gleneagles in about 1890 which seduced him into error.

'I hardly imagine,' said Ludmilla, exhaling with the air of one who could contain herself no longer, 'that tennis and the pianoforte could compete for affection in even the most indiscriminate breast.'

'Ah,' Talbot said, 'I quite misunderstood you.' He was longing for Ludmilla to go all the way, to embark on an admonitory but kindly speech about their not having got off to a good start, but let them both try again, from the beginning. Perhaps she could even go out of the door and come back in again, this time looking like Chloe, or an elderly version, fluted and kindly, still graceful, with plentiful hair swept back from her forehead and coiled at the back of her neck. Lace collar, perhaps, and a faint perfume of Dutch Violet.

'Well, well, well,' said Ludmilla, managing not to be offensive. She sighed, taking her time over it, as though to usher in a few quiet moments during which they would both consider the past. There was a 'let us pray' feel to it. The emphasis of her sigh indicated that this summoning up of the past was also a respiratory process, like breathing on a mirror to create a distance from the immediate image. Talbot shifted on his chair, and lifted the lid of the teapot. Disbelief had stepped between him and his book, *his* book, Flynn's book before that, the two of them together on the right side of the line, and this elderly parrot before him was the begetter of that disbelief, wheeling out of the sky with a fluorescent shriek into his pastoral world – his, Chloe's, Flynn's.

Ludmilla, too, was feeling shocked. She had come prepared to charm, in her own peculiar way. A bit dotty, garrulous at times, but heavily impregnated with her own personal lore, which she delighted to share. With people she liked she played this part most of the time – as a compliment to them – and it gave them an excuse for being interested in her, which would initially save them the embarrassment of being plain curious about her. Now she had not known whether she would like Mr Hardy – she had supposed she would. On the phone he had sounded pleasant and intelligent, and she had imagined that their meeting would be amicable, although she knew there was nothing she was going to share with him which would amplify his knowledge of the world of *Pierrot Lunaire*. Whatever she might have told him was already on open display – the book, the house. A true story? *Let's separate fact and fiction here.*

But of course she didn't say this to him, although the anger which had risen so unexpectedly as she saw the handsome face of Talbot Hardy smiling calmly and, all right, pityingly, into her own as he first beheld her, had almost wrenched a confession from her. She had wanted to squash his smug superiority. It was clear that he thought her an elderly fantasist, laying claim to something not her own, a nursemaid come-lately to the lonely; impostor and freak. Her, Chloe? Her, drifting through the swathes of corn in her hat with the veil against the sun, and the young poet waiting taut with love for her in the dovecot? Ludmilla felt a sudden urge to run from this place, to leave the silly, handsome bugger with his shattered fancy and a tale to tell over dinner when he'd recovered. God, what a monster, he'd say. If I hadn't been so devastated I'd have had to laugh, really. Ludmilla could have kicked herself. Could she really ever have imagined that she was returning in glory? To have lived all one's life without beauty, without love, with the exception of that one brief period, here at Monvanité, and then, after so many years, for a stranger to say, however gently, no dear, I'm afraid you're really not quite right, that can never have happened to *you*.

To give him his due, Talbot had not said this. He was talking quietly, in a tone that seemed to suggest he understood that she was still grieving, about his plans for the film. He was not sure she had a right to know. Time and his own interpretation had made an impostor of her, so that her credentials – her obvious knowledge of the book in particular – read like a faked testimonial. In his ignorance, he had supposed this meeting would restore to the past its true colours, opening up the possibility of an evocation uninflected by change or decay. Change and decay suddenly seemed the better option. Out with the pot of varnish, away with the miraculous substance that dissolves the accretions of time. Someone, not him, had said on seeing restored Dutch masters at an exhibition that time, besides being a great healer, was also apparently a great painter. Of a generation for whom the rhetorical swipe of a new publicity slogan convinces like a hastily adapted chivalric motto in times of sudden political change, Talbot was quick to snatch at epigrammatic straws. His only thought now was to get her away as soon as possible, before her vivid presence emblazoned its vulgar image on his cherished picture of the past. As to the nature of the true facts, he certainly wasn't going to ask her and she certainly wouldn't tell. All she would say was that she had been at the château for a couple of days that autumn, arranging for the piano to be put in storage, when Flynn's effects had arrived from Spain. She had forwarded the book to the only publisher she knew – Isa Fontaine.

'I *could* tell you what really happened,' she had said, and he had already run this scene through his head, with a signature tune of tremulous Ravel. It doesn't matter, he told himself. If that is how Flynn saw her, I must work through his desires. Every man has his notion of beauty, and art spins a truth more accurate than reality. If Chloe lives through Flynn's creation only, that is all the better. He was soon sure that if Ludmilla had been closer to, and she could not have been further from, his image of Chloe, it would have been necessary to assimilate something of the real life character into the part. Now he could dispense with her altogether. They could have a nice polite chat and she could potter off into oblivion. Strictly off camera. She must tire soon.

• Helen Stevenson

It had been meant to be a bright day, a curt blue sky with no lip of cloud. But now the breeze had risen to abuse, and the unhappy couple sat uncomfortably at the table, which was too small, and wobbled on uneven ground. Clouds grew bulbous behind the rooftop, peaking voluminously against the blue. It would have been better if the bright morning had never been. Deceit and disappointment flooded in a grey wash across the scene. Of all the people who might have met in this story, these two should have been the last.

Ludmilla opened her handbag. 'My *sensible bag*, I call it,' she said, and took out a half bottle of brandy. While Talbot went to fetch her a glass she heaved herself up from the table and set off towards the orchard, batting her stick on the ground. She was no more lame than a woman who delicately dabs her eyes is really weeping, but the movement bespoke a kind of submission – she had abandoned heartiness. The orchard was very ancient, but its fruit for all that would be luscious and ripe in July. Now the last of the pale white pear blossom lay in the crook of the branches. As Talbot came out through the windows onto the lawn she was leaning against the wall of the herb garden, her feet splayed, stick propped, or rather propping her, between her legs, the left hand over the knob, like an old vine, spotted and gnarled. In her right hand she was holding a brush of dill, and she trailed it over her cheek then held it close to her nose. Talbot felt as though he had witnessed something not normally available, a hidden harmonic, in the way a dog hears notes too high for the human ear. Suddenly, aware of his presence, she flinched, shuddered in an exaggerated fashion, and ground the herb between finger and thumb beneath her nostrils, sniffing deeply. To Talbot she looked like someone in a perfume factory testing for unfortunate aromatic side effects.

They were standing in the herb garden drinking brandy. Talbot had not refused. Ludmilla had done well to produce her hip flask. It put an end to daintiness and the coffee cups and placed her in the position of being able to offer Talbot a drink. They both felt somehow relieved by this. The herb garden was laid out like a chess board, with camomile spreading its spidery fronds on the black squares and everything else dotted in between. It was neatly tended. Talbot was a keen cook. Ludmilla was standing on sorrel, at a knight's move from Talbot, who had one foot in borage and the other in caraway. The clouds were at the far end of the sky from the sun. He helped her down the stone steps to the bottom lawn, which fell away westwards, out of the light, to the outhouses. By a garden urn, trailing with desiccated ivy, she stopped, lifted her left hand to the back of her head where the perm crinkled abjectly above her collar.

'Ah,' she said, posturing with a smart little thrust of a hitherto undetected hip. 'Weave, weave the sunlight in her hair.' Talbot was lost for words.

'I brought you a photograph of Flynn,' said Ludmilla. He took the picture from her and thought immediately that it had perhaps been as well that Flynn did not live to leave her. He did not usually notice the faces of other men. If asked whether his closest friends were handsome or not, even in the case of those whose appearance fell far short of the standards expected of only the most averagely tolerable female, he would have said he supposed they were quite attractive, although he'd never really given it much thought. His standards for women were extremely high, largely because he found it difficult to meet women he really liked, even though he enjoyed female company better than male – it reflected better on himself. This was almost too handsome a face to be believable. In the days when he used to visit his mother's aunt at a residential home in Blackheath, Talbot had been moved by the pathos of a little spinster lady, unvisited through the years, who kept a framed picture of a young Hollywood star on the table by her bed. 'That's my son,' she would say proudly, 'he works on the oil rigs. He's doing very well.' Talbot had been moved not so much by the attempt at deceit, as by its ineptitude.

This was not the face of a Hollywood star, however. It was the 'portrait' nature of the photograph that made him suspicious, the feeling that whoever had taken it had caught the pose with forethought. It was not a chance snap-take of reality, it was informed with prior knowledge of the subject. He looked older than thirty-four, the fabric of the face was already worn, but it was this that brought out the vulnerability and youthfulness of the features themselves. In his unforgiving use of bright midday light, against which Flynn looked prematurely aged, the photographer had actually brought to the surface the intemporal elements of the facial structure. Talbot looked at the photograph for several seconds longer than is usual for a visual image, the reading of which rarely involves the dimension of time. He took in the whole image, then forced himself to look again, more slowly, seeing no more in it than he had in the first fraction of a second, but committing it to familiarity, for future reference.

Unaccustomed as she was to do so, Ludmilla felt a flush of embarrassment as Talbot took the photograph out of the envelope. Her naturally high colour began to stipple the panstick no. 15 like some rather arty paint finish. It was a very long time since she had felt the prickle of appraisal. It was like having a young man pick you up from the office in full view of the girls. Of course Talbot Hardy was a man, so it wasn't quite the same, but passion of the kind she suspected he felt for Flynn was entirely permissible, a sign of sensibility indeed, in a perfectly disembodied context, and they didn't come much more disembodied than Flynn.

Talbot smiled and handed back the photograph without replacing it in the envelope.

'I see,' he said. He looked up at Ludmilla again, unconsciously but pointedly, she felt. It was the look a teacher in a kindergarten might have given a backward child who had suddenly produced a beautiful and painstakingly painted picture.

'We grow old, Mr Hardy,' she sighed, 'and some of us the years have condemned.' He could tell she had planned to say this. Her delivery was slightly imperfect. It was real sadness getting in the way of its simulacrum. She recovered quickly. One could not have said that her breast was troubled.

Talbot was all tenderness and concern.

'You were very much in love with him, weren't you?' he said, coaxing, as though he had suddenly understood something.

Ludmilla could have withered him, but she was working on her part. They were sliding between the tops and tails of each other's sentences without listening to more than each other's words.

'You only love once,' she replied, acceptably. Each of her words was always quite distinct, so that her sentences ran like dotted lines. She used her whole face when she spoke, bringing every tiny muscle into play. She had decided some time ago that her face would sag less in the direction of her breastbone if she kept it continually in motion. This provided a sound practical motive for her natural loquaciousness, although its origins lay not in neurosis so much as in misplaced generosity – her urge to entertain. Speech left her breathless, however, so that as she continued to talk a background noise like that on a very early gramophone recording mounted steadily in her chest; the deep throatiness of her speaking voice and the rushing breathiness from her windpipe created the effect of a scratch wind ensemble.

'I was two years older. I met him that spring. In Dublin. He came to a concert where a friend of mine was singing. *Pierrot Lunaire*. Schoenberg.'

Talbot appeared not to know that the novel's title came from a song cycle, a setting by Schoenberg of the obscure poems of Albert Giraud. Ludmilla filled him in. The thought of him discovering the fact a few months from now and thinking he'd solved an important clue was too depressing.

'Isa liked his poems – they were her sort of thing: harsh, fashionable, nothing beautiful. She was fascinated,' said Ludmilla, unflinching, 'by their magnificent ugliness. She invited him down here later that summer. He turned up just about the time she left to marry Gresham. After that she never returned. And there we were.' She smiled brazenly.

There was a long silence. Talbot was concerned about his timing. Things were certainly improving a little, but he didn't want to blow it. A fat partridge, which he had often seen before, rose heavily from the undergrowth and scuttled with an unsuccessful beat of wings towards the trees. Ludmilla followed it with her gaze. Talbot began to explain how the château had passed to Posy on the death of her aunt, along with the manuscript of *Pierrot Lunaire*. It had been uninhabited for almost fifty years. Madame Derrault, who ran the café in the village, had come and cleaned once every year or so. Ludmilla didn't comment. When Talbot had arrived he had had to get the key from the local *notaire*, who had been persuaded with a considerable backhander to relocate his wine cellar from the excellent caves of the château. Ludmilla was tickled by this. The brandy was beginning to lift her spirits, bringing on one of her better moods in which she was inclined to form conspiracies with almost anyone not immediately present, and she chuckled with admiration for the wily lawyer. Talbot felt put out on behalf of the Talbot he had just described, who seemed to have been reduced by her laughter, becoming somehow less than the decent, good-humoured but authoritative sort of bloke of the anecdote.

As they talked, and Ludmilla elaborated on the life and times of Château Monvanité, the great cedar of Lebanon creaked slightly. Ludmilla was not at ease. She felt the house and gardens, the trees and the long concealing grass were lending interested ears. It was like telling a story on behalf of a group of others who had also been present, who would not contribute themselves to the narration, but would be aware of and shocked by deviation from the truth. Suddenly the dramatic monologue she had imagined would fall from her lips dried within her. She felt that if she continued to speak she would crack something, her skin, some kind of membrane. It was time to go.

'Do you have a copy of the book, Mr Hardy? I would rather like to take one away with me if I may. Fifty years is a long time, and I have a lot of spare moments these days. Reading is a great joy.'

'I don't, I'm afraid, no. It's sentimental, I suppose.' He smiled a little falsely. 'Superstitious, even. I work from the original. But I could have one made easily enough. There's a photocopier in the village library. I'll be making a few myself shortly. It'd be no trouble to run off an extra copy and put it in the post.'

Ludmilla was grateful. When she indicated that she must soon be off, Talbot's protests were wafer thin. She asked to see the room where he worked. It was the library, where she too had worked. The dust in there was considerable, and, in his delight with her for being so eager to be gone, Talbot found that nothing was too much trouble. At the first sign of a tickle in her throat he was off for a glass of water, and Ludmilla was left alone in the room for a minute or so. Then she met Talbot by her coat and helped herself into it while he held the glass of water. Well buttoned up, she took it and drank.

They were almost chums now. The aurora of parting was colouring their mood, and they were all smiles.

'I shall expect to be invited to the première,' Ludmilla told him coyly. He promised her a front row seat and thought he'd cross that bridge when he came to it. Ludmilla was *not* going to be good publicity. Perhaps she could be sent on a cruise around the time of release. A very long one.

As he said goodbye to her at the car, and gallantly checked her oil level at her request, she took her coat and jacket off and laid them on the back seat like a travelling salesman. They shook hands warmly.

'It's been a real pleasure,' he said. He had planned to call her Chloe, once, but could not bring himself to do it. Ludmilla chose her moment to inform him of the arrival of Laura.

5

Laura wore red to meet the General. She thought, scathing herself, that if anyone had chosen a colour in which to meet someone called Laura they would have gone for lilac or, pushing it, mauve. It turned out, some time later, but not before the confusion had well and truly rooted itself in her mind, that it was the dog who was called the General, and its owner plain Monsieur Hardy. Although she was by now nineteen Laura reckoned that it was only through such mistakes that she had ever achieved any originality in her view of the world. From a similar flaw in her understanding, for example, arose her conviction that the Crown jewels reposed on a velvet cushion somewhere in the restaurant at the top of the Post Office Tower. Such misconceptions were too well established for anything other than factual correction, and persisted like an underlying crease in a sheet.

The *patronne* of the Café du Sport came over to Laura's table, calling greetings to a passing cyclist as she pushed the chairs aside. She was pretending not to have noticed anything peculiar about Laura, resolved not to bat an eyelid at her French, which would no doubt be foreign and pretty, like her face and clothes. Not many tourists stopped off at the Café du Sport, but Madame Derrault would have eaten her signed photograph of Sasha Distel before she let Laura know that.

'Vous désirez, Mademoiselle?' she enquired, mock distractedly, eyes on a door on the opposite side of the square.

'Un café, s'il vous plaît.'

'Un crème,' wrote Madame Derrault out loud, pocketing her

notebook swiftly, as though she had just completed a fleeting, vicious portrait of her customer.

'*Ah, non,*' Laura corrected quietly, '*un café noir.*'

'*Un petit café,*' said the *patronne* flatly. 'Seven francs.' Laura laid a fifty franc note on the table.

'I'm afraid I haven't any change,' she said in perfectly competent French. 'I've only just arrived.' Madame Derrault picked up the note as though she feared it might not have had the right injections.

'*Je reviens,*' she said, pointed at herself, then towards the interior of the café, then back at the table.

Laura wondered why she bothered. On the train down she had shared a compartment with an irrepressible wine merchant from Languedoc, who, with his estate agent brother had recently followed a Berlitz course in English.

'Nineteen-ninety-two,' he had pronounced sagely by way of a preliminary conversational gambit. 'The English speak no languages.' The two comments were obviously connected in some way with his future business strategy. Laura, who spoke a crisp well matured version of his own language which had been imparted to her by the state education system, decided to let him have his Berlitz-worth.

Madame Derrault returned to the table with an ashtray and the coffee. Laura took advantage of the ostentatious wipe she gave the pristine table top (as though she suspected Laura had secretly been salivating over it while she had been away) to ask the question which had brought her into the café.

'How do I get to Château Monvanité from here?'

'Second right out of the village on the road to Soubyrète. Follow the road for 1500 metres and you'll see a sign. It's closed to the public.'

'I know,' said Laura, 'I've come to see the owner. He's expecting me.'

'Too bad, you just missed the General,' the *patronne* said, with no evidence of having to strain to keep the regret out of her voice.

She angled her hip at a gap between the chairs and sidled through, unconsciously dislodging the furniture with the breadth of her beam. Laura swallowed her two mouthfuls of coffee and pocketed the loose coins. She returned to the tiny railway station, and decided to change. Ten minutes later she emerged from the ten square feet assigned by the *commune* for public attention to private functions wearing a short red dress and a gold ribbon in her hair.

Laura had not missed the General by very much. Talbot had dropped him off an hour earlier at the Café du Sport, with his basket and a week's supply of food. Mme Derrault had effected a not very casual introduction to a bitch in the village, Andromache by name, number four of a brood of pouting setters who belonged to Yvette, who ran the hairdressers. Yvette had collected him only in the last few minutes. Driving back home, Talbot was unaware of Laura's presence in the village. In accordance with Ludmilla's recent adjustment to arrangements, he believed her to be due in a couple of days. He was due to meet Sally Fairfield back at the château. She was coming over to show him how to tie up peas, but that was not until four. It was about ten kilometres from the village to Monvanité, a good three hours walk in the heat of the day, but a matter of minutes by car. Talbot thought, as he drove, how much of the countryside around him he now saw through Flynn's eyes. It had been a different season then, of course, the tail of high summer, fluting into an autumn of decay, trailing into mist. It was as though the lovers had arrived too late for merriment. Too late for merriment. It could almost do as a title. How often our most mediocre aphoristic findings are filed under that particular thought. So many people must have embarked on autobiographies with no more justification for a belief in the interest of their own lives than a particular ability to come up with rather trite title phrases. Story of my life. thought Talbot.

The script was still proceeding slowly. There was so little to go on now that Ludmilla had proved such a dead end. All in all she'd proved about as useful as a copy of *The Lady*, providing a so called researcher and general help, although with the kind of reference that probably wouldn't have clinched the appointment under normal circumstances. Ludmilla was the kind of person who aroused not so much suspicion as superstition. He felt that if he hadn't gone along with her request she would have somehow blighted him. She did, after all, have the power to blight the whole venture. He couldn't believe Ludmilla would simply sit back and wait for the film to appear. She would want her recognition, her photo in the magazines, her credit for being the inspiration of it all. He could not afford to offend her. The biographical approach had lost its appeal for him. He was forced back to the story, he had to treat what could surely be not much more than a work of the imagination as though it contained some higher truth, some ideal love that biographical fact could only palely reflect, pastiche, even. It was a game. She held all the chance cards. He must in some way obey. An extraordinary woman. When confronted with her in the flesh he had realised that it was not by close scrutiny that he would discover Flynn's mistress. He would have to screw his eyes up very hard and use his imagination. She had presumably been trying to tell him that in her way, when she stole the book. But of course he had had two copies. Lightning never strikes twice. He wondered whether she had sustained some dreadful and irreversible damage as a result of the trauma which followed upon Flynn's death. And as for her appearance, well, anything could happen over fifty years. She could do with a few tips out of old Sally's book, though.

Posy had offered in a postcard to have a little chinwag with Ludmilla, although it was difficult to imagine how the wagging of any one of Ludmilla's chins could be a small event. He had declined. Posy didn't always do *exactly* what he did or didn't want, but in this case he was fairly sure that if Posy and Ludmilla had talked about his project he would have been the first to know. For the moment he wanted to keep her out of it. There was a slight doubt in his mind. No, his wife wouldn't keep anything like that from him. She was as anxious as he was that he should find out everything there was to know and get filming as soon as possible. She wouldn't want him going off the boil. She'd always encouraged him to believe in his own creative powers. But if Ludmilla really was Columbine to Flynn's Pierrot there was something altogether more mysterious about the affair than he had yet discovered. Ludmilla had teased him and done a flit. And now she was sending this Laura girl, to keep an eye on him, no doubt, to see he didn't find out anything he wasn't supposed to. At the same time he sensed that Ludmilla wanted the truth to come out, that the truth could therefore flatter her. After all, no one had invited her to contact him. She could have ignored the advert in the magazine. The more he thought about it, the more it seemed the only thing Ludmilla had achieved through her visit was persuading him to have Laura. Somehow Laura was connected with Ludmilla's past. She knew something he could use. It was an elaborate treasure hunt and Laura was a clue. He'd known a terribly dreary Laura once. He grinned. Perhaps she'd have a locket with a little spring tucked under the collar of her blouse, or a letter concealed in the walnut case of her Sunday school bible.

6

At nineteen, Laura knew little more about herself than did the two people closest to her: her father, who was also her vicar, and Ludmilla, who was her piano teacher. She had been a good, self-contained child, neat, delicate, composed, her little dresses always hung up away in her single room at the back of the squatting old house that had only recently been made over into a vicarage. Toys, though she demanded very little in the way of toys and expected still less of them, were carefully boxed and sorted, stowed tidily away before early bed. There had been puppet plays (usually biblical stories, in which Pinocchio and a witch doubled as the baby Jesus and his mother), scripted and typed up by her father and handed out to children in the parish playgroup. Afterwards Laura untangled the strings and laid the spent little wooden dolls out in their shoe boxes in a lining of surgical cotton wool. There was no dressing up. Her mother's clothes were dispatched a couple of Oxfam shops away, out of the immediate area, so that Laura, on her way to church, would never meet the familiar rust-coloured suit and cotton jersey pushing some other pram, stopping to wipe some other tearful face.

There was a library in the house though, where each Sunday after morning service she would choose a new book, running her fingers along the cloth-bound spines like a little blind girl, for there was no picture cover, no thrilling précis on the jacket to allure her. Drab 1930s editions, jumble sale remnants, but fine in their way, said the vicar, and slipped a fiver in the till for the lot. She would sometimes take one along in her music case to her piano lesson, to improve the shining hour, as the vicar, if he had been spending too much time at parish meetings, was wont to say. Ludmilla would soon sniff out the keen musty smell of prurience and disappointment emitted by those women authors she particularly despised. The odour of sanctity, she called it, a lingering taint of mothballs: she was thinking of bottling it and flogging it at the next jumble sale. It might really take off. She envisaged an advertising campaign showing a woman dabbing it behind her ears at the pearly gates and being waved straight through.

Ludmilla took it upon herself early on in Laura's life to supervise her reading matter. Once the vicar, who had a theology degree from Keble College, Oxford, and had heard of a lot of books even if his own diet was predominantly ecclesiastical, had confiscated Ludmilla's copy of *The Painted Veil*, for her good, not his own. It certainly turned out not to have been for his own when Ludmilla went and broke up a tea committee meeting to demand it back. 'I wondered whether you had quite finished with my dirty book, vicar?' Ludmilla had not yet introduced her to *Pierrot Lunaire*. For years she had been waiting for the moment to be right.

Disapproving though the vicar was, he had a fondness for Ludmilla, who reminded him of a kind of life he had missed out on through the strength of his vocation. He was not one of those vicars who, on taking up the ministry, is able to carry their units over into the next column as it were, preserving their secular characters for use in their sacred careers. He had once been quite a witty young man, but theological and pastoral worries, of which he had many, and the early death of his wife had wearied him away into a man capable only of a stern kind of adoring love for his daughter and a guilt-ridden and wildly over-conscientious commitment to the needs of his parishioners. Ludmilla always rather thought he liked to linger over his tea when he collected Laura from her lessons. She supposed it gave him a brief chance, brief enough not to be painful, to imagine the way his life might have been. A rural parish perhaps, a shabby gracious sort of living, comfort and conscience, keeping body and soul together. She and Laura used to plump the cushions up for him before he came, and Ludmilla would make her giggle by pretending to have put brandy in the cup cakes. Perhaps she wasn't just pretending. The vicar knew that Ludmilla was in... on sedition with his daughter, on bringing out the imp to match the angel he had bred. But Ludmilla seemed truly to love the child. She foresaw, years before it happened, that when Laura started to grow up, her gravity would come away like an eggshell. Ludmilla wanted to teach her, to have taught her by then, to dance, to read, to make music, to talk, to know the sensual side of her own intellect. She knew that Laura must leave her when this happened, but, without seeing reason to despise her motives, she counted on the return of Laura's gratitude, an acknowledgement. For Ludmilla had never been beautiful as Laura was, and there was so much, if Ludmilla showed her the way, that her beauty could help her to achieve. Beauty makes the cake rise, she used to say, but not to Laura.

Laura had by now established that she would have to walk to Monvanité. Save the penny and walk, she could hear the vicar saying. The stationmaster, who had been looking after her heavy bag, resumed his game of boules under the plane trees. The village elders, tiny people who looked as though they might just have stepped daintily out of last year's discarded chestnut cases, were getting in a little weekday practice. It was the hour after the *heure sacrée* and the stationmaster's wife wheeled her mother-in-law across the square in an antique Bath chair. A coven of beaky old ladies watched Laura's reflection pass in the shaded window of the ironmonger's shop. It seemed to them that Laura's short scarlet dress must be a costume of some sort, but they did not therefore associate her with the General, the General being a dog.

Laura had discovered fashion through the back door. Elements of both her father's utter insouciance and Ludmilla's hideous parakeet-panache had, in a way, influenced the emergence of a deft kind of wit in Laura's clothes. She fell upon the glad rags that were hustled furtively into the upstairs room of the parish Oxfam shop run by church ladies ('Just thought I'd drop you these in, Mrs Budgitt, I'll put them up with the rest') and converted them to her own style, so that faded has-beens became neat pastiches of past styles. Had she been creating from scratch for the catwalk, she might have been credited with something like post-modernist cheek! She was well aware that the effect of her efforts was one of unconscious flair; indeed, she was a girl of whom it was often said that her charm lay in her unconsciousness of that very effect. This was not strictly true, for a child brought up in circumstances like Laura's quickly learns to see herself as others see her, employing all the subtle deceits available to a person of fundamentally pleasant disposition in order to allay suspicion and avoid detection – a means, perhaps, of protecting privacy. Laura's gravity guarded her against becoming the parish poppet, the vicar's little helper, skinny recipient of our Gloria's billowing hand-me-downs.

As Laura passed on the other side of the road, she caught sight of Madame Derrault standing behind the bar inside the Café du Sport, speaking into the public telephone, hand cupped over her mouth, eyes watching the road, rubbing a patch on the counter with the elbow of her right arm in concentration, hanging up swiftly as a customer stepped in out of the sun. Neatly, she retrieved a coin from inside the machine with a toothpick and popped it back in the till. Laura decided against forewarning Mr Hardy by telephone. He was English, of course, she had received a very courteous letter settling the terms of her 'employment'. He had made significant use of inverted commas, as though rather heavy-handedly mocking the English from the fickle remove of the expatriate.

She continued up the road, turning right at the pink sandstone church, to which she would return, she told herself. Dipping into churches for a quick look round was a compulsion in her family, rather like a genuflection. She reckoned it would have been as grievous to pass by on the other side of the road of St Xavier's of Cricklehamlyn or St Mary's of Loadminster as to disregard the dying victim of a mass mugging. She noted in herself a tendency, in these first few unchaperoned hours out of the parish, towards an ironic hyperbole which was an attendant of sarcasm, that proverbially lowly form of wit. (She had never been able to understand why sarcasm should be relegated to such lowly rank in popular statements on the theory of comedy; she could think of far worse: custard-pie humour, and the-vicar-will-have-his-little-joke jokes, for a start.)

As she left the church behind and crossed under the maples to the road leading north-east out of the village she turned suddenly and, shading her eyes against the sun, looked searchingly down the street, as though hunting for jigsaw pieces on a distant table. Her body was very slim, the slight arch backwards as she tilted her head up was balanced by the dark switch of her hair as it dropped in a silky loop down her back. She rummaged for her camera in her rucksack and chose a shot, which she would send home to the vicar. The ochre sandstone houses in view, with their wrought iron verandas and violet painted shutters, leaned at alarming angles creating long reaches of shade in unexpected places. Dusty vans parked under the maples bore improbable advertisements in an odd and charmless typography. Two stray looking dogs slept under the awning of a patisserie, where the shade which drops at siesta time lingers like a long curtsey through the afternoon.

The little village was almost silent; the men were mostly out in the fields. Laura was at once astonished and soothed by the discovery of an entirely different kind of place – it was as though she had discovered an unknown sense. Her nerves were delighted in an unfamiliar way. For the first time in her life the sun beat down on her limbs and face, uninterrupted by cloud or wind, as though unacquainted with grief. Ludmilla, with a burst of almost Old Testament arbitrariness, had brought her to a new world.

She was to give secretarial help to the owner of Château Monvanité, who was writing a film script. It was the early summer of her pre-university year. Ludmilla had fixed it all. She had persuaded the vicar it would be a culturally improving experience for Laura, who like the vicar was a little world-shy. The vicar, who, besides other considerations, thought Laura might have derived at least as much cultural improvement from staying at home to help with the Sunday school anniversary production of *The Burning Bush*, had raised objections. Laura, who never contradicted her father except in matters of chapter and verse, as facts were known in their house, had left it to Ludmilla to talk him round. The Lord knew (it having been confided to him, no doubt, by his anxious servant) what she had said to him, but he had relented and an élite handful of local ladies (referred to by Ludmilla as the usual suspects) had been mobilised to support the vicar during the period of Laura's little desertion. She had only ten days to prepare herself – to pack, fill the freezer, sew her clothes and buy books from a reading list compiled by Ludmilla (with generous book token attached). She had taken the night train from Victoria, in order, she thought, that the experience of travelling might be as dark, brief and unconscious as possible, so that there might be no sense of travelling away from home, of putting distance between herself and her background, that she might be, as far as possible, dealt hand to hand, like a baton. The sad cheeriness of her father's fluttering white handkerchief as the train moved off had given her a lurch of self reproach. The poor widower, alone on the platform in his dark blue 1950s raincoat, which showed the dirt less than it did his age, transforming a gesture of farewell into one of surrender, giving up his beloved daughter to the world of which he was not.

Everything was of course well above board. Miss Pike was a splendid organiser (a pity, in a way, she was an atheist, she would have been a valuable asset to the tea committee) and he was, after all, inclined to worry too much about Laura now that she was almost an adult, in the worldly sense. He felt as though his devotion to her – and he found his devotion easier to examine than his love – would keep her close if he concentrated hard on her in his thoughts, examining each detail of his knowledge of her with the fine scrutiny he applied to his ecclesiastical texts. Until now the shifts in his reading of her at different times in her life had been only vaguely perceptible. No radical internal contradictions, no dramatic changes in style had occurred to throw him. She had never indulged in the kind of undesirable, cheapening activities that seemed so disastrously to beguile other girls of her age. No teen magazines, no streaking her hair, no hanging around in shopping centres on a Saturday afternoon. She had a temperate sort of charm. Her manner was more mature than that which he remembered her mother having at that age. Eleanor had been flippant and untidy, unruly even, when he had married her. He had still been at theological training college when they had met. They had married quickly, and he had taken a dowdy position as a curate in North London, so that she could complete her course at art school. She had been killed by a car shortly after they moved north. Carelessness, the driver said, and the vicar had accepted the verdict. At the moment of impact, Eleanor had actually been thinking with great care about how to broach with her husband the subject of a parish crêche, and had been discussing the matter with her friend Catherine Bates as she stepped off the kerb. Catherine later told her husband that Eleanor's last words had been 'Somehow I don't think Jeremy will approve.' Jeremy soon asked Cathy to take care of Laura in the mornings, when he had visits and business to attend to. In the afternoons, until she was old enough to go to school, she could play on his study floor. He wasn't at this stage sure what playing would involve, but it could surely be conducted in a spirit not entirely incompatible with the writing of his weekly sermon. Cathy agreed, and promptly set up a parish crêche-cum-playschool, where Laura soon assumed a helpful semi-pedagogic role, teaching by serene example the skills of sitting still and reading quietly to oneself.

7

Sitting still and reading quietly was what her father Jeremy should have been doing the previous evening when the phone rang. *The Confessions of Saint Augustine*, perhaps. He might have been better prepared. After he had waved goodbye to Laura he took the train back up north, and arrived at the vicarage shortly after nine o'clock. Laura had left him an amateurish hand-written menu which he was to prop up in front of him at the dining room table. It was meant as a kindness, though perhaps nothing could have been more guaranteed to intensify his sense of his own folly in regretting the absence of a nineteen-year-old daughter than her assumption that a childish gesture of the sort would compensate his loss.

She had left the avocado and the dressing in the fridge, along with a lamb casserole. All the vegetables were in the casserole, so he would only have to heat it up. There was apple crumble to follow. Laura, who could never remember how to cook and always had to refer to a recipe book, which is why she never learned to cook properly, had made all these preparations under the grip of a painful vision of her father dolefully cracking a couple of eggs and grating some cheese into a frying pan. Jeremy, who was not hungry and would have been well satisfied with, say, a cheese omelette, dutifully spread his napkin, specially ironed, on his lap, and bit with the spoon into the avocado. A spot of lamb casserole dripped onto the napkin ten minutes later. Tomorrow when he used it it would be dirty.

Surprising himself, he was almost irked. For the first time he felt her guilt over leaving him, her attention to his needs, as a burden. Unhappy, worried at his failure, but impossibly full, he stretched some clingfilm over the crumble and put it back in the fridge. The washing up only took a minute or so. He picked up the *Radio Times*, where Laura had ringed the programmes she thought might interest him. For the most part they were on the radio. He noticed that she had drawn a dotted line around some Open University programmes which formed the basis for a postgraduate course in theology. Laura had been trying to persuade him to take the course, in the belief, which was in some ways only slightly misguided, that her father was a frustrated academic. He had been tempted to sign up for the course himself, but conscience, rippling through that dark pool in the back of his mind in which resentment of his tedious daily duties grew like luxuriant algae starved of light, had stayed him in the very act of dialling the freephone number. For a humble parish priest it seemed a matter of indulgence, vanity even, something beyond the point of necessity, like the Advanced Driving Test. He contented himself with watching the occasional broadcast. If he found he was following the course too closely he would invent strategies which, in their tedious complexity, prevented him from being at home, or finished in his study, or washed-up in the kitchen, or sufficiently prepared for the next morning's work, or from simply being able to find the remote control device, so that he would, when it came to it, be unable to watch.

It was a wise discipline, he told himself sadly. When Laura was at home, which she usually was, she went to bed around eleven o'clock, and he was able to resist the temptation for fear the television might disturb her. That first evening, the time he normally spent in conversation with his daughter was passed dully in over-fastidious attention to the parish diary and the agenda for the meeting to plan the flower festival, so that now he was an hour ahead of himself and sat looking at the blank screen, toying with the idea of switching it on. Perhaps it wasn't too late for the news. The remote control device was in its little hole in the control panel. He fished it out and pressed. Just then the phone rang. Jeremy ignored it at first, but not because he was one of those people who ever simply let the phone ring – that is not a prerogative of any public servant, be it of the Lord or of some more securely established British institution. Besides, it had always seemed to Jeremy that in some sense once a man is tired of answering the telephone he is tired of life. No wonder the luxury of 'let it ring' was always depicted as a ruse of the very rich in American soap operas. His failure to respond immediately was rather due to the fact that they had recently had a new telephone installed, which emitted a peeping noise exactly like that of a phone in an American soap opera. and which he did not immediately recognise as their own. Then, after three or four rings, he realised that the sound was as inappropriate to the eighteenth-century costume drama unfolding before him on the screen as it was to his own 1930s vicarage. He stood up quickly and crossed the chilly hall to his study.

It couldn't be Laura, she would be asleep on the train. He had all the times of her trains and buses on a piece of paper by the phone. She had written them out in her fine italic hand, in a greeny turquoise ink. Supposing the train had crashed. How quickly would they get through? The study was cold after the warmth of the living room. He had forgotten to draw the curtains. The fluorescent light from the wet street outside seemed to finger the plastic digital phone, recognising it among the musty leathery antiquity of the rest of the room. The old black telephone still sat, solemn and dependable next to the new device. He had not wanted to part with it, old and outmoded as it was, and had retained it, like an old passport with its corner clipped off. Lifting the phone was like putting his finger in a socket. He waited for the shock. It was Ludmilla. Could he meet her for coffee next week? She had recently learned that she had not got long to live, and was anticipating a religious crisis.

Now, sixteen hours later, nine hundred miles away, far from the wet red bricks of Lincolnshire, its swelling dykes, collapsed umbrellas in the parish schoolroom and mosaic of muddy footprints, Laura was walking slowly up the hill out of Soubyrète in the late afternoon heat. The village lay already a couple of miles behind her, and as she stopped to rest for a minute, there was little she could make out beyond the barest outlines of the warm stone building which rose gently up a now distant hill. So close together, the little houses with the church rising above them, looked like figures in a photograph who have had to huddle unnaturally close to one another to fit in the picture. Or perhaps that direct gaze, staring back slightly defiantly at her across the swimming heat rising from the tarmac road, reminded her of a group of women she had once seen in an old war film, sheltering escaped prisoners under their skirts whilst pretending to crowd together under the pull of sheer exuberant neighbourliness.

She heaved the heavy bag up again, a shabby suitcase with sharp corners. Her father had offered her the use of his matching canvas shoulder- and travel-bag set, but she had refused, and not for the reasons he thought. She preferred the look of the shabby case. The matching set her father was so proud of reminded her of petrol coupons. She had a severe sort of censoriousness when it came to her father's lapses in style, which she feared would make people laugh at him, and on the few occasions when she had betrayed this she had damaged his pride considerably. She would try to ring him later that evening, she thought, as she noticed a public phone on the road ahead. It was on the corner where she would have to turn off left.

As she approached she noticed a figure standing outside the phone box, although she couldn't make out anyone inside. It was a man, quite an old-looking man, although at first she mistook him to be very young, about her own age. The she realised that the slouch of his body was not the languid pose of an idle youth against a wall, but a fixed deformity. His body was caught in some youthful movement which had been interrupted by paralysis, giving him the startled, unfinished look of a single frame in an animated cartoon. As she drew near, she noticed his head was nodding up and down very slightly with a chewing motion. The head was tilted a little to one side. He was dressed oddly, as though someone had chosen his clothes and put them on for him, like a child. He seemed to have so little regard for his limbs and muscles that the garments hung like curtains around a faked window – unanimated by light or perspective of any kind. Laura's compassion for the sufferings of others, whether imagined or actual, was based on a mild egotism. Loving herself, the suffering she supposed she might feel in their position of misfortune was so great as to excite an appalled rush of tenderness. As she stared at the figure, drawing nearer to him on the road, until she was only a few yards away, she realised in embarrassment that he was returning her gaze. She felt as people do who have been singled out in a crowd by a pavement clown whom they have been observing in happy anonymity, suddenly to find themselves the object of the crowd's peculiar attention, as though their own ridicule had found not an object but a reflecting surface in the opacity of Pierrot's mask. She nodded nervously. It was hard to find the locus of sense in the face. The eyes seemed to stare at her chin. The mouth chewed rhythmically on an old piece of frayed towelling, but her nod was returned. She nodded back, with a timid smile, relieved. She hadn't offended him. It was he who had chosen the gesture, and had performed it at the proper moment, just as she was drawing level, pitching it exactly right. Once she had passed, she wondered if she had not imagined the nod, whether it hadn't just been part of the general up and down of his apparently habitual jaw movement. What if, like Billy, who sat in the front pew of her father's church every Friday night for six weeks, waving his hands to the sound of choir rehearsal, before defecting to the touchline of the boys' club soccer practice where he was, admittedly, less conspicuous among the doting fathers, he was convinced of his own invisibility? She hoped that by her nod of acknowledgement she had not, as had the lady who did the orange juice for the boys' club in appealing to Billy for assistance, shattered a fond illusion on which the structure of his existence depended.

Laura was tired and uncomfortable and anxious to reach the château. Her curiosity was strong, but she savoured the last moments of not knowing what it would be like. As she stood leaning on the hot grainy stone wall it seemed that she was still leaving, not yet arriving. She was still in the bit before the beginning. But there was no doubt that the beginning must come. Even if she turned back now, it would be to walk into a new phase of the old life. Better to carry on. Ludmilla had told her that the house would be hidden until the last minute, she would think it had disappeared, that she had mistaken the route, and then emerging from a dip in the road, she would see it through the branches of a chestnut tree, retreating behind a swathe of parkland. So it was. She swung her suitcase and rucksack over the gate and scrambled after them, jumping lightly from the top bar into the grass on the overgrown track. Nettles and soapy-smelling cow parsley burrowed among the lower snatches of elder and as she brushed against them, stooping to grasp the handles of her bag, she felt them stitch her skin with little white dots of mild poison. Laura would not use this track again for a week or two. Once she knew the house it would swivel 180 degrees in her mind and she would never approach it again from this angle. If she did, she would know it to be only a back entrance, from which it was impossible to see the character of the buildings.

The scarlet dress flicked between the long grasses as Talbot watched from the dovecot to the right of her path, a hundred yards away. Sally stood with her arm loosely slung round his shoulder, a woman in her mid-thirties, wearing cut-off jeans and an old jersey, her very fine pale hair, streaked by some unknown agency – not worry, not the sun, though her skin was a fine muscat colour – fell lightly onto his shoulder as she leaned forward to place her hand on the binoculars.

'What is it?' she asked, though waiting for him to hand them to her.

'Damn,' said Talbot. 'You'll have to go back tonight. I didn't think she'd be here till Wednesday. It's the girl I told you about. I thought she'd ring from the station.' He had dropped the glasses, but kept them slung round his neck, beyond Sally's reach.

'Sorry? What's the connection?' She stepped away from him a little. Talbot turned from the window. He didn't know. Privacy and secrecy were not brooked by any consciousness of subterfuge in his mind, although he tended to mistake one for the other. He had hardly really believed in the existence of the girl. Ludmilla had told him in parting that she would be sending him an envoy, and his passivity in the face of what was more a point of information than a proposal had given the moment the quality of an annunciation, something promised to one who sleeps. Her references had been so allusive that he had begun to wonder whether they hadn't after all been metaphorical. Had she not perhaps simply meant that she would furnish him with more details of the original of Chloe in some later message? That was ridiculous, he knew – she had spoken explicitly of the need for her protegée to travel and gain some experience of the world away from her cloistered family circumstances, and fitted Laura's organisational abilities over his own avowed blanks in that area with the adroitness of a seasoned lotto player. He hadn't discussed her with Sally, although he had briefly mentioned that Laura would be helping him out for a few weeks and that she was a friend of a friend of Posy's. Something to do with the film. She hadn't questioned him further. She couldn't realistically offer her own secretarial services to Talbot as she lived twenty miles away and had her own business to run. For the moment he wanted Ludmilla's things to stay on the other side of the line.

'I haven't got enough petrol to get back. The garage shuts at six. I'll have to fill up in the morning.'

'It's only twenty to,' Talbot said. 'You'll make it. There's a spare can in the back of mine. Take that in case.' He turned back to the window. The red dress had stopped moving. The girl was standing with her legs slightly apart, head and shoulders bent right over, so that her dark hair hung loosely towards the ground. She held something between her fingers behind her neck, then lifted her head suddenly so that the dark hair fell quickly back off her face and was caught deftly in the ribbon high at the back of her head. She was looking past him. The dovecot was too distant and the window too deep set for him to be visible.

8

To Laura's surprise it was the woman from the café who opened the door. Mr Hardy was in the park. This referred to the two or three hectares of trees which extended away from the château on the north-west side and through which cut the drive by which Laura should have approached the château if she had followed Madame Derrault's instructions correctly. Laura was obliged to explain who she was and what she wanted before Madame Derrault would let her in. Eventually she reached up and undid the bolt which held the second panel of the door shut. With the whole door open, Laura could see past her to a broad stone staircase where the shallow steps ran up and round on three sides to the floor above. The steps were printed with dusty footsteps and the wooden balustrade was rotting in places.

'You follow me,' said Madame Derrault by way of instruction rather than invitation, and picked up Laura's suitcase in a manner which implied disdain rather than deference. Age before beauty, came an echo from the playground. But instead of showing Laura upstairs to her room, she bore off to the right and kicked open a heavy door with her foot. Laura had not noticed at the café, but the hefty movement revealed that her right foot was shod in some kind of orthopaedic boot of the kind worn by those plastic casts of rickety children holding collecting boxes which are still found in unrefurbished shopping centres in England. For the second time in half an hour, Laura found herself caught staring. This was a bit of a record, for she was normally very discreet and managed at least to be covert in her curiosity. It was obvious that whatever Madame Derrault's role in the household was, she wasn't the cleaner, for the expression on her face indicated that she was no more insensible than Laura to the prevailing smell of mouldering straw.

They were in a room about forty feet square with the proportions of an eighteenth-century drawing room. It contained a couple of moth-eaten armchairs, a table with a typewriter, a precarious looking pile of box files, a kicked-about paperback lying face down on the floor in a corner, a pink, eighteenth-century *chaise longue* and a rug before the fireplace on which lay, unmistakably, a pair of gentleman's trousers. The light came through the french windows, which were folded back into the room. In a bay tree just outside, a robin was singing. Laura seemed to have arrived just as Madame Derrault was leaving, having done her bit. She seemed determined to persist in her belief that Laura was either deaf or suffering from comprehension paralysis, and indicated only with a gesture that she should sit down. Perhaps, Laura thought, everyone had to have some kind of handicap around here, it was somehow *de rigueur*. She wondered whether this would extend to the proprietor himself. She began to frighten herself with the thought of spending six weeks with a limbless war veteran who understood no part of speech beyond the imperative. That would not, on the other hand, account for the pair of trousers. Through the window, past the robin, came the sound of a car starting and reversing over gravel.

'He will be here in two minutes,' said Madame Derrault, and withdrew.

It was natural that Laura should also leave the room, which did not feel like a room for waiting in, or if it was, it was for pausing in before passing on to some other stage. She left her two bags and stepped cautiously out of the french window, which even if it had been differently hinged could not have opened out into the garden, for the grass was quite long at her feet and the bay tree, though tall and sprouting at the top, was bushy. It was now warm early evening. The grass grew unscythed and stretched like a fallow field, as far as the eye could see in detail. She was looking south now, towards a freestanding dovecot she had noticed as she approached from the west. It was circular, and mounted by a sort of wizard's hat construction in slate. In each quarter there seemed to be a slit of narrow vertical window. There was one facing the house, looking at her now. She was studying these details with deliberate absorption, aware that Mr Hardy might appear at any moment and see her. She felt very hot and was sure that the long journey, followed by the walk, must have dishevelled her to her disadvantage. There was a certain point of dishevelment, reached after roughly two hours of moderate exertion which could positively favour the appearance, on occasions lending a certain wild bloom to even the most severely potted plant (a riotous session of the tea committee could set the sap visibly rising even through Mrs Budgitt's stiffly-powdered temples). Now, however, Laura felt distinctly beyond her best. Was that why Madame Derrault had looked so disapprovingly at her? Well, perhaps not. Laura did not have the kind of beauty which got easily out of line. As Talbot was later to say, she looked like an untouched madonna waiting there beside the bay tree.

9

Madame Derrault was running late. She had only slipped up to the château with an excuse, prepared to pretend to Talbot if she ran into him, that she had thought it reasonable to give the plants an extra watering in this hot weather. Laura's linen was already laid out, had been for some days, ever since Talbot first mentioned that he was expecting secretarial help from England. It wouldn't be the first time he had had company in the last few weeks. Madame Derrault knew about the comings and goings on the road to the château better than almost any one. Today she had had an opportunity to mark Laura's arrival herself, but Albert would have told her anyway. She was in a hurry now to catch him before he set off down the road himself. His sense of direction was unusual, and although he could easily find the way from home to the phone box alone by daylight, he soon lost the road in the dark. He had been there when she passed on her way up only half an hour previously, so she would either meet him on the road or find him still at his post. 'We call him Albert,' everyone always said, as though he could have brought nothing with him into the village, not even a name. Madame Derrault looked after Albert. He occupied a cottage on her farm, where she had lived alone since her son had left home fifteen years before. The son never visited.

Talbot had offered to take Madame Derrault up to Paris with him some time so she could call in on the son. 'I don't think I'll bother this time, Mr Hardy,' she would say. 'The nights are drawing in.' Or, with the weather so warm, she'd rather stay put. And always there was Albert. Talbot had offered to have Albert to stay. This was a safe enough piece of courtesy, however.

Albert generally reacted to the world in a way that came across as placid, to say the very least, but at the sign of Talbot's red Triumph zipping along towards him, he would flatten himself against the hedge and bend his head back as far as he could, so he didn't have to see him. Talbot resented this a little, but was principally concerned that Albert shouldn't choke on his rag in the heat of the moment. Mme Derrault put it down to natural antipathy.

'Don't worry about it,' she had said. 'It's a good sign, in a way. Good for him, I mean.' But when Talbot had wanted to know more about Albert, she had had nothing to say. 'Nobody knows, poor soul. Nobody would think to ask. He's been there day in day out for years. Rain or shine. Call it a habit.' Talbot called it something more precise than that, but not in front of Madame Derrault.

She was difficult at times, but her spikiness kept him entertained. And she was certainly kind to Albert. Talbot marvelled at her strange gaunt features, once beautiful in her face perhaps, but the face had changed. The strangeness was accentuated by the basketry effect of her hair, which she dressed seamlessly on top of her head. It looked like a covered bird cage. When she had first suggested she do his washing and ironing for him he had agreed because her presence in the house gave him a connection with the village. Having once seen her standing with the laundry basket lodged at her hip, a peg in her mouth, folding one of his shirts, using her one free hand and a combination of chin and bosom, he was hooked. There was, he said, something gloriously antique about her. This was less obvious against the backcloth of a Hoover Automatic and a packet of Persil, but she did that bit out of sight in the washroom.

She spread a white linen cloth on the dining-room table, then collected her bicycle, which was half buried in the hedge at the bottom of the drive. As she wheeled it round onto the track off the gravel she caught sight of Talbot. He was standing still, with one hand on the branch of the peach tree under which he was waiting. She thought he was very handsome. He looked like a photograph. He pushed himself off and started walking slowly, running his hand through his hair, shaking his head slightly and smiling. Laura was out of sight, but looking back as she climbed onto her bicycle, Madame Derrault saw him wipe the palm of his hand on the front of his shirt before extending it in greeting.

'Talbot Hardy,' he said. 'Laura?'

'Laura Cranshawe. Hello.'

'You must be tired out. You should have phoned from the village. Anyway, you're here just in time for a drink. Welcome to Monvanité. Where are your bags? Inside? I could do with a quick one. How about you. A quick snort? I'll just pop these up to your room first.'

Laura didn't know what a snort was, but she indicated that her bags were in the room with the french window. His manner was confusing. She couldn't find the right moment to speak. Every time she thought she was about to, he took up again himself. He seemed to be doing a great number of things at once. He was guiding her through the doors back into the darkening room, emptying his pockets onto the little table, picking up the pile of files from the floor and finding the one he wanted, tucking it under his arm, picking up a piece of luggage in each hand, and talking all the time. The heavy door was swinging back and he stopped it with his foot. What was it about that door, Laura wondered, that made every one kick it? It was the luggage of course. He was wearing a rough blue cotton shirt and light jeans. Laura thought his dress was unusual, though it was in fact standard.

'Madame Derrault showed you in here?'

'Yes,' said Laura, worried for a second that he would think she had just been wandering about the house on her own.

'I expect she was very rude,' said Talbot. 'She doesn't like women. It's almost a phobia with her. You might want to steer clear of the Café du Sport. She's the *patronne*. It is virtually men only. The Mairie keeps trying to arrange social nights to get the young people to mix, but she gets all the men drunk on free cognac early on in the evening, so they never turn up to the dance. They say she even locks the door. The next day, none of them can ever remember what happened.' Laura was laughing nicely. He thought she might have been laughing with relief, but at what he couldn't tell.

'She's like Circe,' she said. She stepped through the door after him into the hall.

He put down the the bags abruptly, to close the door behind them, and looked at her thoughtfully, then said, 'Yes, she's like Circe.'

They walked up the staircase side by side.

'And what you couldn't know,' he said, looking at Laura, who was looking at a portrait ahead of her on the landing, 'is that she keeps pigs. Only two, but it could be significant. That is Lord Gresham, my ex-wife's uncle. He is very ugly, as you see, but I expect he looks a lot worse now he's been dead for a few years. I had to put something up there. This is your room, I'll just put your bags inside here. I'll go and get some drinks ready. Come down when you've had a wash.' He turned and ran quickly back down the stairs. Somewhere a telephone was ringing. He seemed to be on his way to answer it when he paused with his hand on the ball of the balustrade.

'Laura,' he called, and she came to the banister rail and looked over. 'I'll cook a meal for you tonight. Exceptionally.' She nodded and smiled hesitantly. He had said in his letter that it would be good if she could do some cooking for him. She'd been practising her basic techniques. The important thing, Ludmilla had told her, was to memorise the recipes in advance, to give an appearance of competence.

Some days later they discussed the way they could only have met once, for the first time, and whether it was inevitable that it should have been like that, that they should have said those things. Laura suggested that they might have met on the road if, say, he had discovered he had run out of cigarettes, which he was always doing. Talbot said he had been working all day on his film script but had taken a walk about an hour before she arrived. They might have met in the park, where he had been cutting down some branches. She could have rung from the phone box and warned him, but she had been intimidated by Albert. But they were glad that it had been the way it was, Talbot especially so. An hour earlier, he said, it wouldn't have been the same at all. Why not? Laura wanted to know. Oh, Talbot said, it was appointed to be that way. Who by? said Laura, Ludmilla? They agreed she should be their presiding deity, spinning their fate.

'Like a top or a thread?' Laura asked.

'A thread,' Talbot said, after a moment, though he hadn't meant it that way.

Laura sat down on the broad double bed. The vast wooden bed-head bumped against the wall. The bed was covered with a pale blue satin eiderdown. There was a glimpse of perfectly white crisp sheet. Windows from the ceiling to the floor, panelled at the bottom, where the wood was painted a pale blue with a faded motif of edelweiss round the edge, opened onto a tiny balcony with a wrought iron railing. The shutters folded back on themselves several times. It smelled of hot cotton, as though someone was accustomed to do the ironing in there. The ceiling was very high, the floor bare to narrow boards. There was a jug and a basin in the corner on top of a roughly painted cabinet. The jug was plain enamel like the ones they used in the church kitchen for pouring out hot coffee, half-and-half, as the vicar liked it. The bowl was made of porcelain, white, with a very fine gold line around the edge. When Laura bent to open her suitcase, she noticed that Talbot had left his file on top of it. *Pierrot Lunaire*. It was the title of the book Ludmilla had talked about, the one Talbot was making into a film. It had obviously been retyped recently. She looked at the first page.

Tom Flynn, world weary poet of the strictly modernist school, had spent the early weeks of that summer in the magnificent surroundings of Château Monvanité. A strange depression lay over him, crippling his impulse to write. The devotion he inspired in the mysterious Chloe only increased his burden. He resented her beauty, her love of life, her easy pleasures.

One act of selfishness on his part was all it took. Disabled through his fault, lame, scarred, but ready to forgive, she awoke in him a gift for love. His poems poured forth, elegaic and pastoral, unlike anything he had ever done, or felt, before. It was a great love, a powerful love – but it lasted no longer than the season which had seen its birth. With the first signs of autumn, and of the fruitfulness of Chloe's womb, Flynn's love turned dry. The world assumed its old pallor, Chloe's grief repelled him, and he fled southwards into Spain. There, in mourning for his love that had died, he penned this heart-rending tale, which is at once self-indictment and a plea for forgiveness from the woman he had loved.

> *Flynn died, aged thirty-four, near Salamanca, at the hands of General Franco's Falange.*

Laura turned the page.

'It is June,' she read, 'and the weather is perfect. Our opening shot (title sequence) shows Chloe labouring up the drive to Monvanité, carrying something heavy. She is about twenty years of age.' Funny, thought Laura, but not so funny. She was wary of coincidence. It was apt to play you false. There were only a few sheets of paper in the file, all neatly typed. Laura wondered whether Talbot could type, imagining him sitting at a typewriter like Henry Miller, with a cigarette in the side of his mouth.

She washed her face and decided to change. Her father was always teasing her for changing her clothes every five minutes. For Laura it was like running up a flag to test the wind direction. She asked him whether he didn't feel different wearing his surplice, or not wearing his dog collar. She was not sure whether it reflected well on him that he said it made no difference at all. When he wasn't wearing his dog collar he almost always wore his dark red jersey and a pair of old suit trousers. Thankfully the suit trousers were so old as to be positively fashionable. She didn't look forward to the time when he got round to picking out the seventies cast-offs from the jumble sale stock. That wouldn't be for a couple of decades yet though.

She shouldn't have brought the pale silk dress. It was, she thought, considering the secretaries she had known, most unsecretary-like. And yet, she had reckoned, when looking for an excuse to pack it, she would have to be off duty some time, and would need something like this – the kind of thing people dressed up in for dinner. It was the sort of silk that handkerchiefs are made of – handkerchiefs for eyes, not noses, the kind which, if found on a lawn in the early morning after a party, might be kept as a token of an event which could have been a dream. She had only worn it once, and that had been for fancy dress, when she had played the angel Gabriel in a nativity play. Since then she had cut it down to just below knee length, and it fell like a tulip from her waist to the hem, where the silk pleats wrapped about her legs, held close by tiny mother-of-pearl buttons. The neck was cut square and, sleeveless, it fastened on each shoulder, again with the tiny buttons. It was a Grecian dress, copied from a childhood story book. Its beauty was that it was the kind of dress a man would find simple and unremarkable, and at whose elaborateness a woman might marvel. Her father, knowing how she prized it, although he tried to discourage such emotions, would have been horrified to see her wear it on an occasion like this. But there was no occasion. It was just her first night. It wouldn't matter if she never left the room.

She washed at the basin and brushed her hair, beating down the impulse to rush. Her shoes were never quite right, she had never been able to afford, in the way some women can, to buy shoes to match a special outfit. She had a pair of old ballet shoes, dyed ivory which went with most things. Round her waist she tied a faded blue sash which might have been cut from a secret panel in the eiderdown but in fact had come from an old night-dress case. She stepped out onto the landing. It felt odd to make her first unchaperoned steps in the vast house. Something qualitative had changed. She had been guided to the room which was designated for her, and up until the moment she left it her movements were in some sense authorised by her host. To choose the moment to leave it, the manner in which she would find her way downstairs, showed a measure of independence, requiring insouciance where the walls seemed to have eyes. She felt awkward and somehow presumptuous.

10

Talbot was in the kitchen, cooking. He did not seem to notice as she came in. His movements were precise but apparently random. There was something about the way he bent and stretched, reaching for herbs, ducking down to pick some onions from a basket on the tiled floor, which reminded Laura of a class they had had at her school, conducted by a visiting dance teacher. She had insisted on the need to learn to relax. Let your body go, she had carolled prettily over a background tape of what sounded like the school pipes unfreezing slowly. Laura had found the degree of premeditation involved an impediment to movement. She was hung up, a friend told her. No, it's not that, Laura had said. I just can't move if I know someone's watching me perform, even if it's only me watching. Perhaps it was the complete absence of hesitation in his movements, his perfect confidence, like typing without looking at the keyboard. At that moment he left the kitchen by another door, without turning round. She wondered whether, if she never saw him again alone, she would recognise his face in a crowd.

Ten minutes later he joined her in the garden. He was dressed as though he were playing a Shakespearean character in modern dress, as though princely qualities had had to find expression in a contemporary costume. It was not only that his clothes were expensive, it was that he could afford to spend so much money on something so casual. For Laura, money was very much associated with Sunday best, in everything, although as a daughter of the church she had naturally never had one.

'You're in luck,' he said, as he came up to her. 'Madame Derrault has ironed all my shirts, particularly the ones which aren't supposed to need it. It's her way of saying I need her.' Maybe because she looked so much like a figure in a ballet, he felt the need to guide her movements, poised at every moment to hoist her into the air. He took her over to a jasmine bush, and when they were within a yard of it, froze as though the music had stopped. Laura had never smelled jasmine before and was amazed. When she told him he was pleased. When she told him she had never been abroad before, he in turn expressed amazement.

'You must tell me about yourself over dinner,' he said. 'But let's have a drink first.'

They walked slowly back towards the house. The beige-coloured stone walls were cracked and lined like a human face, but here there was no sense of travesty, of the years having condemned. The château seemed almost in a hurry to grow old, although it had already weathered three hundred years of sun and pestilence. It looked older still, but like a child's conception of something old. The three sides of the informal square formed by the main building and its two wings enclosed a shabby lawn, where rusting croquet hooks defined a vague figure of eight. The right-hand wing consisted entirely of farm buildings and a large barn, where it was evident that no serious activity had taken place in recent times – the barn door, collapsed off its top hinge, stood permanently wide open, while the grass grew under its feet, and tools and wheelbarrows lay in the random positions assigned by time and neglect. They were the kind of objects no one feels responsibility for, and which begin after many years to assume a kind of right to their position, though no one could say how they came to be there. A trowel leaning against a barrel, a riddle with rotted sieve, buried in the grass. Wood lice running frantic at the approach of their feet.

He placed a little table by the bay tree and they drank white wine. Laura drank slowly, unaccustomed to the cold sourness. Talbot drank slowly because he usually drank whisky. She told him that she had lived in the same town for as much of her life as she could remember. Her earliest memory was of moving from somewhere else when she was two. She and her father had been alone since her mother died. Talbot did not ask her when that had been. She had begun to learn to play the piano when she was eight, and they'd got Ludmilla out of the phone book. She had attended a small local school for girls, and Ludmilla had paid for a uniform and the occasional extra. Ludmilla had said she must travel before university and she was putting off her application until the next time round. Her father thought she should attend the local university, which was in the next town. Ludmilla was gunning for somewhere loftier.

He topped her up, and lit a cigarette for himself.

'I presume you don't,' he said, peering at the lighted end as he pulled it from his lips. Laura made a confession. She had been offered one on the train by an estate agent she had met, and had taken it to see what it was like.

'They did a demonstration at my school,' she told him, leaning forward with her elbows on the table, looking at a point just above his shoulder, trying to remember so she would tell him properly. 'With a polystyrene head, like in a hat shop window, sitting on a sort of ashtray thing. They stuck a cigarette though a hole in its lips and we each had to go and pump on a little rubber ball on the end of a tube. At the end they passed the ashtray round and it was full of melted liquorice. I'd forgotten about it until today. I don't think it was a very good deterrent.'

He passed her the packet. 'Have another one,' he suggested. 'You don't know till the second one whether you'll like it.' Laura, thinking this was not quite a good argument, refused.

'Ludmilla used to smoke all the time,' she said. 'She used to pretend she didn't when I was little, because she thought it was a bad example, but I stayed the weekend with her once and she couldn't hide it. She didn't want my father to know, though, so I had to wear a sort of sheet thing with a belt and a hole for your head all weekend, and she kept my clothes in a cupboard so they wouldn't smell.'

Talbot was delighted to hear that Ludmilla had not been piling on the eccentricity just for him.

'How old were you then?'

Laura had to think. 'Fourteen, I think.' Talbot was surprised.

It must have been well past nine o'clock, but it was still light. Talbot said he would show Laura around tomorrow, and she could start being a secretary the day after.

Questioning Laura later, in a room dominated by two very

large Dutch paintings and the smell of the tender fish they ate, Talbot was disappointed to find that she knew no more than he did about *Pierrot Lunaire*. Ludmilla had said she must read it in France. Talbot would have a copy. In that case she must ignore, for the time being, the draft of the first few scenes of the film which he had left in her room. He wanted her opinion on his adaptations, but they would only be of use if she had first read the book.

'I know bits about it. She's always talked about Monvanité, but I almost never thought it was real. She told me things about the people, and riding a horse. And Isa Fontaine being her best friend before she married the publisher. And the pink *chaise longue* in the square room there. She called it the library. I recognised that.'

'I'm surprised you did. Madame Derrault had a go at it the other week.' He flashed his eyes furtively around the room and came back to hers, whispering confidentially, 'Stains!'

Laura giggled. It reminded her of Ludmilla's comment on a faded jacket her father often wore – 'Spotless raiment'. It *was* a little patchy.

Talbot came back from the kitchen with another bottle. What sort of messenger was Laura? It did occur to him that in a way she was herself a character, a more faithful representation of the winsome Chloe his imagination had fashioned from the book than coincidence could possibly have been expected to put his way. Laura was a cutting from that old and knotted life, grown to sapling size. The horror aroused by Ludmilla was allayed by his delight in her proxy. One thing was clear. Laura need not lift a finger while she was here. The inspiration of her face would more than outweigh the advantages of a host of capable Miss Moneypennies.

Meanwhile, Laura was satisfied with her dealings with the fish bone. Her employer's urbanity was rippled with an easy disregard for formality, but she was anxious not to do anything which would betray her inexperience – for fear, as much as anything, of being an embarrassment to him or, indirectly, to Ludmilla. The open delight she was able to display in the beauty of the place, the novelty of travel and being away from home helped to conceal her amazement at the more particular details of her circumstances – the food, the wine, the paintings, the warmth of the late sun in the sky as it stole back from the table, and the odd intimacy between herself and Mr Hardy. Years of experience at the vicar's side had provided her with a social confidence unusual in one so young, and a particular skill in the use of the interrogative mode. She asked him about his work in a way that drew him to speak of his marriage, and about his marriage in a way which drew him to speak of his future. He was dismissive about all but the last. As to that, he had great hopes of the film of *Pierrot Lunaire*, that it might make his name. He had a certain renown in his career as a television journalist – he mentioned the fly on the wall approach, which he had partly pioneered – but said he had discovered, late in life perhaps, that documentary truth was not to be achieved through unforgiving realism. In his first brush with fiction and the world of the imagination, however, he had found that old habits died hard.

'Take this book,' he said, as he filled his glass and emptied the bottle. 'The journalist in me wanted to know who Tom Flynn was, what he looked like, whether he really did experience all that he writes about with her that summer before going off to Spain to fight. I wanted to know what she really looked like, how they met, even where, and how often they made love.'

Laura reached for a clementine and tried, failed, to imagine how anyone could wonder how Ludmilla made love in a spirit of realistic enquiry. The thought aroused in her feelings similar to those experienced by early Victorians on first glimpsing the Alps – awful, terrible, sublime. It was, moreover, like trying to imagine the choreography of *Petrushka*, having never seen a ballet.

'Posy gave me the book as a sort of separation present,' he said.

Posy, Laura had gathered, was his ex-wife, great niece of the very ugly painting on the stairs. 'Is she that ugly too?' she wondered, splitting the clementine. Surely not.

'I was at a difficult point, my marriage breaking up ... dissolving my production company ... looking for a new start. She gave me a year, with the book, as a sort of challenge, doing something I'd always said I'd wanted to do, a feature film. The manuscript had been lying around for years and years. Not published, of course. Isa – you know about . . .? – had sat on it for years. Perhaps she didn't think it was good enough. It's badly dated, true, but it's almost as though she suppressed it for some reason. Then when she died it dropped like a stone into water. I've got the rights. Posy sold them to me, or at least I swapped them for a Richard Wilson.'

Laura didn't react. She thought perhaps the name was slang for a sum of money, like a monkey or a pony, and blinked appreciatively. It was the most she could manage. She was watching him talk as she might have watched television, omitting to react with facial expressions of concern, surprise or even interest, though she was riveted by his performance. He smiled as he talked, and played with the cheese knife, testing it warily against his forefinger. He looked up abruptly and she was touched by his face, which despite being handsome, was not always strong.

'I must sound very old to you.' Laura had not had time really to think about how he sounded. She was having a certain amount of difficulty following what he was saying. She was reluctant to confess this in case it seemed like she was drunk, which, although she didn't feel it, she might have been, as she had no past experience to compare with. The sun had quite gone now, and they were sitting in near darkness. As she started to speak, Talbot got up to turn on a small lamp.

'If your wife . . .'

'*Ex*-wife.'

'Well, if she . . . *knew* Ludmilla . . .'

'No, Isa did, her aunt,' corrected Talbot, reaching for his cigarettes. Laura refused. All these names ending in *a*, Laura thought – like a batch of daughters to an eccentric Latin master, who would put them all into the correct case in every instance.

'Oh,' she said, and paused, to make it clear that she realised her mistake, although that much she had always known. It had been a slip. 'But wouldn't Isa have known it was Ludmilla in the book? Wouldn't she have told your . . . um ex . . . Posy? To save you the trouble of tracking her down . . . if Ludmilla is . . .?'

'Good point,' said Talbot, to which Laura knew there was never any answer. It was always still the other person's go. You had to sit there with the pat balanced on your head like a tray.

'I haven't a clue,' he continued, 'except perhaps that even if Posy does know, or suspect, who Chloe is, she felt she had helped me enough already. Something like that. We were only married for three years. I never knew her family at all well, or really got on with them. Letting me have this place is some kind of recompense for that. I don't think Posy has ever met Ludmilla herself. Isa and Ludmilla were inseparable, apparently, during the thirties, their early twenties. They travelled a lot together, as people did then. Women, too, surprisingly. Posy told me that. Isa talked to her in a general way about it all. All sorts of strange people used to turn up here in the summer – artists, communists, particularly. I'm told Isherwood and Auden came here after Oxford. I expect it was all highly immoral.'

Laura nodded sympathetically, looking intentionally stern, until she realised that he was looking over imagined spectacles at her in mock disapproval, while she had been thinking of her father.

'Of course, Chloe's kind of innocence transcends morality,' he said confidently.

'Oh good.' Laura was feeling very tired.

'Just the two of them alone here, when all the rest had gone. A short idyll: love and duty; Chloe, Spain. Rejecting it all.' He put on what Laura came to recognise as his 'I could a tale unfold' face. He understood. 'He couldn't keep his intellect at bay. Or his calling. So he chose death. It's almost too simple to be true.' He was quite transported.

'Except for it being Ludmilla,' said Laura. Talbot had already let her know what he had made of Ludmilla's appearance.

'Quite. Fifty years on, she bears little resemblance. I wouldn't exactly have picked her out on an identity parade. But there's no doubt about it. I have the dedication page of the original manuscript.'

'Really? And it's to her?'

'I'll show you tomorrow,' he promised.

She said goodnight. He refused to let her clear up, saying he would do it himself in the morning as she would want to sleep late. This seemed to Laura an extraordinary kindness, or courtesy, she couldn't decide which. She protested that she always, almost, got up at seven to take her father a cup of tea.

'Is that an offer?' asked Talbot. Laura blushed and said of course not, unless of course – but he said of course not too, and that she should go and get a good night's rest.

Ludmilla was somewhere in the room. Laura could smell her mothy perfume on the pillow. She was moving very quietly, fingering the papers on the desk. A cowl of darkness hid her face, but her hands were light and tricky, sorting by the glow of a night-light. Her jowls were slack. It was a face for the small hours, unmade, unprepared for witnesses. Her hands worked a careful distance from the eyes, as though she were peeling onions. Then she was by the bed, nestling close to Laura's head, whispering hoarsely. It was finished – Ludmilla had destroyed the book and herself would soon be gone. For your sake, my dear, for your own sake. Laura felt the coarse wool of a hairy dressing gown graze her cheek. Let us pray, said Ludmilla. Laura started on 'Gentle Jesus Meek and Mild', and Ludmilla accompanied on a piano in the corner, keeping the pedal down throughout, so that the mincing phrases built up into a bacchanalian chorus of layered sound, echoing ever louder. Silence fell like a new kind of noise, and Ludmilla bowed low in scornful parody. Her dressing gown swung open, uncoiling from her waist to reveal an athletic body, taut and bulky under firm skin, with spoon-shaped breasts swooping down from huge pectoral muscles. 'Re–e–qui–em!!!' warbled Ludmilla, and the falsetto did ring false and mocking from that resonant chamber. Nifty, unencumbered by flesh, she nipped back in under the piano lid, which closed with a shudder – or was she laughing still, inside?

Laura woke with the blanket rubbing her cheek, sweating, the sheet in a knot about her ankles. She had cried out in her sleep but it was a silent cry, it had flown with the dream, leaving her throat dry and contracted.

Daylight slanted left on the floor-boards beneath the fastened shutters like the tail of a letter formed by a sloping hand. Laura punctured the film of her dream, getting quickly out of bed to open the shutters. But Ludmilla's presence in the past was real to her now. The macabre comedy had done its job. In a way that had not been possible the day before, Laura could picture her freely, striding about the grounds, treading the gravel with a careless swagger, tough calves and flowing skirts and a sensible linen shirt. Laura had once watched as Ludmilla wrote an important letter, sent one copy to the addressee and posted the second to herself, which she would keep unopened, as evidence of her act. The unopened letter authenticated the one she had actually sent. Something similar had happened in the dream. She must not try to look too closely at it. But as she picked up the beginning of the script from where she had left it the night before she felt a quick pulse of revulsion. Her head ached and she was thirsty. She poured herself some water from the enamel jug, and pushed the typed pages into a drawer.

Talbot had left a note for her on the table in the kitchen. He would be back in a couple of hours, when he would wake her if she wasn't up and hadn't found this note. Otherwise, she could take the car and drive to the village. They needed milk and something for a picnic. He had left a hundred franc note. 'Have a look for eggs in the chicken run, but make sure the cock isn't around – he can fly at you. Hope you brought swimming things? I'll show you the river later.'

She was baffled by the coffee machine, which was large and white, with bits of chrome at the points which were obviously actively involved in the mechanical process (which left a lot of machine space unaccounted for). She drank a glass of milk, trying not to think about the cockerel. Breakfast at home was a regular eight o'clock affair, with instant and toast. She cleared up after the previous evening's dinner, firmly pinched out an instinct to look for a piano, and set off for the hen house.

Outside it was already cauldron hot. There was no weather, only heat and a fierce blue above black tree tops. Not a creak from the cedar as she passed beneath its branches, skirting inside the edge of shadow on the path, where strange grasses and rusty plantain sucked down into the gravel as though in an aquarium.

The hen-coop was beyond the orchard, where no shade fell, and the black canvas of the roof blistered liquid at the eaves. Some way from the hen-house, the cock pottered, with the idle but critical air of a foreman on the shop floor, jabbing at the ground with his beak. Laura trod softly, holding the basket to her stomach. The cockerel's rump twitched as he ducked and strutted along the path. He noticed Laura and jerked up his head, tipping it slightly to one side, considering her, while his hideous pale red quiff lapped softly with the movement like an abusive tongue in an idle moment. With her basket weightless in her hand, Laura felt a clutch of fright which tapped viciously above her knee caps and she stood helpless, hollow with fear, staring back at the bundle of starchy feathers poised for attack.

Laura could be set screaming involuntarily by the sudden proximity of a bird in flight. The cockerel was the worst, perhaps because she did not quite believe it when she was assured he could not fly, so she was constantly anticipating something unprecedented and shocking. She had tried to overcome her fear, which was compounded by guilt at feeling such repulsion, on the basis of the 'all-things-bright-and-beautiful' principle but without success.

Once, she had realised her own fantasy of flight in a dream but, like a hapless fairy godmother in a story, quickly discovered she had also bestowed the gift on her most fervent enemy. She had been sailing along a few yards above dense woodland, where occasional glades flickered beneath when suddenly out of the sky, fell a blood-smeared feather duster of a cockerel, knocking past her, feathers in her mouth and blood on her chin. She had stopped in mid air and felt the thud in her own body, as it hit the ground, watching as the cockerel twitched in agony on a bed of leaves. As she fought with herself, kneading the first warmth of horrified pity even as her heart recoiled, she had spotted a baby rabbit, limping sweetly out of the ferns, soft cocoa coloured, with bewitching little ears. She had tended the rabbit. Shortly after waking she had written the nightmare down, which far from purging, had deepened its mark, so that now, recalling the images of the dream, she remembered also the very expressions she had chosen to describe them, and they stretched like an imperishable skeleton underneath the surface of her memory.

After a second or two, the beam of attention between them slackened, and she found that face to face he was less frightening than she had imagined. Another dread fantasy in which she wrenched off its feet and flung them far into the distance, was indeed nothing more than a conceit for revulsion. With the possibility of actually inflicting the imagined torture only a step away, she was relieved to find that it was rather that her own toes were curling in retreat. And it was comforting to bear in mind that the thought had first come to her on reading a thoroughly sensible if uncompromising recipe for chicken stock in a publication by the Women's Institute. But no, her toes held no interest for him. Tail turned, he was stalking off round the side of the house, intent above all on a show of overwhelming commitment to a prior engagement. He reminded Laura of several prelates towards whom her father regularly and vainly urged her to show greater charity.

She collected the eggs – only three – and hurried back to place them safely in the fridge. She was convinced that they would hatch within the hour, and she would rather they did so in some kind of incubator than in her pocket. All the time, she was listening out for Talbot. If he had gone out for a couple of hours, why had he not taken his car himself? Was he perhaps a jogging fanatic, or was there a local bus? Or was he lost in meditation, humming cross-legged in some dark corner of the hen house? Recently Laura had begun to feel that the contours and colours of Ludmilla's imaginative landscape had begun to emerge in her own habits, buckling the gentle topography of her provincial mind. Rabbit and cockerel. She looked at her reflection in a copper pan which hung above her head from a nail, the image softened by the smooth curve of burnished metal and for a moment it seemed as though her head were hanging from the nail. Unaccustomed as she was to the visionary mode, she asked herself whether it had been wise to drink unbottled milk in a strange house. Or perhaps it was a delayed effect of yesterday's wine. She resolved to take possession of herself before any more sinister agent undertook the task, and set off with Talbot's car keys and his money.

Her day had not started well. Talbot's absence had left her weightless – it was like waiting for an examination paper to be handed out while the blank writing paper and pens lay expectant on the desk. Without him the château was closed to her. The French manner of closing the shutters against the sun in unused rooms gave the place an air of being shut up for a season, no access to strangers. She was lonely.

The next problem was the phone box, and Albert's vigil. She thought she should have asked whether Albert's pitch was just the box itself or the general area around it. If he had really been standing guard there for the last fifteen years or so, as Talbot thought, it was more likely to be the latter. Laura had bought a phonecard before she left the village the previous day. It had still been possible then to imagine a monstrous Mr Hardy refusing access to a phone, or worse still, squatting in his Bath chair, counting off the seconds on some diabolical timepiece, while she begged her father to come and bargain for her release. But Talbot, who did not seem to count the cost, had made it clear that she could phone home as often as she wanted. Perhaps Ludmilla would like a call as well, he had suggested. She felt it would be an extravagance during the day, though, and her need was to talk to somebody now. All Laura's choices, even those which ought to have required some thought, were made according to what felt right. Up until now it had been a reliable system. One of the choices had usually had some kind of unimpeachable moral mascot waving for her attention (possibly with a face a bit like her father's) and her feelings had always nicely obeyed such directives. But now, with regard to the question of whether to phone immediately, or to wait until this evening, her feelings told her strongly that what she wanted was immediate satisfaction, while some other voice said there was something rather underhand and furtive about the phone box thing. She stopped Talbot's car about thirty yards from the corner.

Albert was there, in his too short trousers and his ill-fitting windcheater. She walked confidently towards the box, while trying to show at the same time that she was aware she was trespassing on his territory. Albert didn't react. He chewed on patiently, yet with no hint of boredom. Time seemed to mean nothing to him, although Talbot had said he was regular as clockwork. Perhaps it was precisely that kind of regularity which required no sense of time, only of timing, and that on the hour. It might have been that he averted his gaze a little, but she couldn't tell from what. His head bobbed like a marionette's. His eyes were never focused.

Her father was not at home. She tried Ludmilla, who was hoovering.

'Fortissimo darling!' she shouted. 'Can't hear a thing.'

'Switch off the hoover,' Laura bellowed, but Albert didn't flinch. Ludmilla found the plug.

'Lovely, Laura,' she wheezed, 'I thought you'd ring. Where are you now?'

Laura told her. 'Where the man stands, you know, the chewing man, Albert.'

'Chewing man, darling, is he American?'

'No, he chews his rag.'

'Write me a letter about it will you, darling, that would be better, I think. And everything else too. I've been mugging up "La Cathédrale Engloutie". That and the hoover together – it feels like a dream of being lost in an underground carpark.'

Laura wanted to tell Ludmilla she had dreamed about her. Instead she told her Mr Hardy was very nice and things were going fine.

'Laura listen to me.' Ludmilla coughed. 'The dust bag's leaking,' she explained. 'Hold him off for a few days, can you?'

'Who?'

'Mr Hardy. Don't read the book. I assume there is a copy there? Ahah! Thought so. You're not ready. It will be too soon. How much money have you put in?'

'It's a card,' said Laura. 'Too soon for what? It's my job, I have to type it all up and help him with the script and everything. That's what I'm here for isn't it? Why can't I read it?'

'Because,' said Ludmilla in a sudden moment of quiet – was she changing the bag? – 'I don't want you to know the ending. And you can tell *him* that.'

'But I *know* the ending already. He told me. He died in Spain.'

'Dies. It's a book, not an obituary. And not *that* ending, *this* one.' There was a pause, a very quiet one, and then the noise started up again and it was necessary to shout.

'Do it for me, darling,' yelled Ludmilla. 'Whose service is perfect freedom, remember. Tell him any old thing. Tell him I had a dream you shouldn't read it. He thinks I'm barking anyway.'

The way she said it, Laura thought she knew Ludmilla *had* had a dream.

'Ludmilla, can you ask my father to ring tonight?'

'He's hopped it,' Ludmilla said mischievously, unbelievably.

'What?'

'Ecumenical conference in Harrogate. I think he said he'd ring you from the hotel. If the deaconess lets him, of course. He's due back tomorrow. We've got a date next week. Have you got my letter yet?'

'No, when did you post it?'

'The other day. It's very important. Check it hasn't arrived. I don't want snoopy Hardy poking around after it.'

Laura told Ludmilla she was thinking of another Hardy, the one who had taken up the piano late in life and always arrived five minutes early for his lesson so he could peep in Ludmilla's engagement diary while she was upstairs powdering her nose.

'Quite right, darling, association of ideas. I was only going to say . . .'

There was a rap on the side of the cabin. Laura leaped. It was Albert. Ludmilla was sailing on regardless. Albert was pointing, jabbing at the air with his finger. She turned. He was desperate, his face all pulled about. His rag was screwed up in his hand and where it generally tugged there was a dent in his lip, like the lip of something. Talbot was walking towards her, his jacket slung over his shoulder. He didn't seem to have seen her. He was still about two hundred yards away.

'Ludmilla, I have to go. Could you ring me soon, please? Tonight?'

'Will do, darling.'

Laura had scrambled back to the car before she wondered what on earth she was doing. When Talbot drew near, he gave a sideways salute to Albert, who was gaping at the sky and growling. Talbot shrugged, and was delighted to see Laura. He didn't ask what she had been doing. Later she told him and he laughed. She never thought to ask where he had been.

12

'I'm afraid I haven't been to the village yet,' Laura said, as Talbot climbed into the passenger seat. He was happy to let her drive. It gave her something to do for him. They decided to shop straight away and then drive on to the pool. It was a river really, explained Talbot, but a pool at the bit where he swam.

'I haven't got any swimming things,' said Laura, 'I didn't think.' When they came out of the supermarket, Talbot said he was going up to see a man about a dog, and handed her a two hundred franc note.

'What's that for?' Laura took it and tried not to examine it like a stamp sent by a Japanese pen-pal. Talbot put his hands on her shoulders and pointed her up the road.

'Second shop after the boulangerie, ladies' clothes. Swimsuit. Off you go.'

'I can't possibly,' said Laura quite firmly.

'What are you going to do? Go without?' asked Talbot with interest. 'Okay,' and he made to take the note back, looking pleased.

Laura smiled. 'All right. But it will have to belong to you afterwards. I can't possibly keep it.' Talbot solemnly agreed that it would be kept in a special drawer for future secretaries.

'Let's hope I never have a team of them,' he said, 'or I shall have to organise nude running races on the lawn to see who gets it.'

Laura took the cheapest one they had, all in one, orange with blue bits. She showed it to Talbot as they drove out of the village.

'No belly button?'

'No,' she said, 'I didn't think . . .'

'Quite right,' Talbot said. 'Pop the change in the glove box.' For a moment Laura thought he had said she should change in the glove box. Nothing would have surprised her.

'Now get out the map. See Courtes? We're going right at Fleurac, just before the village. Follow the tiny blue line down to the *n* of Maurillon. That's where we're having lunch.'

It was extraordinarily hot. Laura had never been so hot outside before. Once she had fainted in an English lesson, but that was because the sun was coming through glass.

'You know,' she told Talbot, 'like a greenhouse.'

'Oh yes,' he said. 'Greenhouse. I do understand now.'

She realised that she explained too much. That was because her father never understood ordinary things she said. 'Whose greenhouse was that, Laura dear?' he would have asked, with concern. 'Are you working in the allotments this term?'

They would swim immediately, Talbot said. 'You'll have to do a wriggle over there.' He pulled off his white shirt and the long creamy shorts he was wearing. Laura, who was not acquainted with the boxer short principle wondered if he came here every day and dressed in preparation. It was the first time, too, she had seen a man's body. Jeremy did not believe in displaying God's handiwork unnecessarily. Talbot would have looked dressed with nothing on. She did her wriggle and slipped after him down to the water's edge. She was stronger than she looked with her clothes on, but as with Talbot, there was a place for every inch of flesh on her body, and none left over. He had swum to the other side and was sitting on the opposite bank watching her.

After the swim Talbot brought the shopping out of the car. He had packed it in the supermarket so that every thing they needed would be in one bag. Laura and the vicar did take picnics out once in a while in the summer, when the vicar himself usually made the sandwiches as a special treat for Laura, crab paste with a slither of cucumber often, and wrapped them carefully in greaseproof paper, secure with a rubber band, a hard boiled egg each and a Blue Riband biscuit. On cooler days, of which there were many, they took the camping-gaz and brewed up in the boot. Talbot had bought slices of fresh cut meat, rabbit paté, cheeses, one blue, the other creamy and set with bitter walnuts, a whole jar of gherkins, dusky black olives, two long loaves of bread and a bottle of almost black looking wine. They unpacked together. So much of it was new to Laura, she wouldn't have known where to put it on a table. They were like items in a Christmas stocking, with no clear relation or hierarchy.

Talbot's hair had dried in the sun. Laura's was still wet underneath and at the ends, where it lay in damp licks against her skin. Ratstails, Ludmilla would have tut-tutted and reached for a brush. As Laura had no mother, Ludmilla was the only person who ever touched her hair. Laura detested it. To have hair down to one's waist seemed generally to lay one open to the advance of intimacy by those with whom one was really only half intimate. And people imagined that the touch was imperceptible, that a stroke of the hair with a light, loving finger was a caress to which only the performer could be sensible, a Pygmalion touch, outwards only. Laura had always been too shy to duck or protest, too afraid to hurt Ludmilla's feelings by rejecting what was after all a fairly standard way of saying 'pretty thing'. Now Talbot was watching as she threaded the plait in a seam from the top of her head, like rough embroidery of the skull.

'It will dry frizzy,' he said knowingly, and offered her the loop of cotton which had tied up the parcel of ham.

Over lunch it became clear to Talbot that she must become his lover. The idea was the more irresistible because he had known it, and dismissed it, when he first had seen her from the dovecot with Sally. It was not a fascination with her body. If anything, Sally's was better, stronger, more winning. Anyone who did those exercises of hers three times a week could probably crack Laura's skull between their thighs. It was, he had to admit it, her face, or more particularly the look on it as she turned, time after time, to meet his eyes, answer his thoughts, querying, hapless, entirely new and trusting. Everything he said was new to her, the epic self-narration of an average, worldly, clever man who had travelled and met some people. Perhaps because he was rather more handsome, slightly, but only very slightly, cleverer than most men, and certainly than any Laura could have met, he could have said 'Look, Laura, a blade of grass', and she would have applied her attention, solemn and slightly worried, as though afraid she might not understand exactly what he had meant. 'Look Laura', he would say one day soon, and point out her naked body to her in a long, distant mirror. And she would somehow be surprised, and turn to him for explanation. That was the nature of his desire for her. It was almost pedagogic in origin.

This was surely exactly what Ludmilla had known, and exactly what she had intended. Had she not herself had her initiation at the hands of a worldlier, crueller person than herself, indeed in this very place, and did she not believe that where she had failed, a glorious beauty like Laura could wring triumph, inflict, where she had suffered, pain? And would it only be because of beauty? Was there not also ignorance? Poor Ludmilla, the lovesick clown, romping along, trailing a wounded side, afflicted by what guilt? Does she really need to know?

Laura was beginning to open up. Like her extraordinary clothes, her charm was so particular to her, unimaginable on anyone else, that it seemed to have nothing to do with commonly recognisable brands of the same thing – so that to be on the receiving end of it was an intensely personal experience. Talbot was not the first person to have felt that he was alone in recognising Laura's allure and therefore in at the start of something which promised to be big. Her strangely hesitant composure was like a gift she was not certain you would care for, but which she had chosen with instinctive taste. Talbot was greedy for it, but played it lightly for now. He lay back on one elbow, letting a peach drop from hand to hand.

'So,' he said meditatively, as though he were facing it for the first time with her, whatever it was. 'A friend of Posy's phoned this morning. He may be putting some money into us.' Laura thought at once of piggy banks. Posy Piggy Bank. 'Posy's obviously had a go at him.'

Laura couldn't get used to him talking about Posy as though she had been a mutual friend of theirs. Perhaps the impression was heightened by the diminutive-sounding name, as though it had been 'Mummy' or 'Daddy', some family character to whom they bore a common relationship. She felt it was an improper intimacy, one that the woman would feel had been thrust upon her. Laura wanted badly to know what she looked like, that is, whether she was beautiful. How would it reflect on Talbot if he had been married to someone as plain as a rich tea biscuit?

Talbot was torn between telling Laura about Posy's energy, which seemed to be derived from some mysterious process of fission, perhaps in her personality . . . her long crinkly red hair, eyes the colour of silver firs and the long, slightly bent nose, and letting slip, out of curiosity about Laura's reaction, that Posy's initial desertion of him had been in favour of an English don who looked like Katharine Hepburn and dressed like Calamity Jane. He had a problem with that. It was sexy. Damn.

'Great girl. Gets things done.' Laura's enquiry had been only indirect, but it had obviously not been a *good question*.

'Sorry,' she said, 'it's none of my . . .'

'Oh it might be,' he replied smoothly, she thought it might have been airily. He rolled onto one side and bit into the peach. How he dared! She almost looked away, out of habit. He caught her eye.

'What's up?'

'With me? Nothing at all.'

'Christ,' he said, though she thought it had been quite an unremarkable response. The way he said the word (it was hardly a word to Laura) was so slow and unashamed, with a kind of juicy reverence broken by an underlaugh, it sent a ripple through her. 'You're quite something.' Was that good or bad?

He had the sort of face you always thought the man in the holiday photos next to Princess Diana ought to have, but of course didn't. It was a face to inspire confession. They swam across the river again and sat on rocks on the opposite bank, looking back at the picnic. Talbot said if she half-closed her eyes she would see them both sitting there still by the cheese and the pieces of fruit.

'Look,' he said, 'I can see you sneaking another glass of wine while my back's turned!' Laura was indignant, but her eyelashes were so long and dark that she couldn't half-close her eyes without blocking out absolutely everything. She was condemned to walk round with her eyes wide open. He told her it was a disadvantage in life. When they had swum back again Talbot went to the car for a light and came running back with his cigarette in the air like the Olympic flame.

• Helen Stevenson

Laura waited till he had sat down again.

'I've got to tell you about this morning. I phoned Ludmilla from the phone box. I did mean to tell you, but she was so funny I felt furtive about it. I'm sorry.'

Talbot was delighted with this sub-plot. It was a case apart, in which to pre-rehearse the intimacy he planned. His response seemed to suggest the opposite.

'You don't have to tell me anything. You're not answerable to me. You do exactly what you like, when you like.' It seemed to be a point he wanted to stress, as though he were counting to a hundred and closing his eyes. He *wanted* her to steal away and do these things.

'Is she well?'

He chucked the peach stone over his head. It hit a tree twenty feet away. 'Prufrock eat your heart out,' he said, and winked.

'I don't know. She was hoovering. I suppose she must be. The thing is, she made me promise not to read the book yet. I'm really sorry. I couldn't help it.'

'And you're going to keep your promise?'

'Well, I suppose, yes.'

'Shit.'

'Talbot, I'm really sorry, I just got—'

'No, it doesn't matter. We can get round that. It may even be a good thing. But why did she ask you that? That's what I want to know. Did she say why? Give you any clue?'

'Only that she didn't want me to know the end. Not of the story. Of this.'

'Of *this*?'

'That's what she said.'

'Might she,' asked Talbot, with no view to pursuing the question, 'have been talking about the hoover?'

Laura wondered whether she was faking naivety, or whether it was her genuine naivety that was fabricating a complication between them. After another swim they thought of moving on. He was in a slightly strange mood.

'Can I ask a question?' It was a device, a rhetorical one, for interrupting her father at work.

'Certainly not,' said Talbot swiftly. 'You're paid to keep your bloody mouth shut.'

Laura gave a tiny gasp and sat up on her knees in alarm. It was as though the legless veteran had just wheeled out of the bushes and it was all about to start.

'Laura! I was joking! For God's sake sweetie, it was a joke!'

She had gone quite sick-looking. He held up a towel round her shoulders.

'Joke? Please? Thank God for that. Now. Go ahead.'

Laura pulled the towel around her. She looked like a ten year old who had come last in a swimming gala. After a little while she said, 'I just wanted to ask about Ludmilla.' She had drawn a tent around her body. Even her toes were inside. 'Why did she really send me here? It's not just the secretary thing and my, you know, *horizons*, is it?'

Talbot smiled at the thought of Laura's horizons. 'I don't know, love,' he said. 'Perhaps she's just old and lonely. She wants a lot for you. Things she couldn't have herself.'

'That doesn't make sense, though, if she was Chloe. You said it was the most wonderful part for a girl. In your film. Or . . .' she almost clutched at his arm, 'do you think she isn't?'

'Oh no, I'm sure. There doesn't seem to be much room for doubt. She didn't tell me, and I didn't ask. She wanted a little doubt for me, a little mystery for herself. A little gauze before her eyes stops her confronting what we can all see. What she was and what she is. Time is very hard on people, Laura. You'll have to learn that one day.'

It didn't seem a very complicated thing to learn. Laura thought she might as well slot it in to her knowledge now, since he was telling her officially, to save room for something else later on.

'My feeling is,' Talbot went on, 'that she doesn't want much more than a background seat at the moment. That's where I like her personally. Chloe alive is a dream for me. The backers will love it.'

'And Ludmilla? Will they love her?'

'Now you're learning! Like hell they will!'

Laura waited to learn if that meant yes or no.

'No.'

'But Talbot, she so wants to be famous. She missed all her chances in her career. It would be so wonderful if she could get some pleasure from being Chloe again. Some recognition, you know. She could have been a world class pianist if she hadn't been ill.'

'Something to do with her hands?' He sat up. Laura was looking at him across the remains of the picnic. There was a great deal still uneaten. She didn't know him well enough yet to speak to him without looking.

'It could be, I suppose. I hadn't thought.'

Talbot was measuring his hand-span with a blade of grass. Insects were beginning to swarm over the water, suspended in one pocket of evening air, as though held aloft on some invisible waiter's platter, pricking the stillness like a fault on a screen.

'It sounds hard. Trust me, though.'

That old line. 'Trust you!' Ludmilla would have said. 'Typical!'

'She's an old woman, Laura. Films aren't made in a day. Let's face that one when we come to it.'

Laura rubbed her ankles and said nothing.

'Don't hate me, Laura. I'm a realist. It's the old old story.'

Laura was lost.

'I know it sounds rude,' she said, and she was only ever consciously rude and then apologetically, 'but in a way it is more Ludmilla's story than yours. She's in it. You didn't invent it. So . . .'

'"*The true artist is known by the use he makes of what he annexes.*"'

'Oh.'

'And I'm annexing that towel. Hand it over!'

Laura passed it and started to pull on her shirt.

'And besides, I haven't said this before, but the book is only a springboard. It's got no commercial value. It's all very dated. I'm keeping it quiet for now. That doesn't mean I don't believe in it of course. Do you see?'

Laura, who had only heard this expression in connection with ghosts and God, said nothing. She wondered whether he intended to let her keep her promise to Ludmilla. It sounded like letting her keep a kitten or something she had stolen from a shop.

There was no sign of sunset, but the leaves of the beeches and the white birch had lost their light, which, in the middle of the day, had seemed not reflected but evanescent; now the scene was lit entirely from the outside. They packed the picnic away. He was scrupulously neat with all the little parcels. As they left he looked back for a moment and saw a piece of paper lying in the grass. He put down his bags and walked back to pick it up. It was something that surprised her. You wouldn't find him at the head of a paper-chase, she thought.

13

Ludmilla was a bit alarmed by the number of new departures in her life. Aeroplanes, religious crises (she'd have to think of something to say to the vicar), Intercity 125s heading for the border. My *late* life, she thought, gloomily. Late train, late in the day, late Ludmilla Pike, spinster of this parish. She stood waiting for the train-leaving-from-platform-three-now-standing-at-platform-12b. Please make your way to platform 12b, where the train is now waiting to depart. *Leave*, she corrected irritably. *Waiting to leave*. Depart this life. *Leave* the station. Fortunately she had nothing heavy to carry. This was a round trip on her Awayday saver ticket (blue).

'No bags, love?' the ticket man had asked cheerily as she waited to go through the barrier.

'No,' she had replied firmly, taking the ticket back from him. She held it up in the light to check he'd done it correctly. 'I shan't be needing any bags on today's journey, thank you.'

There was something a little Anna Karenina-ish, she hoped, in the way she said it. The scuttle over to 12b put the lid on the requiem in her head, though. By the time she was safely up the steps of the waiting Intercity 125 to Edinburgh – via York, Darlington, change at Wakefield for all East Coast stations – the sound track of popular classics in her head had found a cheerier groove. Could there be a glimmer to the East for her, she wondered: could life's relentless train not be diverted for a few unscheduled hours, to tarry in the morning glory of Scarborough, Filey or Brid'?

'Plenty of seats to the rear of the train! Tea, coffee, toasted sandwiches, light refreshments.'

A uniformed official came brushing past her as she dithered in the gangway. She'd just rest here a moment. Get her bearings. As the train picked up speed out of the station she watched the official's gait grow heavy, as though the air were thickening and repelling him. She fancied he might have looked appealingly at her in passing, grasping for some solid feature of the visual landscape by which to measure his progress.

She had her reservation. Seat 15b, next to the window, carriage fourteen. Non-smoking. Posy had insisted on that.

'I shall be wearing a green linen suit and reading *Cranford*,' she had said, and Ludmilla had felt as though her acquaintance-to-be had not been deciding this at the moment she said it, but that that was the way it had always been meant to be; she was simply doing a quick check in her wing mirror to see herself sailing confidently past to catch the appointed train at the appointed time on the appointed day. 'There I go,' she was saying, 'Tuesday next, sensible green suit, same one I wore for the funeral of that uncle of Talbot's. Good choice.'

Ludmilla, true to form, had spontaneously replied that she would be wearing a full-length plastic raincoat and carrying a first edition of a novel by Colette. Maybe not so spontaneously. A lifetime's practice in the art of being funny-old-me, first-thing-that-enters-my-head, gave these pearls of eccentricity a distinctly cultured feel. She had found the plastic raincoat in a railway carriage years ago, and was hoping to round things off with a pleasing da capo by leaving it behind her on the train. As for the first edition, she was old fashioned enough to think that Posy, who was travelling north to a feminist writers' conference, would be shocked by the Colette. In fact she was shocked by the state the first edition was in.

In the end, none of this was necessary. Neat little redhead in a window seat. Her identity was confirmed by the predicted accessories but Ludmilla would have recognised Isa's niece in a pair of tartan dungarees down a pothole. The same gilt-flecked green eyes, sickle brows, cheek bones like Striding Edge, no make up required. As Isa would have done before her, she had forgotten and was reading *Silas Marner*. An eager reader, Ludmilla noticed, one of those who gets their finger and thumb around the next page turn at some point near the top of the left hand side. A little greedy. The glass door between them slid open just as their eyes met. It occurred to Ludmilla that here was one kind of door you could not close by standing still. You had either to retreat or advance. 'Tally ho, Ludmilla,' she had said to herself on similar occasions in the past, and it helped to have had a few drinks, but this time she had lost the tongue in her head.

There was a difference, though, between aunt and niece – apart from age. Isa had been twenty-five years old when Ludmilla had last seen her, discounting the odd sighting in tittle-tattle papers, and Posy was closer to forty, though in mint condition. Glacier mint, Ludmilla thought, despite the warm gleam of her well-styled hair. The really striking difference was there. There had been a duskiness about Isa which had nicely blurred the sharpness of feature, an oily chiaroscuro where Posy was pen and ink.

She slipped a bookmark between the pages of *Silas Marner*, put the book to one side of the table and stood up to shake Ludmilla's hand. They swayed slightly as the train swung to one side and Ludmilla was reminded of an early rock and roll routine she had never quite mastered.

'Good morning.'

When she smiled Ludmilla could see why Talbot had married her. It was a near laugh which went up and down and round about her face, even into the corners of her eyes and the tiny muscles below her ears. Ludmilla approved of people who said good morning. She liked to be made to feel like a public meeting. It justified her taking up so much space, she said. She took off the plastic raincoat

'Just park myself, dear,' she smiled, and Posy watched as she unzipped her little fur booties for the comfort of her ankles and slapped at the seat with a suspicious sniff. Her gloves were attached to a piece of elastic which must have run up her sleeves and round the back of her collar, and they danced up and down on their strings as she went through her motions. Ludmilla was slap happy. People winced to watch her read a newspaper. Smack! she would go as she opened out a new page. She showed a similar contempt for the disposables of modern life in her treatment of paperback books. There wasn't a spine in her collection that had not been ceremoniously broken.

She held up a waggish finger to indicate that Posy should say nothing further until she was properly settled. Once she was safely berthed she seemed to wait a few rather theatrical seconds, as though to allow time for the ripples in the extremities of her body to subside. It was a physiological memory, in a way, a mannerism left over from the days when she had been so much larger than she was now. She treated the weight she had once carried like an amputee his long lost limb. Perhaps it was the voluminous nature of her garments that kept the feeling alive. She would have argued in one of her Alice-in-Wonderland moments that you didn't see one legged people going around in half a pair of trousers.

'*Enfin*!' Ludmilla said, when all was ready, clasping her hands in front of her and suddenly smiling like someone who has just read the stage direction before her line and realised it was supposed to have been spoken jovially. Posy resolved her own smile into a well-set, interested little grin, biting off the loose end of her discomposure with her neat front teeth. 'Go on', Ludmilla's expression seemed to be saying, 'you've thrown a six. You to go.'

Posy's voice was surprisingly nervous.

'Well, so you're Ludmilla Pike. What a thrilling surprise! Not to see you, of course, you know, but I don't know, somehow I didn't expect you . . . well, so . . . *soon* . . .'

The train had picked up speed and passengers were making their way forwards to the buffet car. The door thudded back and forth in Ludmilla's ear. She was looking at her hands.

'Now now,' she said, unpursing her lips, but not looking up at Posy, 'you don't *really* mean that do you? Oh, unless of course this isn't Retford after all . . .' A carefully measured rallentando lept suddenly into prestissimo and she was pretending to make ready to leap up from her seat. 'Good Lord, do you mean to say I got *on* at the wrong stop? That *would* be an interesting mistake to have made.'

She looked up at Posy, who was laughing, not least at the idea of Talbot coping with *this*. It was rather an affecting glance. Ludmilla sighed and put her book down on the seat beside her. It was a way of saying she was dropping pretence, unclipping the inverted commas around her charade of herself like a pair of earrings.

'What you meant was you didn't expect me *like this.*' There was a pause without a sigh in it for once. 'I know, I know.'

Posy leaned across and took Ludmilla's hand. 'I don't quite know what I meant. It's lovely to meet you and nice of you to come. How long have we got?'

'Four stops. On reflection I think it probably wasn't a terribly good idea of mine about the train. It felt rather Graham Greene-ish at the time, you know?'

No, no, Posy thought it was thoroughly sensible. She'd been quite relieved Ludmilla had fitted it in this way, although she'd been prepared to invite her down to stay. Talbot had phoned her from a café the morning before. In the background she had been able to pick up a parrot saying *'oh merde!'* over and over again. Even at that distance it seemed to her, in her rather fragile state, that the verbal skills of parrots were striking not because they were so advanced but because the act of mimicry had the effect of undermining the original act of communication, making a mockery of language. It was a beautiful day – he was off for a picnic. With Sally? (No real third-party risk there, she was sure.) She scented a change of mood in his voice, he was excited but assured – she missed a note of panic which had become familiar and, frankly, rather comforting. The call had unsettled her. Nothing distinguished it from the other recent conversations they had had so much as the manner of his ending it – she had no plans to come down – good, no, that was fine, look, he had to go . . . She had replaced the receiver thoughtfully and sat for a couple of minutes staring past her knees at a tuft of glue on the carpet. If anyone had asked her what she was thinking she would have said she was wondering whether the glue would come out with a dab of spirit.

She realised, as she identified her disappointment, that Talbot's call had been a kind of depth charge. He had been assuring himself of a clear head of water, where she was listening out for a scraping of rocks. They had called it a trial separation, but Posy suspected that while she had all but exhausted her fantasy of transgression, Talbot, who had been a bit slow off the mark, was now making good speed. She decided to call in Ludmilla, and was all the more pleased she had done so when Ludmilla told her that her time was very nearly up.

On discovering Posy would be travelling north the very next day, Ludmilla had decided to pretend to an engagement which would make it convenient for them to meet on the train. She had some vague feeling that anything you said at a speed of over one hundred miles an hour couldn't in all decency be used against you.

Ludmilla felt suddenly doleful. 'I've taken rather a shine to locomotion recently. It seems to give some direction to my life. Especially,' and she looked mournfully at Posy's pretty hand grasping her own, 'when I'm sitting with my back to the engine.'

'It's a wonderful idea. I think if we're going to be conspirators we should behave like them.'

'Quite so,' replied Ludmilla, smiling broadly. 'Shall I put my face-concealing rain-hat on?'

Things began to run smoothly. Ludmilla told Posy she would be well cast as a female Robin Hood in a pantomime. 'You know, one of those little tunic affairs in Lincoln Green with scalloped edges, flitting about from tree to tree with a bow and arrow, trying to make your voice sound deeper. Go on, say "halt sirrah!".'

Posy giggled and tried. She was about to tell Ludmilla in return that she would be good as a male Widow Twanky, but stopped herself in time. Other occupants of the carriage were intrigued by the sight, not of Ludmilla in her rain hat – Posy didn't believe she had one, and she didn't – but of the two women, drawn close together in easy good humour on the short threads of a new acquaintance, comfy in their first class accommodation towards the middle of the train.

It was Posy, quite rightly, since the meeting had been her idea, who brought the conversation round to Talbot, and how Ludmilla had come across his advert. Pure chance? Absolutely. She asked how she had found the château after all these years, whether and how much things had changed.

'Not much,' Ludmilla considered. 'A bit smaller, perhaps, to me. Dustier. That's your husband, I suppose. Ah . . . ex!' she added, holding up her hand like an indian chief before Posy could get there herself.

Posy was not complimentary about Talbot although she was

apparently still quite fond of him in a pat-him-on-the-head sort of way. 'It's rather pathetic to watch, really – of course I don't have to now, but I've got a friend who lives out there near him. A good friend. She sees quite a lot of him. Says he's like someone who's got God for the first time – you know the sort of thing – starry-eyed naivety basking in the light of a revelation. With him it's the countryside. *Birds* would you believe it? And wild flowers. Oh, and *literature* of course. Poet *manqué*. The worst breed.'

Ludmilla was wondering who had dropped whom.

'I do feel it's a shame. He's rather gone to pieces. He had so much bite, you know, to start with. Hard-nosed journalist – not an intellectual, by any manner of means, but bright in an energetic sort of way. It's mid-life crisis point, of course, post-divorce reversion to adolescent values. You see it all the time. He was determined to prove he was an artist at heart. Perhaps he thought it would make him feel younger. I told him, there's more to it than turning up on time with your crew and running an efficient Filofax. But I thought, why not? Let him have his little fling. I wanted someone to house-sit while I sorted out what I'm going to do with Monvanité. There's a syndicate of independent PR agents interest – for conferences and the like. And I thought that way at least I'd know what he was up to. But *Pierrot Lunaire*. You've read it I suppose? Of course you have. Well, I ask you! I should have realised that was the beginning of the end.'

'In what sense?' Ludmilla asked. She found Posy's way of talking very modern, a cross between reportage and dramatic monologue. She supposed it was the idiom of the age.

'Oh come on, it all fits together! Classic fodder for a middle-aged none-too-literary playboy like Talbot. Alain Fournier for the wine bar crowd. Let's face it, it's your archetypal trite romance with a few trimmings. And, if you ask me, tongue in cheek from start to finish. It's never written by a man in love! I'd bet my bottom dollar. I couldn't keep a straight face!'

Ludmilla kept her eyes on her hands. Posy's voice was sharp, so that her words fell and died without being softened by any kind of resonance, in a way that seemed to heighten their impact on the mind. Not to react. Not to let it show. Not to spit. Not to weep or to howl. The secret of private dignity. To dissemble, to smile, to whistle a merry tune. She broke apart the clasp on her bag, rummaged with both hands inside, like a dog digging for a bone, and produced a large linen handkerchief doused in some eucalyptus related scent. She gave the end of her nose a punishing polish using a technique traditionally associated with the care and maintainance of brass door knobs. Her mouth was covered by the cloth, her clotted-looking eyes fixed on the window in a way that suggested that more than the world outside was passing before them. They were covering ground at a terrifying rate. She looked up at Posy, for whom nothing would have changed, and took up her invitation to face it.

'Oh, you're quite right,' she agreed bluffly. 'I must say I was surprised at the revival of interest. Still, all the best to him.'

She brandished the hanky in the air as though toasting Talbot's feeble-mindedness. Posy was staring at her, struggling to integrate a new piece of evidence into her scheme of things. She had been so sure this wasn't Chloe. That was why she had laughed – to think, on seeing Ludmilla, that Talbot might have had a moment's doubt. But why else should she be so upset?

Ludmilla was back in order. 'Please try and control that child,' she snapped at a man over the way, and both father and child flattened their backs against their seats as though hiding from the sandman in a dark alley. Ludmilla apologised sincerely to Posy.

'You were saying?'

Posy was back in possession, feeding strands of hair behind her little ears with their perfect diamond studs. She put the half finished subject to one side for a while and tried a different tack.

'It's so strange the way things happen,' she said wonderingly. 'Somehow, somewhere, I just had a feeling you'd crop up. Talbot'd never heard of you, you know that? He rang me just after he'd heard from you, to give me all the gen. I didn't let on. Just *ah*! and *really*! and *Well I never*! You don't get the chance to say "Well I never" very often, do you? It seemed it was time for you and I to meet. And in fact I felt I knew you already, as they say. Aunt Isa's version, of course.' Ludmilla reflected that this was what it must feel like to be a composer and be subject to poor performances.

'What did she say?' It came out rather sharply.

'Aunt Isa? Oh, well, that you had always frightened her a little,

I think.' She wondered how far she should go. 'That she felt she might have let you down. That you made her laugh. That she had loved you in her way?'

'Is that an answer or a question?'

Posy had a slightly American style lilt that sometimes sent a statement pitching over into the interrogative. Ludmilla preferred to let her own question go unanswered.

'We *were* close, yes. Isa certainly had a knack of being close to people. Sometimes it could be lethal.'

Posy laid her hand on Ludmilla's arm. 'Your fingers. That was terrible. She told me about it. It wasn't an accident at all, was it?'

'Oh, we were only children. She apologised. Years later. It was very hard for her, a strange, ugly companion thrust upon her because of the war. The attention her parents gave me – a blundering refugee in her way all the time, playing with her things, forcing friendship with her.'

'Your parents were both dead by then?'

'Of course. I'd been living with Isa's father's cousin – she was a nurse in London. She was fostering me after a fashion. Rather as you'd foster an illusion . . . It was her car in my parents' accident. Their fault, of course, I'm not saying it wasn't, but she felt it was hers. There seemed to be nowhere else for me to go. Then when she signed up for the Red Cross it was off to Lincolnshire and Isa's family. Quite a change.'

'And Isa resented it?'

'As a child would. I adored her of course. She was such a perfect little girl. Then her parents topping themselves like that. Finish!' She smacked her right fist into the fleshy palm of her other hand, 'Finish!' and then said belatedly 'Bang!' addressing the remark to the scolded child, who was watching her in terror and fascination. 'Orphan Annie number two.'

The child looked up at her father who was reading a newspaper.

'Not you,' Ludmilla said. 'Get on with your crayoning, dear.'

She waited, as it were, for the audience to settle. Herself.

'A rich orphan, of course, which helped, but in a world her own parents had already found too painful to live in. They obviously thought she was tough enough to cope or they'd have taken her with them to the bottom of the lake. They left me the little house – I still live there by the way, did you know? – she could hardly begrudge me that. They had places all over Europe. But it didn't help. I never told anyone. Said it was an accident. I could hardly point a finger.'

She lifted her hands, palms upwards, fingers crooked, and looked from one to the other with a cross-referencing glance. She wriggled the fingers experimentally then turned her wrists and tapped out a flourish on the table top. Then she brought them up again, back into the crooked position, examined her nails with a nervous, trivialising gesture. She blew on them and turned her hand face down again, stretching the fingers as she could. Poşy, watching, saw the hands as a thing apart, dislocated from the forearms, like hands thrust into a tank of water, slit at the wrists by a trick of the light. Sympathetic in her timing, she waited for Ludmilla to begin again, which she did, laying her hands aside and looking back up at her audience, as though she had been reading a quoted passage from something printed and was now returning to extemporised speech again.

'I always said it was an accident. I could hardly point a finger.'

She laughed and leaned a chalky cheek on her hand, looking out of the window for a second. She wore a man's watch, with large arabic numerals, for good sense.

'That's a hoot,' she said, and really semed to think so. 'All ten of them were in plaster for five months. But I wouldn't have mentioned it anyway. By the time I was out of hospital the war was over. She was ten, I was eight. She was in school in Switzerland, I went to another foster home – oh, a very nice one dear, very suitable, don't you worry. The Red Cross nurse was past it. Piano playing was a therapy to start with. Later on it earned me a living. Shall we have a cup of tea dear? My throat's a little dry now.'

She had done some rather bludgeoning pencil and powder work around her eyes by the time Poşy got back with the teas. Ludmilla stirred her sugar into the darkish liquid, which looked, she said, like something which had been drained off from the Sunday roast.

'I'm sure it will taste just the same, though,' she said comfortingly, which left Poşy wondering at the use of the word *though* and whether this extraordinary woman often washed down her grief with just a little dripping from the joint. That was the way Ludmilla often got people. She was a kind of Red Queen.

Outside the carriage window, the flat surface of the world slipped past. Cooling towers and churches. High roads and low roads she would never see again. River-banks, some bonnie, some too close for comfort to the cooling towers. 'Twas here that we parted, she thought, then remembered that the Anna Karenina bit had only been for fun. It was a round trip saver ticket after all, and there were things still to be settled.

She snapped the lid back on the little plastic cup and slipped it into her bag.

'Very useful those little things. Do you mind if I take yours?'

'By all means.'

Ludmilla, aiming at archness, raised her eyebrows towards her hairline. 'So. Do you want to hear the rest?'

'I think I know a lot of the rest.' Posy, watching the time on Ludmilla's watch, decided on a change of pace. 'You came to Monvanité by chance. She said you turned up as accompanist to a singer for a summer concert there. You had no idea it was Isa's place until you got there?'

'None at all.'

'And you became friends?'

'Yes.'

'For long?'

'As long as it took.'

'What? What took?'

'For her to feel she had paid me back. Paid her dues.'

Posy edged on. 'Are you sure that's fair? Do you think that's really how she saw it? I wouldn't be so . . .

Ludmilla's anger came down like a butcher's cleaver.

'Listen to me, young lady,' she snapped, but slowly, with almost a little menace, 'I've waited over fifty years to tell this story. You wanted to hear it. You wanted to know – and now here you are, squeezing it out of me like dirty dishwater. Bide your time, be quiet and listen. I will *not* be interviewed!'

Posy was a little taken aback, but she was a working woman, and used to arguments. Besides she did not want to hurt her. 'Please Ludmilla,' she wheedled, taking her hand again. 'I don't mean to hurry you.' She paused apologetically. 'But we have just gone past Darlington.' Somehow the line sounded comic.

Ludmilla was clipping those earrings back on again. 'Well, well, have we really,' she exclaimed, 'what a shame. I might have looked up an old pupil.' She actually took out a compact and started to powder her face. Posy, who was of a generation who didn't do such things, was touched. 'Her husband keeps a pub. I believe she leads the community singing on the piano every Friday evening. Don't you love that? *Leads* the singing. *She trained our leaders*. That's what they'll say when I'm gone.' There was a tell-tale sign of bitterness in the muscle that pulled in a sudden tiny movement to the right underneath her bottom lip.

Posy looked at her wryly.

'Lud*milla*,' she said, and those wonderful eyebrows did the trick. Ludmilla smiled, but something in the smile reminded Posy of the naughty-child mime she had on occasion seen performed by one of her campest authors.

'Oh, all right. Can I tell you the story my way?'

The train was waiting at signals. The guard announced a delay. Never say die though. The buffet was handsomely stocked with tea, coffee, toasted sandwiches, light refreshments . . .

Posy gave a little sigh, and hesitated, as though to indicate that she was not unaware of the pain she might be about to cause. Underneath the table she was putting her two tiny high-heeled feet tidily together, perfectly aligned. If she was right in her suspicions, it was her duty, she thought, to point out to Ludmilla the implications of her situation. She might stand to gain a considerable sum. She had quite forgotten, in her excitement, that Ludmilla would soon be dead. She folded her arms and sat forward a little in her seat.

'The thing is,' she said, unnecessary words, 'I think – aren't I right, Ludmilla – I think you've already told it.'

In the seconds that followed Ludmilla felt she had to decide an awful lot very quickly. On the one hand she could choose deception: I'm sorry, I don't know what you mean; forgive me, you couldn't be more wrong. On the other, friendship, perhaps a reconciliation, relief. The funny paper party-hat she had donned so many years ago, scrunched up in a ball and tossed from a moving train, the love-sick clown restored to ordinary human status as one who had loved and lost, and grieved in an everyday, unsmiling way. No, she could never do that. Fifty years' bravado had done the trick, even if the ridiculously sentimental tale she had spun was still capable of bringing tears to her eyes. She had overcome. *Quod scripsi scripsi*.

She gave Posy a rueful smile. 'I'm sorry. Forgive me. My little joke,' she said.

There was nothing to forgive. Oh! Quite the opposite. Don't apologise!

'I think it's a scream!' said Posy, and there was a little touch of truculence in her voice. 'Talk about giving Talbot the run-around! There he is, out with his shovel and spade, digging up the past, ferretting about after his little worms of truth! Oh dear me, he'd better get on with his Great Imaginative Project, hadn't he?'

Ludmilla was fearless in her anxiety. She wasn't bluffing now. 'You won't tell him?'

'Me? Of course not – what do you think I'm going to do, get straight on the phone and tell him it's all off? You must be kidding. This is the biggest laugh I've had in years.'

Why so funny? Ludmilla wondered. Funny that she might have fancied herself as Chloe? A hoot to have been the author of, what was it, a piece of trite romantic fiction? Hilarious that Talbot thought the book expressed something of the truth of anguished love? Posy was unstoppable, already well into the second lap of a fearless exegesis of *Pierrot Lunaire* as a post-feminist satire *avant la date*. Ludmilla sat tight and counted the minutes, wondering whether 'exegesis' came immediately after 'execute' in the dictionary.

'So what happened to the real Tom Flynn?' Posy wanted to know. She was all wriggly with curiosity and the sleeves of the green linen jacket were riding up over her shirt cuffs.

'Executor,' thought Ludmilla.

'Did he really end up in a trench with his toes turned up? Nothing whatsoever to do with the case? What a *shame*, I really quite fancied him!'

Ludmilla thought that if she told Posy much more she would end up not liking her very much. As it was the feeling of friendship she had had was beginning to look very much like a milk tooth ready to be pulled.

'Don't jump the gun, young lady.' It was impossible to treat Posy like a grown woman. Like Isa before her, she played the little girl game to a tee. She was all flushed and eager, and to hear her giggle you would have put her at twenty years younger. A proper little vixen. She'd met her type before. Oh yes, she had. But they had a lot in common. For all that nature had differently endowed them, they might have been Juliet and her nurse, yet they were both lonely women of a sort. The subject of Laura, of whom Posy had known nothing, was Ludmilla's sweet, accidental revenge. She pretended not to notice the burn of colour on Posy's cheek, but she remembered it, and it was the image that recurred in the days that followed, as surely as if for the whole of their meeting her eyes had only flickered open the one, fractional photographic moment. She had no time to go into details. It was the faintest graze of a poisoned arrow.

'This is your stop.'

Posy started up. 'Oh my goodness,' she said lightly, and started gathering her things together.

They had done a quick demonstrative shuffle round each other's cheeks, and Posy banged her way hurriedly off the train. Ludmilla pushed down the window.

'It all happened for real as well!' she called. 'To other people. Flynn's dead, just the way I told it. But you haven't asked about Chloe.'

Posy put her bags down and came up close to the window.

'She *is* still alive?'

Ludmilla bobbed her head to one side, weighing up the accuracy of the guess.

'Not in so many words. What would you say to a neo-Chloe?'

Posy suddenly had a change of mind. She marched back onto the train, picked up Ludmilla's things, not forgetting her plastic rain coat, and bundled her off onto the platform. She pointed towards the Traveller's Rest.

'Give it to me,' she said. As they made their way across the platform Ludmilla filled the gap by telling her that the plastic cups could be converted into very jolly party hats for her little ones, with just the addition of a bit of elastic under the chin.

* * *

Another table, another little confrontation. Between them a flimsy tin foil ashtray, the kind of thing you might bake a miniature tart in. Posy sucked on a gold tipped menthol cigarette.

'There's the child,' she opened. 'Chloe was pregnant.'

Ludmilla explained what she knew about the child of Tom and Chloe. 'It's a little dynasty of foundlings,' she said. There wasn't much interest there.

'Is it male or female?'

Was she going to ask for age and occupation?

Posy went on to outline her plan. Okay, so Ludmilla hadn't long to live – personally, she said, she didn't believe it for a moment, but it would probably put Ludmilla's own mind at rest if they took her demise as read and worked backwards from there.

'It's early days,' she said, and when Ludmilla protested, added the qualification, 'in the broad sense.'

Ludmilla took note, picking up on Posy's extraordinary lapses of sensitivity and carrying them off mentally to a distant corner for burial and later recovery – that bone again.

'Of course we can't bank on Talbot finishing what he's begun, but it seems more than likely he's going to make a go of it – yes, two teas please.'

The waitress wiped the table with a gentle movement, as though washing an elderly invalid. It was a pleasant intermission, reminding Ludmilla of the existence of tenderness. They both watched closely, following the movement of the cloth about the surface of the table like an ice puck. Just before she turned to go and collect their order, the waitress picked up the ashtray and wiped underneath. She was about to swap it for a clean one, but Posy leaned across and stopped her. 'That's fine, just leave it there—' and as she held out her hand to retain it, knocked over the pepper pot: it lay on its side rather feebly secreting fine white pepper onto the table. Ludmilla righted it. It was clear that Posy was not in a happy state. Perhaps she had rushed in a bit over Laura, but in Ludmilla's condition there weren't many places where you feared to tread. She wondered why she felt unable to offer Posy any comfort. It was partly, of course, her determined affectation of immunity. Posy sneezed violently.

And again. Ludmilla offered her her handkerchief and suggested they change places so that Posy would be next to the radiator (Ludmilla was so hot in the seat that she felt you could have skinned her and turned her hide into a pair of pink and white pyjamas). No, no, said Posy, it was just the pepper.

The tea was, as Ludmilla put it, strong enough to trot a mouse on. She noticed that Posy managed to filter out most of her conversational gambits by affecting not to have heard her at all, a technique which she felt was fundamentally flawed, as a certain measure of perception, however derisory must, in the order of things, precede such unequivocal rejection.

'When Talbot's film is ready,' Posy said carefully, 'you and I go into action.' Ludmilla, who had supposed this would be a *sequitur* upon her mouse comment, waited for Posy to make a bridge between their respective remarks, but it turned out there was none. 'What I want you to do is really very simple.'

Ludmilla was a bit disappointed to hear this. She had been hoping for a hard one. 'Concentrate!' she told herself, but she was feeling slightly light-headed. In my condition, she tut-tutted in her head, and told herself she should most certainly be in bed. She began wondering where the hot water bottle was.

Posy was explaining that when Talbot's film came out Greshams would be publishing the book. She twisted her earring cunningly in its hole. She had regained Ludmilla's attention.

'Of course, now we can be sure Flynn has been dead . . .'

'These fifty year or more,' chimed in Ludmilla in her most Hardyesque accent – Posy stopped and looked at her sternly. Ludmilla was brought back into line. She bit her lip and picked up her cup of tea.

'. . . there will be no royalties to pay.'

Ludmilla brought her cup to her lips amd found it was empty. She put it back in the saucer and pushed it away.

'Unless . . .'

'Ah . . .'

Posy smiled. 'Unless.'

Ludmilla didn't need the money for herself. She had already paid for her coffin – she'd been putting a bit by over the last few years – and her original estimate (six by four by two) had come down a bit as she had cast off the weight of the years. Nor did she need Posy's flattery, she told herself. What she needed – had always craved – was complicity, which, *faute de mieux*, came in fairly close to love.

Posy's idea didn't seem all that simple, despite the claims she was making for it, but as a Red Queen, Ludmilla could move in all directions and was really pretty flexible. Posy explained that it was necessary to act immediately in the view of the fact that she – you, she said – would probably not be around for the publication of the book. 'We're looking at the end of next year,' she said, and Ludmilla felt like replying that they might well be, but that she – I, she said – could not see it for the life of her.

'Exactly, but we will be able to see you.' said Posy sweetly. 'Get the picture: Talbot's film comes whooshing out to an accompaniment of sickly violins, Kleenex shares go through the roof, and Greshams time it perfectly so that the book comes out at the same time. We point up the satire in the blurb and Talbot falls flat on his face. Now what I want you to do is help us make a little video – just tell your story – I'll write it for you if you like.' It appeared that Ludmilla was to be a sales tool. Posy had to repeat the expression several times over, as Ludmilla had got it into her head that it was some spooneristic rendering of toadstool. Her posthumous glamour would be transmitted nationwide. She could wear the yellow and black striped trouser suit.

Back in London the next evening, Posy bumped into Hugo Grears, an ex of Sally Fairfield. 'You're an ex of Sally Fairfield, we've met before,' she challenged, and Hugo felt rather insulted that the prefix was not to be awarded a susbstantive. The fact that he was no longer whatever it was he had been in relation to a mutual friend of theirs seemed to be enough.

Hugo was an actor. Posy wondered if he had ever played a conman.

'It doesn't matter, it doesn't matter,' she finished, as he began to describe the moment in Macbeth when the first murderer (whom he had recently played – Posy, listening with half an ear gained the impression he was talking about some inter-thespian sports event) says to Macbeth, 'We are men, my liege,' to which Macbeth answers, 'Aye, in the catalogue ye go for men,' and this was an idea Hugo would have liked to have expanded on, but as Posy said, it didn't matter.

'Anyway,' he said, and he was someone who used the word to stand alone. It seemed to stand as a signifier of hopeless eloquence, which was one of Hugo's better cards.

'Put that down and come with me,' said Posy, and she took the glass out of his hand and propelled him from the party. Hugo allowed himself to be rolled out of the door, feeling he was being rather bundled off the stage at a moment when he really could have been ready to make an impression on the evening, until she told him they were going to dinner round the corner from her flat in Beauchamp Place, when he decided it was time to stop worrying and loosen his belt.

14

Talbot recognised several people in the Café du Sport. Madame Derrault herself, of course, who was reading classified advertisements in the local newspaper. She was looking for a second hand bicycle to replace her present one, which was too cumbersome and heavy. She fancied something a bit more modern-looking – made by Peugeot, or Renault, perhaps. Talbot was afraid this would involve her in a serious clash of periods. The glint of chrome and metallic blue and the busy little wheels, no more than two hand-spans across, and the white plastic basket would not sit well with the billowing skirts and the canary cage on top. Such disparity would not get past the continuity man in his head. In the corner of the cafe, the parrot, Le Touquet, hung upside down from pebble coloured claws, his wings half opened upwards. like a prophet's arms. His colours were definitely English preparatory school – a smart dark grey, with scarlet details, and a black emblem on his brow. He would not talk for Talbot. Otherwise there was the priest, of whom Talbot had an irrational fear. He was oily silky and sat with his legs wide apart. You could see the tracery of a string vest under his smooth black front, which swelled like a fruit towards his belly. Talbot had a bit of a thing about any profession which required its practitioners to wear seamless shirts, the type that doesn't button down the front. Talbot was a nonpractising Anglican. The priest discomfited him. He wondered for a moment about the Reverend Jeremy Cranshawe. Father Bénoit had just been served a pastis. He lifted the water jug and filled his glass. The drink clouded up like dirty chalk. He was deep in conversation with Norman Davies, an Englishman in his sixties, who ran a bookshop in the village. Talbot knew Norman vaguely. He kept meaning to invite him round, but was unsure of himself. He doubted whether there was a gay underworld in a place the size of Soubyrète, but was loath to risk appearing to want to sign up. In fact he was quite wrong about Norman, and it was probably Talbot's loss.

Talbot shook hands with Madame Derrault over the counter. She poured him a cold beer. They agreed that the weather was very fine and that the north-east wind had subsided for the season. News on the General was less bright. Andromache could clearly afford to be fussy, as she was, and they had thought the General would be getting somewhere near her class. But although the General was keen, in fact he was devoted to Andromache, she was clearly holding out for something better. Yvette had apparently said that things were looking more encouraging than they had done and that they should let the General be for another couple of days.

He was Talbot's first dog, bought off a friend of Sally's in the Dordogne. He was first generation French of stalwart English stock and already two years old. Talbot had never had a dog before, and found all this blind dating a bit public. He felt for the dog, who had to suffer not only the humiliation of having Andromache forced upon him and falling for her on the spot, but being a widespread subject of gossip.

Madame Derrault wanted to know about Laura's linen.

'I can manage it if it's only once a week,' she said, 'but if she's going to be wanting it more often than that she'll have to have a spare set. I know what these young girls can be like. My sister's daughter washes her hair every morning and evening, which can't be good for it. Those sheets can't go in the machine. I'll do them once a week and if *more* is necessary she can take the *linge ordinaire* from the cupboard.' Madame Derrault had that way of talking about cleanliness which always made you think immediately of its opposite. Talbot was sure Laura could fit in perfectly well with Madame Derrault's weekly wash of linen.

'I'll show her how to use the machine, though, so she can wash her own clothes.' Talbot was squeamish about Madame Derrault's prurient eye and washed all his own underwear. He wondered sometimes whether Madame Derrault might not think he, or Englishmen in general, didn't wear any. A couple of months ago it had become clear that Andromache was very much on heat and Yvette had slipped a pair of her husband's underpants round her to keep her clean. For a time Talbot had been wary of open discussions with Madame Derrault in the bar, but there had been no embarrassing association of ideas.

Epuration was a bit of a speciality with Madame Derrault. Besides being responsible for the laundry of a number of single men in the village, Norman included, and very possibly the priest as well, she was a member of the committee which was to organise the cleaning of the church sarcophagus in the autumn of the following year. This was a ceremony performed only once every couple of hundred years. The sarcophagus contained the relics of two Christian martyrs, brought to the village from Rome in the ninth century, hidden for safety in barrels of drinking water. Ever since, the sarcophagus had produced copious volumes of purest water. Sealed and free-standing, lifted clear even of the cobbled courtyard where it stood supported by two blocks of marble, it had defied the examinations of international scientists and its gift of water was widely regarded as a miracle. Every year on the fourteenth of October, the date on which was celebrated the arrival of the relics in the village, the priest distributed water to the sick. This year, after the sarcophagus had been emptied, a team of four local women were to give the marble a gentle scouring and rinsing to remove the slime which had built up over the centuries on its interior walls. On the last occasion when this had been done, in 1794, after the tomb had been desecrated by passing troops, it was recorded in the church annals that women had wiped the tomb dry with clean linen, only to find that as fast as they wiped, the sarcophagus produced its pure mysterious water to drench their cloths. Each of the women had recounted the incident in her own words, and the accounts had been transcribed and signed. Although the cleaning team had reputedly been chosen by the priest for their virtue and faith, Talbot felt that Madame Derrault, who regularly wiped the floor with the reputations of other womenfolk, had been largely recommended to the priest by her professional competence.

The public telephone behind the bar began to ring and Madame Derrault answered. As she talked she tickled the parrot in slow motion with her forefinger, and it swung lazily from the roof of the cage. Talbot thought of its blood rushing to its head. The conversation was rapidly concluded. A plumber in another village was selling his late wife's bicycle, a recent model, immediately available for collection, without a scratch. Her earlier call had foundered on the subject of the price. He was ringing back to say she could have it at the price she wanted if she could come and collect it herself. They reached an agreement.

'Said he thought it was worth more than that.' Madame Derrault's shake of the head suggested it was not for herself that she lamented the way of the world, but for others, the little ones to come, the gentle and meek.

'I told him it was worth as much as I was prepared to pay, no more than that.' She was lost in linen. 'Verteuil, now, how am I going to get myself up *there*, I wonder. The bus isn't what it was.'

Talbot, whose French was sometimes a little slow, wondered what it was now. Madame Derrault's next gesture was so far from being spontaneous she looked like a magician at a children's party who has just clicked that there might be a rabbit up his sleeve. She opened her eyes wide and stared very hard at Talbot, as though he were giving her an idea.

'Yes?' Talbot queried sweetly, holding out his glass for more beer. Madame Derrault dismissed the whole idea of the rabbit as too absurd for contemplation. Just put that rabbit right out of your mind, she was saying, and started to wash the glass.

'Another ... little ... beer perhaps?'

Oh it was too much, she would let herself believe it might just be possible.

'I'm not one of these people who *likes* to ask a favour, Monsieur Hardy,' she explained, 'but then it's difficult ... oh, very difficult ... for a woman on her own.' Half a minute later, Talbot had agreed to pick up the bicycle. After all, as Madame Derrault pointed out, his lady friend, oh, what was her name now, *la blonde* lived over that way didn't she. Talbot deflected her with a proposition. He would do her the favour in part exchange for her own old bicycle, which he wanted for Laura. She agreed, but held out for door-to-door delivery – in his own time, of course; he'd probably be wanting to get back for whatever the *jeune anglaise* had made for lunch about now. Perhaps he could get over there some time this afternoon and then Albert could bring up the old bike and collect the new one this evening. Talbot said all right, but he couldn't be too precise about times, his movements were a bit hazy.

'Albert is very punctual,' said Madame Derrault. Yes, agreed Talbot, that was one of his strong points.

As soon as Talbot got back to the château he took the phone into his room and called Sally. She was delighted to hear from him.

'You remembered!' she cried. Talbot had not remembered at all, he had even forgotten what it might have been she thought he had remembered. It turned out to be a dinner party she was giving that evening for Nancy Dingwall, an American naturalist from the University of Southern California who was researching a guide to the natural history of South West France. Sally had met her on a canoeing trip on the river. Talbot was slightly intrigued by Nancy, whom, since she was American and academic, he suspected of being an evangelist for the women's movement and kooky to boot. It was difficult to drum up any French guests. Home entertainment seemed to be a concept unknown, or at least wisely ignored by the French, so that an invitation to a dinner party would be matched on their part by a meal in an expensive restaurant. Such reciprocity became embarrassing for both parties after the first few occasions and Sally had had to restrict herself largely to the expat circuit, which was notoriously dull and amongst whom conversation tended to revolve around recent developments on *The Archers* and the impossibility of buying gentlemen's relish in France. Sally was feeling optimistic about this one, however. She had managed to invite a rather celebrated female novelist who lived not far from her village. She was mugging up on her books. It was all about magic realism, and mythic transpositions of desire. The novelist's husband was coming, which would be good for Talbot, since he was extremely rich and looking to invest in films, well television, but it was all related, she said. The last thing Talbot wanted to do was scoot over to Sally's for a whole evening. The thought of leaving Laura on her own while he knocked back martinis with Sally and her friends who weren't even her friends and, worse still, of having to go into all that with Laura, held no appeal. He had imagined a quiet evening at home with her. He meant to cut the tennis lawn and rig up a net. They could drink Pimms and lemonade by the laurel tree and he could work up to telling her she looked like Chloe. But he would have to go to Sally's, otherwise Sally would get suspicious and start to ask questions. She seemed to have forgotten about Laura, or was delicately avoiding mention of her.

'I won't be able to stay long, Sally. It's a long drive back.'

Talbot and Sally's relationship was actually very new. She was very much his type, good fun to be with, gossipy and excitable. They got on well together. Talbot would never have considered making any long term commitment to her – that would not only be the last thing he wanted right now, it would also be quite out of order, he told himself, considering she was herself only quite freshly divorced. He was happy to keep things ticking over as they were. He had not expected Laura to interrupt anything there. He had reached an age where he had almost forgotten about girls in their near twenties. He didn't come across them all that often. Some of his friends' daughters were coming up to their late teens, but they were a dull, pasty lot, bread dough like, who would emerge from the oven of marriage and foreign holidays in twenty years time looking more like themselves. When Ludmilla had talked about Laura, her shyness, her many talents, her sheltered life, her need to see beyond the limits of her father's parish, the picture which had sprung into his mind had been of girls of the bread-dough type, plump and bitchy, pulling the hair of a plain little mouse, in an A-line skirt and lilac blouse, who wouldn't even know how to play backgammon. She might be useful about the place. She could sleep in the garden room if she was a real pain. She would frown at his cigarettes.

'All right, but I'm sure there's a reason why I shouldn't,' he had told Sally over a refill of Armagnac one evening. And then at breakfast, 'I've got this girl arriving soon to do some secretarial work. A friend of a friend of Posy's. I'll have to get Madame Derrault to sort out her room. It probably hasn't been slept in for forty years. We don't want her getting earwig shock on the first night.'

'Or worse,' said Sally, who had recently been dealing with

rats. 'I'm sure she'll be ... very robust,' she added coldly, as though she were delicately finding a circumlocution to prevent her openly predicting a pair of whacking thighs and a doughnut fixation.

'She'll be frightfully efficient and jog to the village for *pain au chocolat* every morning at six.' After divorcing an acquaintance of Talbot (to whom she now referred in Talbot's presence as 'your chum', a near relative of the 'your father' device he remembered his mother using in unworthy moments), Sally had traded in her girlish enthusiasm, which was wearing a little thin, for a form of withersome wit, which glinted with polish and was certainly no longer running in. Talbot had only mentioned Laura in passing, which was unusual, because they didn't have that much to talk about and the arrival of domestic help, as she called it, was the kind of thing she could be relied upon to make much of. Besides the fact that the film script and Ludmilla Pike were a sore point – had been ever since Ludmilla's dreadful visitation – he felt reluctant to open up on the matter to Sally. He didn't fancy Sally on the subject of his domestic inadequacies and his need for a female hand about the house. One never knew where that might lead. She was a nice enough girl, but her finger nails were too long by half, and, despite her intense interest in the domestic arts, was distinctly lacking in the interior design and furbishings of the cranium. The exterior finishing was well achieved, however. She looked the way wealthy no-longer-young women had started to look in the last ten years – radiant with yoghurt. He couldn't help feeling there was something rather *fin de siècle* about the relationship between that surface sparkle and those roving, live bacteria within. Such middle-aged youthfulness was unnerving. His father had once compared his own mother's face to a book, densely written and full of wisdom and picaresque charm. This was probably something he got out of a review in the *Daily Express*, which he read on the way to work and put carefully in the bin as he got off the train. Sally's face was more like a sheet of recycled paper.

Though Talbot was, as he was wont to say, the wrong side of forty, he was not yet showing any signs of physical deterioration; at least, those which he bore worked to his advantage, like signs of distress in the kind of furniture Sally sold in her expensive little *atelier* in Montmarcy. A child, perhaps even Laura, might have called his hair grey. He thought of it as greying and that at the temples. His face, with its long swooping nose and dark skin, was sensitive, and it was not difficult to imagine him weeping. He often wore an anguished expression in unguarded moments, but it could lightly be interpreted as a squint against the bright mediterranean sun reflected off the distant snow peaks of the Pyrenees. On the morning of the week before, as he had sat for the first time drinking black coffee with Sally, it was probably that his hangover was beginning to emerge like a rusty spring through the lavish upholstery of Sally's breakfast. She had looked nice at that breakfast – swathed in a generous drapery of pastel hue, well tuned calves coiling winsomely about the legs of the garden table. But he had had to be off. He had taken a quick look inside her aga, which she said was playing up, and promised to bring along a new oil filter for it next time he came over. He was struck by the intimacy into which such discussions could lead one. His view of her until quite recently, perhaps until the night before, had been fairly dim, though so was his memory of how the glow of desire had crept up on him in the half light and the haze of the drink and the gradually softening pallor of her perfume. In the bright morning, even with every noise quivering like an electric eel in his ear drums, and her body fresh and showered and looking pleasantly clean and ordinary, he had felt in danger of liking her slightly more than he didn't not like her. The memory of a gaping oven door leapt out from childhood, the fairy-story punishment for greedy boys and girls, suddenly flashing up as an image of marriage. The goblin peered out at him from the aga and he quickly slammed the door shut and hurried out to his car.

So much had changed since then. The thought that he would have to leave in six hours time to drive the twenty or so kilometres over to Sally's house was an impediment to his present happiness. He wanted to close the gates and wall himself in with Laura, say 'now it begins', but with a closing of curtains against the world.

15

Laura was in the herb garden, reading a letter. They'd discovered it lying on a table in the hall that morning. Talbot had handed it to her with a quizzical look, recognising the handwriting. He said that Madame Derrault had brought it up from the village on her way home the previous evening. The postman never went as far out of his way as Monvanité, and had come to an arrangement with the proprietress of the Café du Sport by which it was agreed that she should deliver Talbot's letters when she passed. Talbot did not know what the postman had come up with to match this generous gesture.

It was the third time Laura had read her letter. Her skin was already darker; a dust of freckles had appeared on her shoulders and the bridge of her nose. She was wearing a single piece of fabric, peacock colours, around her waist and a plain white sleeveless shirt. Her clothes had been thoroughly and frequently washed, which had taken some of the colour and all the ostentation out of them. She was glad to get the letter. The day before she and Talbot had been to collect wine from a cooperative half an hour's drive away and they had been out most of the evening. When they got back he had shown her how to siphon the wine out of the big red plastic barrel into bottles, and when she had put the corks in and drunk her first ever second glass of red wine she had gone straight to bed. The phone had rung while she was still folding up her clothes, but Talbot did not call her.

Ludmilla's letters were always rather difficult to follow. Her handwriting, which had once been striking, was fragile with age, and around the time when she had given up style and taken up with crimplene trouser suits she had also abandoned the fountain pen in favour of the throwaway biro. Even so, this one looked like a fair copy compared to her usual off-the-cuff communications, and Laura wondered whether she had kept the original. She imagined Ludmilla sitting at her painfully small writing desk, licking the envelope with two sharp flicks of the tongue and smoothing down the edges with her fist. The only piece of furniture which really fitted Ludmilla was her grand piano. It was just the right size for her, although the little drawing room was far too small for it. The notepaper had its usual garland of pretty flowers which wove delicately around the border, accentuating the thorniness of the script.

On the first page Ludmilla had copied out a poem. Laura looked at it quickly then put it to the back.

De sinistres, de noirs papillons géants
tuent l'éclat du soleil.
Tel un grimoire fermé repose l'horizon muet.
D'une fumée venue d'infinies profondeurs
se dégage un parfum, meurtrier de la mémoire!
De sinistres, de noirs papillons géants
tuent l'éclat du soleil.
Et du ciel vers la terre
s'abattent de leurs lourdes ailes
invisibles, ces monstres
sur le coeur des hommes . . .
De sinistres, de noirs papillons géants.

(Sinister giant black moths
block out the sun's bright rays.
The silent horizon lies
closed, like a book of spells.
Smoke, released from deep darkness,
gives off perfume, to blight memory.
Sinister giant black moths
block out the sun's bright rays.

Wheeling down from the skies
Beating invisible wings
On the hearts of men . . .
Sinister giant black moths.)

Dear Laura,

You cannot fail to have arrived before you receive this letter. I am planning that it should be waiting for you when you get there, but one never knows these days. I have laid all my best plans out, but I shall have to accept that I cannot command the postal system.

In my mind I can see you there. Did you take the peacock skirt I gave you out of the attic, and wear it with the white shirt? I know you will choose your colours with your usual *élan* (this is a very good word for charades, dear, particularly for 'Catalan'). If Mr Hardy has been in television, perhaps he will like to photograph you. You will be the old and the new, as usual, black and white in face and hair, but resplendent colour in your lovely clothes.

The poem I quote, from memory I may say, no copying, for my poor brain is not quite addled yet, there must be some particularly efficacious brine within this old skull, is a sad one for me. It comes, of course, from *Pierrot Lunaire*, the poem cycle by Albert Giraud. I never cared for the Schoenberg. I shouldn't be surprised if you were getting an earful of that now or some time soon. Frightful noise, if you ask me. For once in my life, my teaching life that is, I can say to you – concentrate only on the words. I remembered it today because I was reminded of butterflies by the imminence of death. More of that later.

I was once quite an expert on butterflies. (Do you remember when you learned the Grieg, 'Papillon', and we looked at those plates in the museum?) Those *grands papillons noirs*? I suspect Giraud is thinking of the Giant Peacock Moth, *Saturnia pyri*. They are certainly large, with a wingspan of up to fifteen centimetres. People often mistake them for bats. They fly in May – they like the blackthorn; perhaps that is why you should never bring it into the house. Found mainly in Southern Europe, occasionally as far north as Paris. Or perhaps it could be the closely related Emperor moth (*Saturnia pavonia*). A strange species – only the female flies at night.

I meant to talk to you before you left, but when you popped round I only had those couple of minutes for you before Mrs Beech came for her lesson. How I hate adult education, but she pays well. Her husband, you know, is an accountant and is going to fiddle my books for me. I am afraid that very shortly I shall be dead – natural causes. There, now I've said it. I am going to leave my piano to you, and something else too, if things go well. Mr Beech is advising me wonderfully – never be shy of opportunism, dear, treat it as a gift of the gods and have some fun on the way. I say shortly – well, I'm not all that sure when exactly – but I am already feeling like a great old soggy butterfly which should have died out years ago, heaving myself from pillar to post. Your father is to become my spiritual adviser, on death, that is. What a charming man. If I am not careful I shall allow myself to be seduced onto the tea committee. Another butterfly – why didn't I think of it before? – Old Lady, so called because its wings resemble the dark shawls worn by elderly Victorian ladies.

What a wonderful time it must be for butterflies and moths at Monvanité in June. The Giant Peacock likes orchard trees, as well as blackthorn, so even if Mr Hardy has neglected to prune for fruit, you may yet find something luscious there. It was always awash with lepidopterae in my day, and things like that shouldn't really change, at least, they must repeat themselves sometimes, it depends if it's a good year. You will have noticed how I like repetitions. My memory has faded. Perhaps, as the poem says, a certain perfume has extinguished it; a misremembering of a fragrance can make all the difference. I hope you wear no perfume yet. And you may be a plain Peacock, *Inachis io*, with your blue eyes edged with brown, and your fine feather dresses. It has an almost black underside, which serves excellently for camouflage, particularly during the winter. Did you know that some butterflies may hibernate and emerge in the following spring, although by this time they are often torn and faded? But let me not be morbid. I picture you, just emerged from your silk lined chamber, flitting through the garden flowers.

The caterpillar of *Inachis io* feeds on stinging nettles, I'm afraid, but let us not dwell on the past.

What shall we choose for Mr Hardy? Perhaps you will not know him well enough yet to say. Spanish Gatekeeper, Grizzled Skipper? Dingy Skipper, Death's Head Hawk, Coxcomb Prominent (I like that one)? Feathered Footman, Striped Grayling? The Drinker? Yes, there is even a butterfly called The Drinker. Two-Tailed Pasha?

I having been telling myself I should have briefed you more thoroughly when I last saw you. But I wanted so much for you to be free. Freedom *to* is so much easier to arrange than freedom *from*. I should perhaps have tried to warn you against Mr Hardy, which I must not do, for I am a biased old lady and you a very sensible young one . . . It is good for you, you know, this travel, and Mr Hardy, however poor a fish, may teach you a thing or two.

Yes dear, I'm sure you think him very fine. I should not wish to discourage you from falling for him, he is attractive enough, for the short term. Cut your teeth on him a little. See what he can teach you, but do not forget that men are in the end poor whippets, and as easily duped. Did you know a male butterfly will fly up to greet anything at all which is about the right size and colour? Now I am not suggesting that you are not the real thing, but take that from me, darling, who know you of old, not from Mr Hardy and his like.

And now I come to what I most want to talk to you about. (Goodness. five pages gone already, this will weigh a ton). When I returned, a month ago, to see Mr Hardy at Monvanité, I had no thought in my head other than to help him, in whatever way I could, to realise his project. It had always been a sadness for me, particularly in the light of the great intimacy which, before her marriage, existed between myself and Isa Fontaine, that she had never seen fit to publish *Pierrot Lunaire*. I have tried to explain this to myself in many different ways. Perhaps, in the end, it was jealousy. She was not a jealous woman, except I suspect that perhaps after her marriage, she came to resent the freedom I retained, living the way we had always lived, carrying on in my own way. *Pierrot Lunaire* must have shown her quite how much that was the case. We had quarrelled bitterly by then, as only women can.

Still, something moved her. They say her marriage was not unhappy. Why did she leave the manuscript to Posy Hardy if not that she at last forgave me? I welcomed all this, and crossed the channel in great haste to celebrate the new life which I foresaw for that old story of ours.

This is the difficult bit.

I always held myself responsible for Flynn's death. I have to tell you darling, that I drove him to war (that is as in 'Ah me, I drove him to it', not as in 'Hop in, I'll give you a lift'). What I mean is that we had a rather violent falling out one day, about his work really – he had written nothing for several years, and his talent was withering. He was always full of grand sentiments, political ones mostly, he was a communist you know – we all were in those days – but for months he had done nothing but drag himself round Europe sponging off rich friends like Isa. I hit home pretty hard, I suppose. I packed my bags and left for Italy. A month later, Flynn was killed in Salamanca – a very beautiful place to die in, there is that. I returned to Monvanité, knowing nothing of his death, en route for London. It was early autumn then, and I wanted to check that the piano was safely in storage. Isa gave it to me. I had the feeling none of us would be back for a long time. It was like tidying up a corpse, you know, the cotton wool in the cheeks and all that. A telegram had arrived, and later Flynn's effects. That's where I got the photo from. It was the only address they had for him.

Anyway, Isa wasn't interested in the book. End of story. Until I got news of Mr Hardy's project, it seemed that there was nothing further I could do. She did not return the manuscript I sent her, and I myself was too dispirited to enter into any correspondence with her. It occurred to me, I think, that one day she would forgive me and that eventually the book might even see the light of day. It has taken all these years for that to happen.

Imagine, then, with what joy I rushed to your Mr Hardy's side, anxious only to help in whatever way I could. And then, you ask, and then? (You will perhaps notice a certain similarity darling, between the wistful tension of my prose and that of *Pierrot Lunaire* – or at least you would if you had read it; take my word for it. Consider, if you will, that it has rung in my ears these fifty years and more). Well, and then I changed my mind. I had a change of heart, as they say, which in these days in which we have come to expect so many wonderful things of medical technology, would not actually go amiss.

Talbot Hardy bears a resemblance to Flynn. Not physically, so much, although there are certain things. An attractive man, as I have said. But that arrogance disguises a baleful lack of courage (and I know it is not my place to reproach Flynn for lack of courage, but we have talked about cowardice and foolhardiness, and the mean which is courage, before). Greater love hath no man than this, said the Son of Man (Son of Man, why won't they get it right, must bring this up with your dear father) that he lay down his life for his friends. No doubt that is how Mr Hardy will show it in his misty soft focus wrong end of the stick way. But remember that I was not Thomas Flynn's friend by that time, and he did not lay down his life for me. Full stop. No, I am not dictating this to my daily, but I do find the American way of writing punctuation telegraph style effective on occasions. And his emphasis on the biographical – where, when, what, how and so on. These journalists are all the same. Representing the truth my foot! Do you believe, as Plato says, that if they understood the things they represent as well as produce images of them, they would seriously give themselves up to making these images and take that as a completely satisfying object in life? Here we go, page 322 in my copy darling, beginning to read at the very top: 'I should imagine that, if he had a real understanding of the actions he represents, he would far sooner devote himself to performing them in fact. The memorials he would try to leave after him would be the noble deeds, and he would be more eager to be the hero whose praises are sung than the poet who sings them.' You will notice that Plato is talking of poets here, although for my purposes that is not so far removed as to make the quotation inappropriate. You might think that would give the lie to my statement that I lost my sympathy, admiration, what have you, for Flynn. Not so. But I am sure he made a wonderful soldier. Let us imagine he died a noble death, it will uplift us, darling, as well as him.

You know what else old Giraud says? *'Le rayon de lune est la rame, un nénuphar sert de nacelle; là-dessus Pierrot vogue vers le Sud avec bon vent.'* (The moonbeam is the rudder, nenuphar serves as boat, on which Pierrot goes southward, wind behind his sails.) We girls were the same, but for us it was more of a physical malaise, literally exiled in some cases (more of this one day), while for them it was a spiritual one, I think.

Oh, Mr Hardy will get his hard facts, as he calls them. I shan't begrudge him documentary evidence, as he calls it. He shall have every last bit of it. It is important that the order of events should be correct, however, that we should not spill our beans before time. Spilled beans, as a little horticultural experience, which it is to be hoped you might acquire this summer, would tell you, tend to grow alarmingly tall in quite the wrong places.

Must dash now. Feet need a soak.

Cheers darling,

Ludmilla.

Laura could not understand how so long a letter could still seem cryptic. It ran to over sixteen sheets of paper. No wonder it had been late arriving. Ludmilla had no sense of economy. The final sentence just tipped the top of the last sheet of paper. Laura's experience of intrigue was very limited. The kind of letters she was accustomed to receive were short and newsy from friends who had moved away or from her pen-pal in Lille, whom Laura had never met, and who wrote with more panache than accuracy about her older brother's birthday parties and Dutch rock groups who were touring northern France. She had never realised until now how a letter at the moment of delivery entails the recipient in inescapable complicity. A blind eye was a much more difficult thing than a deaf ear, in this case.

Talbot was watching Laura, fondly, he thought, from the top of the steps which led down into the herb garden. A herb garden is rarely aromatic. The scent is held close within the leaves of the plants until the sun moves off it in the evening, when the secret phials seem to ease a little open and release their tangy flavour onto the air. Talbot had meant to pick mint for the pitcher of julep he had made up in the kitchen, but mistook the plant and gathered leaves of lemon balsam. He went over to Laura with his cuttings and interrupted her reading, offering her the leaves as a mock posy. Laura slipped her letter back in its envelope.

'It smells of mosquito repellent,' she said correctly. Talbot sniffed with a cross expression and realising his mistake, turned it to his advantage in taking Laura's wrist and rubbing the herb across it like a dock leaf on a sting.

'That should keep you safe then,' he said rather weakly and knew that he was stylistically committed to retaining her hand. He turned it over and looked at the back. 'I shall have to study the back of your hand before I can say I know you well.'

Laura told him that Ludmilla had said that the people she could say she had known like the back of her hand were the people to whom she had most often waved goodbye.

'That is a little like what I meant,' replied Talbot.

Laura's hands were not things of great beauty, and it was rather that thought than the idea that Talbot might not be allowed to hold her hand that made her detach her fingers and stand up.

'I'm sorry I wasn't there when you got back. There wasn't anything left to do – I sorted out the books for you and put them in the cabinet.' Talbot had a large collection of mostly twentieth-century novels, some in rather fine editions, others simple paperbacks, which he had not, until now, got round to unpacking. There were over five hundred or so of them. He was finding these tasks for her to do, things which seemed to suit her, because he did not want her to read *Pierrot Lunaire*. Nobody wanted her to read it. Talbot had begun to feel that it would be like showing her a photograph album in which she found pictures of herself, pictures he might have taken the day she arrived when she paused to adjust her ribbon, or eating by the river, or just now, reading her letter, pictures he could not possibly have taken without her seeing him do so.

He had once spent a month living with a family in Buckinghamshire, a wealthy old English family who had 'welcomed the cameras into their home' in order to allow a discreet study to be made of their fading lifestyle. Talbot, as director, had done his job well. The family had gradually begun to forget the presence of the cameras and to lift the veil of circumspection and propriety which at the beginning of the experiment had blurred the prurient lens a little. It never happened completely though. Talbot had felt in the end that it had been less of a social study than an essay in the nature of observation. He thought that was probably why it was useful to believe in a god. He felt that a television crew in the house could perform much the same function. The mother of the family had sought grace on one occasion when she feared that a row between herself and her oldest son had been caught on film. He had been able to bestow the gift upon the supplicant and rip the film from the camera and put it in her hands. She had run it through her fingers like a rosary and thanked him with tears in her eyes. Things got a little complicated when Talbot started to receive nocturnal visits from the mother. Luckily he knew the time and place when it was appointed that the camera cometh, so omnipresence was put on hold for a bit.

'I have to confess,' said Talbot, wanting her so much to know, 'that I was spying on you just then. I think I shall have you cast in stone to sit there even in wet weather. Like the little mermaid.'

'Oh, that's such a terrible story,' Laura said, and she said it for herself, but then added, 'Ludmilla says it could never have been written by a woman.'

'Oh come on, Laura,' exclaimed Talbot angrily, notching up their second moment of intimacy by ripping a young spur from a tree, where an insect later brought disease to the clean, open wood. 'Why must you see everything through her eyes? Stop hawking her round like some scraggy old familiar.'

Laura's hand tightened on her letter, and she felt Talbot look at it in exasperation.

'Sorry,' he said, shaking his head and putting his right hand on her right shoulder, standing behind her as she looked blankly away from him. Then suddenly he gripped both her shoulders, then shot his forefinger past her ear. 'Look! Green woodpecker!'

'Where?' Laura whispered back, never having been aware that she wanted to see a woodpecker in her life before, and surprised by how much she wanted it now. It was easier to follow Talbot's gaze than meet it. She saw the woodpecker fly once more before he disappeared into the park. By that time Ludmilla's letter was well out of the way. Once again, Talbot had prepared lunch.

16

She watched Talbot's car disappear down the drive with some relief. He had been very nervous about leaving her on her own; at least that was how he said it. What he meant was that he didn't want to go. That was clear even to Laura. At the same time, though, she realised that he was actually grateful for the opportunity to leave her. It allowed him to make this reluctance to be parted from her explicit. He actually kissed her on each cheek before he left. It was a long time since he had kissed a cheek which was not dusted with stale-smelling powder. He tried to make it an automatic thing, a familiar sort of cheerio but be back soon, but as Laura was not used to double kissing she did not know to turn the other cheek, so that Talbot had to duck round to the right of her to affect the second half of the manoeuvre. For a second she thought he might have seen another green woodpecker.

She had stood there thinking that if she blushed or touched her cheek she would be the guilty one, for making it obvious that this seemed to her more than a purely social performance. Yet she knew there was something strange about it. It was clear that she was not being allowed to slip into the role of his employee. He was doing everything to prevent that – cooking for her, wine at meals, commenting on her clothes, saying that he must show her this and that, and that he wanted her to come and look at a painting he wanted to buy. And yet if he had wanted them just to be really comfortable together and rub along well, which was perhaps a kind of intimacy whose rules she could easily have adduced by drawing on the experience with her father, he would have behaved towards her in a less stately fashion. There was a delicacy and restraint in his manner which made it seem all the more intimate. There was less awkwardness of the day-to-day type than she encountered in life at home. When Talbot spilt red wine all over his shirt because he tripped over the telephone book while trying to reach a catalogue he had wanted to show her at the same time as dialling a friend in New York, he had pulled off the shirt and poured half a packet of salt over it before the phone was answered at the other end. He never seemed to hesitate, or rather any hesitation was voiced out loud with such a well paced command of the rhetoric of 'either-or', or 'perhaps on the other hand', that he never seemed to be personally at a loss of any kind. Laura was impressed by such displays. He would never say 'I didn't know that', but rather 'Christ, I'm completely ignorant about the whole thing. Tell me about it.' This had happened twice that she remembered. Once when she had told him that she was interested in stained glass windows, and the second when she said that most of the cooking experience she had had at school had been in baking. He was going to see if they could get hold of some fresh yeast. He never said 'get', always 'get our hands on' or 'get hold of', which made it feel an altogether more vigorous and exciting undertaking.

There was no doubt that life with him was exciting. Whenever he told her about things he used a tone of voice which might have been appropriate if he had been describing to a sceptical fellow gourmet the extraordinary subtle and sensational flavours in a particularly *recherché* dish. If something required her special appreciation, he would lower his voice dramatically. Perhaps, it suggested, the information he was imparting was so sensitive, so private, that although he would gladly share it with her, she being the kind of confidante he might in a different life have raked the entire earth's surface for and never found, it would not do for any old leaf or passing housemartin to pick up on it.

Maybe it was Laura's clothes which encouraged his theatricality. What struck her as strange was that the thing he was apt to paint most vividly, with recourse to the greatest range of facial and manual gestures, of vocal dynamics and general adverbial activity was the truth. 'I'll tell you something, Laura . . .'; 'Believe me, Laura . . .'; 'What in actual fact turned out to have happened . . .'; 'The thing is . . .' It was probably because he thought her so naive that she couldn't be expected to accept anything plainly, only if he surmounted her provincial incredulity with the full rhetorical weight of his sincerity. Because she found the implications of this awkward she tended to meet it with a slightly exaggerated calm which made her respond in rhythm with the metronome in her head – miss a beat after his last exclamation mark, then one, two, think, speak, draw a pattern in the dust at the same time with a slightly unsure smile to indicate that she wasn't giving the full weight of her attention to her own response, even if she was being maybe a touch over-earnest in delivering it. Ludmilla would have come straight out with it and called it sexual tension.

When she was sure that Talbot wasn't going to come back for anything he had forgotten or to announce a puncture or an insufficiency of petrol, she went upstairs to her room and fetched her diary. She meant to go and write it in the walled garden where the herbs grew. She had four days to catch up on. In the kitchen she looked inside the fridge. Talbot had said she should 'fix' herself some supper. The word implied to her the probability that some unenvisaged frustration would arise during the course of her preparations which would have to be met with a slightly out of the ordinary, even not quite natural solution. This proved to be the case, although she never did come up with the solution.

Talbot had come back from his shopping expedition with enough food for a fortnight, he had said. Putting it like that sounded as though he were stocking up for a period of incarceration, or as if, associating with the old Germanic derivation, they were to have fourteen sumptuous midnight feasts. Even so, there was hardly anything in the fridge she recognised. Shallots, where she was familiar with onions, huge red peppers looking like pantomime noses, a carton of blueberries, sheaves of chard, flat field mushrooms, mange touts, tiny potatoes no bigger than the ones her father planted in the autumn, slices of translucent ham, pickled baby cucumbers and a bowl of delicate little pale blue eggs. There was no bread, no milk, no butter. The cheese was not the kind you put in a macaroni cheese, the only Italian dish Laura had come across, which her father had learned to make during the war. It was difficult to know what to do.

She looked about the kitchen with a caricature of a puzzled expression on her face, as though half afraid Talbot might be watching her through the window. She wouldn't like to disappoint him by looking ordinary and vacant when she thought she was alone. It wasn't so much through vanity as because she knew he expected a certain enchantment. He had made a point of that. She generally found that if she acted her normal self he was pleased enough, but doing it to a fault was not always as easy as you might expect. She found some brown rice in a jar in a cupboard. No label. No instruction. It might need some special treatment. She might burn the pan. Better stick to something cold. She was uncomfortable at the thought that whatever she used from the stock of food would be noted missing. What was no longer there would be the thing she had taken. There was something disturbing in that. Talbot had caught her somehow on the hop, and yet it was the very simplicity of the food, the finished quality of each fruit and vegetable which prevented her from being able to see any of them as ingredients. She sliced a cumquat down the middle. The fruit was so tiny that without its skin it could be of no possible nutritional value. The cartwheel of orange flesh was no bigger than a fingernail.

In the end she ate an apple, then washed the white silk dress she had worn the first evening in cold water. Her hands were brown from the sun and looked oddly dark and unfrivolous against the fabric. On her way out to the garden it occurred to her that the copy of *Pierrot Lunaire* was sitting around somewhere back in the house. She could go and find it, read the words which no one wanted her to see. Laura had been so raised on good discipline and stringent rules of behaviour that she had never actually had to consider morality. It had never really cropped up. To do or not to do a thing was a question of whether or not it was proscribed or encouraged. Nor had she had any experience of temptation to practise on. New situations, which up to now had rarely arisen, required an empirical approach, a precedent by which to categorise the nature of the difficulty and the correct way to deal with it. Still, Ludmilla had asked her not to read it, and Talbot said that he had a funny superstitious feeling about it, that something would go wrong with his plans if she, of all people read it. She was like a charm, he had said. He hadn't said what plans. She closed the heavy front door behind her. It had weathered badly and the wood splintered and squeaked dryly against the stone entrance step.

Laura hung the dress from a line which ran between the medlar and the magnolia. With no pegs to hand she fastened the tiny mother of pearl buttons over the slack rope. It was like dressing a marionette. It sagged like a stone in a sack with the weight of the water. She had not liked to squeeze it out too hard for fear of damaging the threads. She did it all very neatly and properly. The hanging up of clothes was such a familiar action, and yet so unlike anything else, with the water trickling backwards up your wrists.

At home it would never have occured to her to hang washing out as darkness fell. In fact it was so unthinkable that she wondered whether there might be an old wives' superstition that night could stain the washing. Perhaps, she thought, it was more that the neighbours might pop over the fence in the dark and pinch your knickers. Knickers was a Ludmilla word. Sometimes Ludmilla's soul flitted through her head like a swift at dusk. She could never be sure she had seen it.

Three stone steps, not enough to call a flight, connected the herb garden and the paved walkway which ran round the inside of the wall. Laura sat on the bottom-most step. The west side of the garden was unwalled and she could see the dovecot in the distance. She had not been as far as the dovecot yet. There was no path from the house across the field to where it stood among the tall grasses. Talbot had said there were rats. Country rats were different from town rats, but rats all the same. It was their fleshy pink tails whipping round corners she remembered from the time they had had them in the school room at her father's church, a kind of backlash. Like the cockerel's legs, they would be easily severed. She wondered if they were there now, scuttling purposefully about, bowling stolen potatoes along the stone floor. The light was too far gone for writing. She laid her diary on the step above and watched the slow drip of water from her dress form a pool on the hard baked earth, listening to the squawk of the birds – an orchestra before the overture, each player practising his party piece, trills and runs and dismembered snatches of tune, while there was still time for virtuosity. One by one they subsided, over perhaps three quarters of an hour. The tiny flowers Laura could not have recognised, pink campion, yellow spurge, and white meliot had buttoned up against the dark. Only the huge white arum lilies caught the light of a sickle moon. Their stout pollen bearing batons glowed in the dark while the desiccated bouquets of ransom flowers already brushed the ground like burned-out party lanterns from a different age. There was no possibility that she was dreaming. The air was growing colder about her face and she had been thinking about Talbot at his dinner party. And yet when the figure wheeling the bicycle appeared in the shadow by the wall her eyes almost drifted over it. She recognised Madame Derrault's bicycle. The front wheel cut half into the moonlight on the wall, so that when it was lifted away you might almost expect to see a pale print on the stone. The visitor had not seen her. Feet splayed, not with the nonchalant stance of the orator at ease with himself, but like clock hands painfully stuck when the mechanism has moved on. Head nodding not in emphasis but vacantly, lost for a meaning. Hands fiddling for buttons at his throat. A whimper escaped him as he bent forward to touch the dress, and for the first time Laura saw Albert smile.

Slowly he moved his hand up to the right hand shoulder and his fingers felt the three dull glassy buttons in a row. The tip of his forefinger covered two of them, and he did not seem able to bring his thumb up to close the movement. He shuffled forward to gain a better balance, then hooked his wrist over the washing-line, drawing it towards his face. Laura didn't move. With a neat movement, like a seamstress biting off a finished thread, he nipped off the buttons one by one and let them fall gently from his mouth into the pool below. The shoulder slipped from the line, and the dress hung, swinging very slightly with the hem brushing his knee. Laura moved her foot deliberately against the stone step and he started with the same movement of fear that she had recently stifled and saw her sitting there in the dark. She said nothing, but with a strange, half flirtatious gesture, stepped over to the dress and held the free shoulder against her own. It was her dress. She could not put it on for him, it was still wet, but she could hold it against her body and animate it vaguely with her form. For a moment she thought Albert might run for it. He covered one eye with his hand and swayed backwards and forwards a little, peeping through his fingers. It was a show of delight. Laura smiled back at him, suddenly wildly happy with their meeting.

The noise of a car made Albert jump. He had been looking steadfastly and shyly at the different parts of Laura's face, as though he did not expect her eyes to move when his own did. She felt she was witnessing a process of unforgetting. As the headlights beamed up towards the house Laura touched his arm.

'I have to go,' she whispered, but he was already away, stumbling up the bank, making for the field and the long grass. 'The bicycle!' she cried after him, but he did not seem to hear.

When she looked down she could only find two buttons on the ground. The third he had kept concealed beneath his tongue. Later she wondered whether it was really true that he couldn't talk, or whether it was just that he had a precious store, hamster like, of things which wouldn't let him open his mouth.

Back inside the house Talbot was rushing from room to room, banging open doors, calling her name. She ran up the stairs after him and met him coming out of her bedroom. When he saw her his whole body suddenly sagged and his panic seemed to leave him like a pain. A bat swooped down the stairwell and was gone into the night. Talbot circled her with his arms, and still holding the car keys, pushed her gently against the wall and kissed her.

17

The telephone in the bedroom rang early. This was bad luck. It forced Laura and Talbot to turn and face the outside world immediately they woke. It would have been much better if they had been able to rehearse in daylight, just for a few moments even. In a split second of wakefulness they became a couple side by side, not facing one other; like flat paper dolls, a matching pair, joined at the wrist, looking outwards. Talbot was grateful for this.

It was Posy calling from London. Three of the four potential backers were in Cannes and wanted to come and see him at the château next week to discuss *Pierrot Lunaire*. She was going to try and get in touch with the fourth, but he was thought to be off philandering in Belize. She also had rather an interesting proposition to put to him. 'Stop picking your toenails darling, and listen to me for a minute.'

Talbot was irritated. Here he was in mid-production of his own very real *Pierrot Lunaire*, with the sun on the shutters and his Chloe in his bed, and here was his ex-wife chivvying him about some pale facsimile he had once dreamed of mocking up. Posy sensed as much.

'You haven't lost interest have you darling?' she asked anxiously. For a moment one part of Talbot's mind flicked independently to falling bank rates and back, and he was brought back to heel. He was lying on his back with one leg stretched straight out in front of him and the other with the sole of the foot on the bed and one brown knee pointing up at the ceiling. The sheet, Madame Derrault's laundry, their linen, was doing a good job of concealing what at this point was best concealed and setting off the walnut tan which made Talbot look so good in bed. He swivelled the speaking end of the phone round through one hundred and eighty degrees so that it stuck up into the air like an ass's ear and rolled onto his side. Posy talked on. Talbot leaned down and silently kissed Laura's cheekbone, where the face is most vulnerable beneath the eye. She smiled and bit her nail. Her hair seemed twice as long against all the sheets and her white cotton nightdress, and it hid the right side of her face. She had to keep very still so that whoever was on the phone wouldn't hear her. The conspiratorial nature of this display of discretion further sealed the fact, not yet discussed, that this had all happened and would happen again. She would have had to have made alarm her first reaction if she had wanted to bring it up at all. It was too late now. Stealthily Talbot slid his arm underneath her and settled her against his left shoulder as he stared back at the ceiling again. She had no choice but to stare at the ceiling too. So that was how the whole thing was normalised, giving Talbot yet one more thing to thank Posy for.

Posy seemed to have had a lot to say. Laura, who didn't know it was Posy and didn't know enough about Talbot's life to make even an educated guess, felt intruded upon and intruding. If this was what she was to do, if this was her place, she could only suffer it to be so if it were in isolation, totally abstracted and unconnected to any other part of life. If she was to be an awakened sleeping beauty she wanted those trees to keep growing higher and higher, and the broad green belt of undergrowth to thicken and darken. Talbot clicked the phone down, telling Posy he'd think about it and call her back.

'Morning princess,' he said very cheerfully. His face was slightly rough against her own. The whole world of men in the morning, unshaven men, men flat on their backs in bed, men smelling of sweat and biscuits, men contrasted against swaddling white, men debating whether, if ever, to get up, began that morning.

The night before, when he had kissed her for long enough to reassure himself that she was there and that she would let herself be kissed again, he had taken her down to the pink *chaise longue* in the library and sat talking to her, holding her hand. She had listened with her chin in her other hand while he stroked her hair and talked into her eyes. He had been an hour and a half late for the dinner party – had got the time wrong. He never wore a watch and had told Laura to take hers off when she arrived. It was still sitting in the dining room on a small bamboo table. He had checked the time on it before he left. It had been set still to English time. He had been extra late because of Madame Derrault's bicycle, which was now in the back of the car. By the time he arrived they were well into the wood pigeon in red wine, which probably meant that the evening was not going well, that conversation had by no means impeded the consumption of Sally's food, which was not usually of such tip-top quality that it could actually stop a conversation in its tracks. Sally obviously blamed him for this and made matters much worse by being rude to him from the moment he arrived.

'How was she rude?' asked Laura.

'In her own way. She knows my ex. She came up with the story of why I was here. She made it sound as if it had all been Posy's idea.'

Timidly Laura asked if Sally was Talbot's girlfriend.

'Oh no,' he was able to reassure her. 'Just an old acquaintance. We've known each other on and off for years. But she likes to make out there's something going on. She's a good girl really, one in a million – like a green bottle left on the wall.' He laughed. Laura wasn't quite sure what he meant.

'Is she pretty?'

'Is she *pretty*?' Talbot wondered. 'Not bad. All form and no content, though,' he said vacuously.

Then he told her the tale of his discontent, how he had felt a physical compulsion to come back and find her, to be able to see her again. He had driven like a madman along the twisting roads the moment he could escape the after-dinner patter – which, he told her, was an interesting word usually ascribed to the cheap running-commentary of conjurors and other practitioners of low forms of entertainment, deriving from the low mechanical fashion of a priest's delivery of the Paternoster. The priest would only pipe up loud and clear, he said when it came to not leading us into temptation. Talbot called this emphasis heathen and Laura was so far from understanding what he meant that she wondered if the word had a secondary meaning.

He explained about the bicycle, and Madame Derrault's updated image. Laura told him Albert too had come with a bicycle and left it in the walled garden.

'Jolly good,' said Talbot. 'That's for you. It's a Chloe bike. You can sit up and beg on it.'

Laura didn't tell him about the incident in the garden, in case it got Albert into trouble.

Talbot had come clean with her. He told her that since he had first seen her he had known his life would be changed, purified by meeting her.

'I'm just a cynical old divorcee, at least that's what I thought till last Tuesday,' he said. 'When I saw you standing by the bay tree I knew that all this preoccupation with Flynn and Chloe was part of a search for innocence. I'm not a corrupt man, but I was tired of the way my life had turned. I knew too much perhaps. Meeting you like that, it was like shedding layers and layers I just didn't know I had, but at the same time remembering something I had forgotten, some kind of memory unpeeled. It's as though my love for you already existed before I met you, and seeing you standing there was a revelation of it. I can't believe I'm talking like this to you. You're going to think I'm mad.'

Laura was a bit embarrassed – not by his confession of love, she loved him too, he was the only man she knew – but by the way it made him look at her, made them both look at her as some kind of pre-existing figure. After all, he couldn't have loved her all his life without knowing who she was, since she wasn't anybody at all until he was well into his twenties. Talbot told her not to be a pragmatist. He talked about her beauty. She had not heard this from a man before, only from Ludmilla, and considering some of the things Ludmilla found beautiful she had always been unable to feel flattered. Their conversation was endlessly trivial and absorbing and revolved around themselves and the tiny things that had attracted them to one another, and the extraordinariness of having met at all. Laura could think of nothing, would allow herself to think of nothing but that Talbot loved her and Talbot was the only man on earth she had ever known, forgetting her father, and that she saw no reason ever to know another. He was all men to her and the trees would grow higher and higher. His worldliness was all she would need for life, his knowledge would be enough for her, the rest she could choose out of old books. She could not see that it would be wrong to say yes when he asked her to lie with him. In bed he had kissed her and let her sleep. There would be time for all manner of things later on.

Talbot's room was above the library and down the corridor from Laura's. The walls were white, pocked with tiny blue fleur-de-lys stencils. On one wall was a huge engraving of Château Monvanité, seen from the park. In the foreground a shepherd sat with his back to the viewer, looking over to the château through the trees, as though waiting for someone to emerge. A large bookcase with glass doors and a key stood against the wall opposite the door. They had not closed the shutters the night before. Laura asked if she might get up and look out of the window. Talbot, thinking of the light passing through the cloud of white cotton, laughed and said she didn't need to ask him for permission. Laura was slightly put out. It hadn't been permission she had wanted, so much as leave, which was a different thing.

She went out onto the little stone balcony with the wrought iron railing. The stone beneath her feet was already hot. From here she could not see the dovecot – it was not in line with Talbot's room, unlike her own. She could see straight across and down into the walled garden though, where the black bicycle still leaned against the bricks. On the saddle was a shower of red rose petals. The white dress was still hanging there, bone dry in the sun. It was too old and pale to fade. Strangest of all, there was Madame Derrault, snipping down chives to a stubble with a brutal pair of scissors.

Laura turned to Talbot, who had come up behind her and placed his arms around her shoulders.

'What's she doing here?'

'I've told her she can take whatever herbs she likes. Things will only bolt if we don't use them up.'

Laura wanted to get out of Madame Derrault's line of vision. It would be all over the village. 'Why not?' Talbot said. 'Give them something to talk about.'

'Because they'll talk about it all the wrong way.'

'What's the matter, we've nothing to be ashamed of.'

Laura's heart dipped a little. This was the kind of adult shorthand that made you fear that the original complex thought behind it had suffered the years' decay. Shorthand was riddled with ellipsis and error in her mind. Perhaps living innocently in a prurient world all her life had taught her a proper respect for malice. She turned back into the room. She wanted to cry. She knew it wasn't that she was Talbot's mistress. She knew there was a proper enchantment. She didn't want anyone else to give it so much as a moment's thought. Of course they all already had, and it wouldn't have made much difference what scenes Talbot and she played or suppressed there alone in Château Monvanité, although Laura didn't know that and Talbot probably did. Wanting to cry wasn't disingenuous, no more so than running up a flag or wearing black, deliberate as they are. It would simply go to show that she meant what she could not say she felt. She slipped back to her own room, where the shutters had been open all night.

Talbot shouted to Madame Derrault that her new bicycle was in the back of the car. She should go and help herself. She stopped nipping at the herbs and looked up at him standing in the wrapped-around towel at the window. It was the look of a hitherto impossible-to-charm housewife who has just been given a wink by a celebrity game show host. Then she seemed to recollect what he had just said. The bicycle had been outside her house this morning, she said. Hadn't he dropped it off last night? Me? No, said Talbot, he had been back very late and hadn't been able to get over. She told him Albert had been up in the garden with the old bike for Laura. He must have hung around in the bushes and found the new one. They were both rather worried by this. Albert would have to have an eye kept on him. He seemed to be developing a capacity for independent action unknown until now.

Laura could still hear them chatting. She came out onto her own balcony and could see Madame Derrault looking up at his window. As Talbot withdrew, she turned away smiling, then caught sight of Laura watching her from her own post. They must have looked to her like some kind of Swiss timepiece in a market square. Laura nodded and withdrew. Talbot popped out again.

'I was wondering if you'd be free to do some cooking for me next week,' he called over to her. 'Six or seven people.' Madame Derrault thought that could be arranged.

'And the *Anglaise*?' she inquired a little slyly, peering up at Talbot with an expression that would have been coy had she not put about forty years on it by pulling her chin in sharply and raising her eyebrows, so that the skin between chinbone and throat blew out and back in again like a frog's. Talbot assured her Laura would be around to give her a hand. Laura, who overheard all this, felt put down. She had yet to understand the nature of her privilege in being loved by her employer. It was not vanity, nor in the least a disinclination to work which had somehow led her to feel that Talbot's ecstatic recognition of her qualities, his falling in love with her, his placing of her far above him, his claiming to be unworthy so much as to gather her up in his arms, might have precluded his speaking of her with someone like Madame Derrault as though she had been little more than a scullery maid who might well bungle the washing up. Such hyperbole *was* vanity, on the other hand, but the thought was not worked out in sufficient detail for Laura to notice.

18

It was Ludmilla's shopping day anyway. She liked to go to the market and get a bit of fish once a week. All the serious shopping was done at the superstore by her daily, but Ludmilla kept a few things in reserve for her own expeditions. Her house was near the town centre, so unless it was raining she could easily walk. On the day of her meeting with the vicar she closed her front door behind her at ten o'clock in the morning and set off, towing her little shopping trolley, with a determined spring in her step. She had an hour before she was due in a small, rather chintzy tearoom at the other end of town. Aware that the shopping trolley on its little castors was ridiculous, she made a bit of a game of it and pretended it was a sort of little dog.

'Hup! And *over!*' she encouraged, bumping it over a huge crack in the pavement where a tree root had erupted through the surface. Some of her fellow shoppers took well to this little conceit, others gripped their children a little tighter by the hand and hurried past with eyes fixed well ahead. Ludmilla felt it was a case of more fool them; if they actually believed she thought a shopping trolley was a dog they must be well on the way to barking themselves.

When Ludmilla had said, both to Laura and to her father, that she was shortly due to die, she had not, for once, been exaggerating. She had a clot on the heart and the young doctor at the hospital had had no qualms about giving her the news straight. She was the type who would much rather know.

'What makes you think that?' Ludmilla asked him after he had broken the news to her. People had been making this sort of mistake about her all her life. 'In retrospect I should far rather not have known. But I should probably have died of curiosity first.'

She was not feeling particularly ill, in fact she was fine. She felt mentally alert and wondered whether that might not be a sign that her body was indeed in an advanced stage of inward decay. The bit about anticipating a religious crisis had been untrue, but she wanted to be sure Laura's father would turn up. Nothing like the prospect of bums on seats, even aged ones, to get a preacher going. She had already decided that she would pay for their morning coffee and, knowing that the bill would be presented to him first, she relished the moment when she would say, 'Pass the plate, please, vicar.'

It was a grey Lincolnshire town. Flat and woldy, with a hint of salt breeze come from miles and miles away to the east. The traders were mostly local, though a few came down from the fishing ports of Hull and Grimsby with refrigerated lorries. Tuesday and Friday mornings, come hell or high water. High water didn't happen all that often, thanks to Dutch engineering. Hell happened most days now, with the mess they'd made of the ring road, but the lorries generally seemed to manage to get through. Ludmilla fancied a bit of mackerel for her supper, and a few gooseberries to make a sauce. She made for her favourite stall. She favoured this one in particular because the trader wore a boater and a white apron which was invariably smeared with fish blood. He knew Ludmilla well, although only from fish selling. He had an adroit way of smacking the fish around which reminded her of a circus seal. She wondered whether fishing smacks were so called because of the sound made by walloping them out of consciousness on the side of the boat.

'Good morning Mr Lipton,' she said.

'Ah, morning Miss Pike. Be with you in a minute love.'

Ludmilla didn't like his knowing her name – she suspected it encouraged him to feel a rather macabre professional interest in her. They did a deal over the mackerel, with a few cockles thrown in. She looked away as he brought the cleaver down on the fish head. It always brought her mind back to the sash window and she crunched up her knuckles protectively as it fell. The filleting was done in no time.

'Time a lady like you learned to do it herself if you ask me. Nothing to it.'

'That is precisely why I consider it not worth learning,' she replied, but in a friendly enough way. Anyway, it was squeamishness, not ignorance. People never expected her to be squeamish. 'You're too big for that,' they would probably say, although what size had to do with it she didn't know.

Passing a bric-à-brac stall she was attracted by some old printing blocks laid out in a tray. She ran her fingers over them, picking past the familiar old chestnuts – telephone, acorn, horses running (a little worn), till she came to a little cameo of an eighteenth-century tea party she had not seen before. The stall holder was fishing brass candlesticks out of a cardboard box beneath the till. She slipped it stealthily up her sleeve while he was rummaging and moved casually along. It was the first theft of her life, oh no, the second, but the last one didn't count. It was a thrilling feeling, but a little bit frightening. The thing would probably only fetch a pound or so, though, and that would have been daylight robbery. 'You know I'll beg, steal or borrow (yes I will!) to bring you sunny days!' she hummed lightly, swinging her little cart round the corner after her, for all the world as though she had been fourteen and playing the Artful Dodger in *Oliver Twist*.

'Oh, hello,' a little flustered. 'How are you?'

'How are you?'

'How are *you*?'

It was Mrs Colderstone, mother of thirteen-year-old Gavin, whose fingers she had rapped a little too sharply during last Monday's painful, G-sharpless rendition of 'To a Wild Rose'.

'Blooming, thank you.' Was it a reference?

'And how's Gavin this week? Practising hard for his exam?'

'My husband was going to ring you, actually, Miss Pike. Gavin won't be coming to you any more. He wants to play badminton for the school and he can't spare Monday nights. I'll put a cheque in the post for what's owing.'

Mrs Colderstone was clearly embarrassed. She was wearing a pale turquoise Marks and Spencer turtle-neck through which her breasts stuck out like glasses under a magician's concealing cloth. It was a real meeting of the titans in that respect.

'Well, now,' said Ludmilla generously, 'I suspect that with a little shuffling of my *hectic* schedule we could fit . . .'

'No,' said Mrs Colderstone emphatically. 'No, he won't be needing any more piano.'

'No more piano,' Ludmilla mused. 'I see.' She was fingering the printing block inside her cuff, which she had pulled down to cover her hand. 'Well, all strength to his shuttlecock. He probably *is* better to stick to something one-handed. Give him my love.'

Mrs Colderstone was left standing as Ludmilla towed her cart off with all the dignity of Mother Courage after the news of another defeat for the army. Someone touched Mrs Colderstone's arm. It was the man from the bric-à-brac stall.

'Scuse me, Missus,' he said, jerking his head after Ludmilla, who must have been out of earshot, 'what do they call her?'

'Why do you want to know?'

'Just lifted something while I weren't looking. M'wife saw 'er at it.'

'Ludmilla Pike. Did she now, would you credit it? What was that then?'

'Ludmilla Pike, eh. Right, well, we've got her number all right. I'll see her coming next time. Sorry to bother you. Don't say I asked.'

Mrs Colderstone doubted whether she would have the opportunity to do so, what with Gavin's pianistic career coming to such an abrupt halt, and under such circumstances. She might happen to let something slip at the next parish council though. Old bitch. 'I 'ate her,' she said to her husband that evening, with fish-fingers.

Ludmilla carried on past the stalls, picking her way as daintily as nature allowed through disintegrating chip bags and the odd smear of lettuce leaf. So Gavin Colderstone was to be withdrawn. Well, he was no loss. If she had had to listen to 'To A Wild Rose' once more played without the G-sharps it should have and with the D-sharps it shouldn't, she would have taken a hosepipe to him. Interesting though. A little unsettling even. Tell Laura. No, she couldn't do that. Couldn't. Could . . . not . . . Stupid child. My God, she was crying. Plop! went a tear onto her cheek, and charged off like a downhill skier straight out of the hatch. She couldn't go down into the Ladies under the road. It was unspeakable in there, and there was her trolley. Nice comfy looking dress shop.

'I'll take that for you dear. Did you want to try that on?' It was a pink dress, the kind you'd wear to someone you didn't like very much's wedding. Ludmilla pulled herself together.

'Not just now thank you,' she said grimly. 'Perhaps in another life. They say fashions come round.'

The girl gawped, turned to another customer like a little bird: 'Er, canna – *heelp* – yooo. . .?'

The sing-song of this familiar phrase cheered Ludmilla, reminding her of the opening bar of the Bach *G Minor Fugue*, to which she had always sung 'My Aunt–ie Fan–ny–'s got a huge pair of tits!', as she liked to tell the schoolboys. Schoolboys, whoops, Gavin, whoops, better get along and bevvy with the vicar.

The Tulip Café was next door to a herbalist. 'Can't be too close to the smelling salts in my condition,' she told the vicar as he commented on the pleasantness of the setting. The vicar was looking very well. She told him so and he said he couldn't complain.

'Ah, Vicar,' Ludmilla said, 'you know your responses!'

'I should hope so,' he replied gallantly to her little jest.

This was one of the few times, possibly the first, when they had met on a social occasion without Laura, although they had known one another for years. The meeting had a slight air of festivity about it, and there was a whiff of courteous flirtation in the air. When the coffee had been brought and Jeremy had helped Ludmilla to sugar – 'and another, and another, . . . and, yes, just one more . . . lovely, thank you' – he waited for her to speak first. He was actually a very good vicar, sensitive and very kind, and was not going to jolly her along with a 'now what's all this then you look as fit as a fiddle'. For a start, she didn't, she looked distinctly streaky, livid and blanched in unpredictable patches around the eyes, which were tired.

'I want to talk to you about Laura. I'd like to make provision for her before I die. I haven't any children, although my pupils have always been my children and I've loved some of them very dearly, as you know.'

She stirred her coffee, watching the spoon go round and round as though mesmerised. Then a sharp tap like a knuckle-rap on the side of the cup.

'But when it comes to Laura, well she's my special one. You know that. And not just because she's a good pianist. I've had better, though not for some years. But we've shared a great deal. I've taught her a lot, and I hope she won't forget it. A girl with her looks needs all the support to her intelligence she can get. And no . . .' she raised her teaspoon at the vicar, 'far be it from me to say she's not a bright girl. Of course she is, but that will never be the main thing in her life. She will have to cope with the way she looks for the rest of her life and I hope I have armed her for the fight. Now I've given her books, and I've had a go at teaching her the things she needs to know. A proper little Miss Pygmalion she'd be, though she had a good start, gutsiness, from her mother perhaps – no offence intended, but, trusting in the Lord as you do it would be redundant, like an appendix, talking anatomically. What was I saying. Shall we get another pot?'

The next pot arrived with alarming speed. 'Keep the kettle boi–ling, miss a loop you're out!' chanted Ludmilla and ducked an imaginary skipping rope. She poured.

'You have done splendidly for Laura,' Jeremy said quietly, in his lovely Church of England voice. 'But she is an ordinary girl, you know Ludmilla, she will always cope. She would be devastated, of course, if anything were to happen to you. I know she is terribly fond of you. But she is resilient.'

'Of course,' bridled Ludmilla, 'I do not imagine that she will crumple up like some dehydrated piece of oasis and stay by your side arranging flowers in memoriam for the rest of her life.'

Jeremy smiled slightly. He had such a *nice* face, the waitress was thinking. What was that old woman talking to him about? She didn't look the churchgoing type somehow.

'This book,' Ludmilla was saying.

'*Pierrot Lunaire*.'

'Precisely, and a nice accent if I may say so, Vicar.' She had a music hall way of saying vic–ah that made Jeremy wince a bit. The coffee was very bitter too, with only that UHT cream in a little plastic carton. Utterly horrible taste. A couple had heaved themselves into the chairs at the next table and were discussing whether it was too early for Welsh rarebit.

Ludmilla raised her voice and drawled slightly. 'There could be some money in it Vicar.'

Talk of the Welsh rarebit ceased abruptly.

'That would be very nice. Shall we squeeze the pot?' Not for Ludmilla. Jeremy watched the last few grains trickle into his cup.

'I can't tell you about it in any detail just yet, but my involvement with the *project*' (she highlighted the word for the prospective Welsh rarebiters) 'is sufficiently close for me to be able to say at this stage that I see at least a few thousand in it for Laura. My heir, that is. I haven't much else to give her. She'll have the piano of course. Now what do you think of that?'

Jeremy had been afraid it might be something like this.

'Ludmilla,' he said to her gently, 'what you do with your money is entirely up to you.' Then, with a slightly embarrassed air, 'I am sure He will show you what is best.' The capital 'H' was not achieved in speech.

'Who's that?'

'I mean, do what you think best. But,' and he laid his hand on her arm, 'pray for guidance. I think that is the best I can say. Laura has to find her own way in the world now.'

'You mean you don't welcome my offer.'

'I didn't say that. I would just like you to reflect on what is best for her.'

At this moment an attractive woman in her fifties walked up to their table. She had a merry face, healthy hips and a good smile.

'Ah, Gertrude, my dear,' said Jeremy, with open relief. 'This is Ludmilla Pike, Laura's splendid piano teacher. Ludmilla, Mrs Herbach.'

'Pleased to meet you,' Ludmilla said stiffly, and moved her trolley so the lady could sit down.

'I had meant to tell you before, especially as you are so close to Laura and might have an opinion on how she'll react. Mrs Herbach and I have decided to marry one another.'

'Good Lord,' Ludmilla said flatly. 'Let me congratulate you both,' though she didn't proceed to do so. 'How long has this been going on then?'

Mrs Herbach said, with a faint German accent, that it had only been going on a short while. 'But long enough, we both think. We met at the ecumenical conference last year and had some very interesting talks. And again this year. It wasn't quite out of the blue. It is a pleasure to meet you, Miss Pike. You are quite a feature of this town, I understand.'

'Yes,' replied Ludmilla, 'I'm due for sandblasting next month.'

Mrs Herbach was on the evangelical side of the church. She too, Ludmilla soon discovered, had a tendency to refer to God simply as 'Him', which occasionally led to confusion. But she was no fool. She had come to evangelism through the strait gate of genuine theological enquiry and a tough Catholic upbringing and was a good match for Ludmilla, and undoubtedly, in a different sense, for Jeremy. At the conference they had admitted to one another that theology had come to a dead end. They solemnly abandoned the historical Jesus for the Jesus of faith. Experience over authority.

'Well,' Ludmilla said, quite forgetting her little joke over the bill and leaving a couple of pound coins on the table, 'I must be off. When's the happy day?' She made it sound like a church fête on a wet weekend.

'September,' said Mrs Herbach. 'I shall hope to get to know my new step-daughter a little better first.'

'Not if I get there first you won't, Eva Braun,' thought Ludmilla. 'Will you be writing to her?' she asked Jeremy.

'I shall ring her when we get back from Suffolk on Saturday. Gertrude has a little house there. The curate is happy to deputise at this very special time.

'I did wonder, Ludmilla,' he went on, 'whether you might be able to do a little ground work for us. You've always been so close.' Ludmilla felt herself turn puce somewhere near the centre of her heart.

'I have been telling Jeremy he should not worry so much about Laura. She will look after herself, I'm sure. It will wait. What a wonderful opportunity for her out there in France.'

Ludmilla tweaked out a smile.

'I'll be off then, er, Mr Cranshawe.' She couldn't get the music hall tone back again. She'd got her last laugh out of that one. 'Come on Fido.' She gave a doleful wink at the trolley and tugged it off towards the stairs.

When she had gone there was a pause and they looked at each other wryly.

'I *see*!' said Gertrude, signalling for a refill of coffee.

'Poor thing. She doesn't enjoy good health, I'm afraid.'

'No,' she replied a little tartly, 'but perhaps she is very much enjoying ill health.'

'Now, now,' said the voice of caution and of the church, 'she's a good woman. Very talented and devoted to Laura. We have that in common and you will too, I hope, my dear. She's been like a mother to her. Not long for this world, though, I'm afraid.' He told her what he knew of what the doctor had said to Ludmilla.

'I have a feeling she may change her atheistic spots before very long. Not that I mind whether she does or not. Can't stand last minute conversions myself. I think she thinks I'm trotting up and down the touchline waiting for this one. As it were.'

'I have understood you are speaking metaphorically. Very good too.' She patted his arm amiably and they began to talk of other things while Ludmilla wandered home alone.

They were free to proceed. Posy was ready. She could not leave everything to coincidence, although her confidence in *Fortuna*'s sense of timing was well placed. It should really have been rather a triumphal morning. The little trolley's wheels whirred busily as she bumped along the familiar streets. No rain fell and she was dry-eyed by the time she reached her familiar front door.

19

Talbot's plan for the day was for them both to keep busy. With the lunch coming up next week he had his preparation of the synopsis of *Pierrot Lunaire* to finish and get run off at the copier's. He suddenly switched into professional mode and went off into the library with a cup of instant coffee. Up to now he had always drunk meticulously prepared, freshly-ground coffee the like of which Laura had never tasted, except once or twice in a Berni Inn. Drinking the watered-up granules with a dash of cold milk obviously took him back to a time when he was too rushed for anything more elaborate and put him in a frame of mind to concentrate on higher things. He was whistling as he bore it off into his office though. Laura recognised the final movement from the *Emperor Concerto* and wondered what had put that in his mind.

Alone in the kitchen she knew that the enormity of what had happened to her needed to be ignored. If she started thinking of the fifty-first psalm, which she had been taught to do, but which would have been a poetic rather than a pious indulgence, for she was more apt to be moved to guilt than persuaded of it, she would be placing at risk the whole of her present happiness. It would require serious and, worse still, proper consideration of her conduct. She was better at deep than at serious feelings. The intensity of everything that was happening to her at Château Monvanité was so absorbing that it would be a crime against all Ludmilla had taught her about feeling and responsibility to suddenly, as it were, change the record in mid-party. That was a terrible thing to think. Try to look at it from the outside. Well, she hadn't actually, you know, *done* anything . . . No, that was feeble and jesuitical (which she thought meant non-reformist and therefore wicked) . . . Oh dear, she thought, as she squirted some Lux Citron under the running tap, *Wash me thoroughly from my wickedness: and cleanse me from my sin.* It wasn't working. Water off a duck's back . . . *Thou shalt purge me with hyssop, and I shall be clean*: . . . No response . . . *Thou shalt wash me and I shall be whiter than snow* . . . It wouldn't wash . . .

'Laura!'

She looked up from the soapy water. Talbot was rummaging through some papers on a telephone table in the hall. Her stomach swooped. Had she left her correspondence lying around?

'You haven't seen *Pierrot Lunaire* have you? I left it on here yesterday and it's vanished. Where the hell is it?' Apart from the fact that *he* would have said 'where in heaven's name', he sounded just like her father.

'I don't know,' she said, slightly timidly. Perhaps she should have emulated Talbot and said, 'I've got abs–so–lute–ly no idea at *all*!' Perhaps she would have done, and he would have liked it, but he was looking really very cross just at this moment so it didn't occur to her. 'You must have moved it. Things don't just disappear on their own.'

'Oh thanks Laura, what's this the new age of enlightenment? Go on, tell me God is dead will you? I know things don't just disappear – someone's shifted it.'

The whole world of men at work, men losing papers, men losing their tempers, men thinking you've lost their papers, men slamming doors. Men opening them again and saying, 'Look I'm sorry love, it's just very important. We've got this meeting next Tuesday.'

'We?' said Laura sweetly. 'I know, I'm practising washing up.'

Talbot wasn't one of those men, if there are any, who look furious for a moment and then throw back their heads and laugh. He looked at her for a second, while she panicked with inner hysteria that he was going to throw her out on the spot, as he would have called it, and then came up and kissed her with something like awe.

'I'm really sorry.'

'That's all right,' she said, 'I thought you were putting it on.'

Ludmilla had never got round to telling her that authenticity was no prerequisite for a full blooded display of righteous anger in a man. She must have meant that she thought he had been joking.

'Okay?'

'Bit shocked.'

'I'm a bugger when I'm working. You should ask my secretary.'

'I *am* your secretary.'

'No, I meant the one in London.'

'But here?'

'My muse.' Laura thought this a frivolous comment, which it was, but not because, as she thought, it was somehow etymologically related to 'amusement'.

'I can *type* and things,' she said. 'I want to be useful. That's why Ludmilla wanted me to be here. To help you with *Pierrot Lunaire*.'

'PL, darling, please,' he said grinning, 'PL to us in the trade. Now where's that bloody book?'

Twenty minutes later, they sat at the top of the great staircase, where they had recently exchanged kisses, sure that the book was not in the house. Talbot was by now philosophical. There were only two possibilities. Either Laura had instructions from Ludmilla to suppress it, or Madame Derrault had walked off with it by mistake. There was no other possible explanation. This was the second copy that had disappeared. Last time he had known what Ludmilla was doing while he was out of the room, and indulged her little piece of stage villainy. She must have realised when he didn't pursue her that he had been lying when he said he had only one copy in the world. He didn't tell Laura what he was thinking. Besides, he was also thinking that it was a hell of a relief to be liberated from the book and to be able to write the script off the top of his head. It took all the difficulty out of the problem which had been bugging him for months. Laura was thinking that Talbot must have trumped the whole thing up, possibly with Ludmilla, although she couldn't imagine why.

Talbot observed that there was a tide in the affairs of men which taken at the flood led on to fortune. Laura's gloss on this was that Talbot was going to make the best of it and turn the disappearance of the book to his advantage. Relief at his liberation from the text had dulled his curiosity. It was as if in a dream, he had been waiting for a bus for hours on end, when suddenly a flying elephant appeared and told him to hop on. In such circumstances a man's sense of zoological enquiry might quite easily be subdued by his momentarily much keener sense of serendipity.

'Got anything blue with you? Simple dress, and a ribbon, perhaps? Pop it on and go and wheel that bicycle away from the house, quite slowly, you know, dreamily, as though you were thinking of . . . ah . . . what it might be like to fall in love for the first time. Yes. Reflective. Stop and pick some of those poppies when you get halfway down. I'll be watching from the tower room. I've got an idea for a shot.'

Laura panicked. 'I can't act for *anything*, Talbot! Please don't ask me to do anything like that, I'll only mess it up for you, make it look all wrong.'

'Don't you believe it, sweetheart. Just be yourself. You *are* Chloe.'

There seemed to be an incompatibility between these last two remarks, but Laura was just about won over by his emphasis. 'I'm too self conscious for stuff like that, honestly, the only thing I could ever act would be someone acting badly, and then I'd probably do it so badly it would look like someone acting well. Or something.'

Talbot missed what she said. He was already off down the staircase. She was sitting miserably on the top step. She was already *doing* it, she thought. Talbot was straightening the picture of Posy's ancestor, twitching from left to right to get it to sit straight.

'What about all that puppet theatre business you told me about? Cinderella by the crib and Rumpelstiltskin wrapped in a white hanky. That's acting isn't it? Go on, get your kit on.'

Kit on, kit off, thought Laura, and went off to put on a blue dress Ludmilla had given her as a leaving present. It'll come in useful, she had said, although it wasn't that sort of dress at all.

The shots came out well. Luckily for Laura they were all from behind. Talbot had a fancy sort of video camera you could plug into the television immediately after shooting. This came in handy for trying out his ideas on the spur of the moment. Laura refused to watch.

'Pure magic,' Talbot told her, coming into the kitchen where she was starting to make some bread. 'You were wonderful.'

'Don't be silly,' Laura said, 'It could be anybody from behind. Anyone can push an old bicycle. Even Albert.'

'Albert would *not* look good in a blue cotton dress. Which reminds me, someone rang from the Mairie. It seems Albert's got a new job. We've got to watch out for him.'

'What happened to his old one,' Laura asked, alluding to his post by the telephone box. 'Were they over-manned?'

'Watch that tongue,' Talbot warned her.

He kissed her avuncularly, in a cloud of white dust as she poured out flour into a bowl, and did an impression of an uncle patting her bottom. 'Albert's job,' he continued. 'Position of monumental public responsibility.'

'Good,' said Laura. 'Is he going to *be* a monument? I'm sure he'll be very efficient at that.'

'Not quite.' Talbot was loving moving about the kitchen with her in it, talking to her over his shoulder instead of looking directly, moving away into the hall so he had to raise his voice, or pause slightly before answering. It was the luxury of the newly-married man who gets a kick out of continuing to read the newspaper after hours. 'They're widening the road between here and the village, a few hundred yards down from the telephone box. It'll be narrower while they're doing it, so cars can only pass in one direction at a time. Albert's going to hold the lollipop with red and green on it and turn it when the traffic's to change over. Every four minutes. They've given him a stopwatch.' Laura was pleased for him. She had had a couple of theories about Albert, that he watched for a lover who had once gone on a journey to another village and never returned, or that he had a premonition of peril, a huge black dustball of danger spinning down towards the village, which only he could hold back. Pathetic or heroic it had to be. It couldn't just be senile dementia.

She had cycled down to the village to get yeast just before the shops closed at midday, and arrived slightly sweaty at the baker's two minutes before time. The lady was delighted to sell her some and they had a little chat about what astonishing stuff it was, although the shopkeeper was glad more people didn't know how easy it was to use or she'd be out of business. She cut off a corner from a large block in the back of the shop and wrapped it in waxed paper for Laura to take home. Laura carried it in her hand, where it crumbled like a long-dead living thing at a human touch, hot-smelling, powdery and salty sweet. As she passed the hairdresser's a dog slipped out from a side passage which led down to the church and followed her all the way down the road. A huge red setter she had heard spoken of by his master. Andromache was still holding out against him. He was looking like the original hangdog. It was a pretty hopeless situation for him with Andromache, and for the poor, unread beast there was no savour in the cry of her namesake's lover. (*Je meurs si je vous perds, mais je meurs si j'attends*, Talbot had sighed for him the night before, and they had considered sending Andromache a card on the General's behalf.) He was now sniffing after her hand and the edge of her skirt, intrigued by the sweet odour. When she got home she held it out to Talbot.

'So strange,' she said. 'It smells like nothing else,' and Talbot laughed for quite some time at that and asked why she thought the General had been sniffing at her skirt. He watched as she stirred it with a pinch of sugar and it ran to liquid in seconds. When she had kneaded the dough, embarrassed by the gracelessness of her movements, though Talbot said she looked like Werther's Charlotte, she laid it in a bowl in the sun, covered with a cloth against the flies.

'Come on,' Talbot said casually, 'let's go up and lie down.' If it hadn't been that there was for her something biblical about the bread, while for him the silent swelling of the dough was altogether associated with different things, she might have said yes. As it was she couldn't bear the idea of closing the shutters against the sunlight and creating a false darkness. After that he had to say he was going up anyway, so she felt awkward and wrong-footed while she sat by the bowl outside and could almost feel the warm air swelling in pockets under the darkness of the cloth. She longed for him to come down again and announce a plan, as a child lies in bed waiting for the first noises from its parents' bed, the sign that play may begin. But he kept to the house until early evening and she sat for hours after the bread had been baked, with her head on her knees, watching her legs turn brown in the sun.

20

There are certain things, Talbot told Laura that evening, that if you can't cook, you don't cook, because if they go wrong everyone immediately knows you don't know a bain-marie from a chip pan.

'That,' he said, nodding rather censoriously at the cake of dried out mince on shanks of spaghetti, 'is one of them.'

Laura felt there was still a slight chance he might be being unfair – after all, it had been meant as a propitiatory lunch, and Talbot hadn't come down until shortly before six.

'What's in it?'

She stuck a finger in it, prepared to show that she too had not much respect for it left.

'Well, you know, mince beef, er . . . a sort of tomato paste thing, oh yes, onions, um, stock, from the cube things. Talbot, *please* don't look like that, I can't *help* not knowing. I know I shouldn't have pretended I did, but I can do *some* things, it's just not knowing anything about food that makes it so hard. Ludmilla said it would be all right if I used my common sense and we used to have this at school so I thought there couldn't be *that* much to it.' She stared glumly at the untouched meal on the plate. 'I don't know how it got to look like that.'

He put his arm round her with the hand that was holding a little green bottle of beer. 'Don't worry sweetie. Tell you what,' and he sounded as though he was going to try and make her forget her doll's house had been lost in a fire. 'Let's go out for dinner. Somewhere nice.'

There was a place he often went to where everything was very simple but perfect. The chef was – he made a circle with the index finger and thumb of his right hand and seemed to pluck a kiss from his lips with them – 'mwauh!!', and at first Laura thought he might have said *'moi'*, although she was almost over believing absolutely everything might be possible.

'Go and grab me the phone and the book and I'll give them a ring. What day is it?'

'Thursday.'

'Good girl. Just testing.'

She wanted to say, *'Don't* call me good girl like that,' but thought he was probably being deliberately old rakish to make her feel more at home about everything else. She hoped he realised she only had seventy francs. She supposed her salary, slight as it was, was off now.

'Great, we'll go there then, and I'll explain everything we have so you could come back and cook it here on your own tomorrow if you wanted. We'll soon get you going. Talbot Hardy's Easy Learning Guide. Stage One. Go somewhere really expensive and pig out. Stage Two, learn to fantasize rewardingly about it. Stage Three, with a little practice you'll find you can quite easily recreate the experience in your own kitchen at home. Its smells, its colours, its succulent textures and haunting flavours . . .

He was circling Laura, twisting his arms around her head like a cross between an ice skater and a sorcerer when he caught sight of Madame Derrault coming round the corner with an empty laundry basket and a packet of washing powder. He skipped up to her and laid hands on the packet.

'Are you happy with your washing powder madame?' he cried.

Madame Derrault replied firmly, but almost smilingly, that she was.

Talbot fell back into his normal tone of voice.

'That's a shame,' he said, 'I was going to offer it to you in exchange for this tempting little preparation of Laura's here. I'm sure it has excellent cleansing properties, if only for the lower stomach and bowel.'

Laura found it difficult to follow his French. They hadn't done parts of the intestine at school. Madame Derrault picked the plate up and scraped the contents into a plastic bag. Perfect for the pigs, she said. Laura felt from that she could probably gather the general drift. She thought petulantly that it must be really quite nice to be old enough or confident enough to be able to make fun of other people without being deliberately cruel, just imagining that they were immune. It must mean you were immune yourself, or simply knew you were never going to come in for criticism. She wondered if there was anything Talbot couldn't do that she could. She could hardly challenge him to stand on his head and recite 'You are Old Father William' here and now.

Talbot stayed outside talking to Madame Derrault while she went inside to find the telephone and the book. The telephone was one of those ones that charges up overnight so you can carry it round with you during the day. At first she had felt she ought to try to walk in a straight line with it so as not to tangle up the invisible thread that connected it to its little pad. She was standing by the door into the garden with it when Talbot came in, loitering in the shadows like a stage hand with a vital prop for the next scene.

'The telephone.'

He took it from her quickly. 'For me?'

'No I mean, just the telephone. For the restaurant.'

He gave her a very funny look. 'Oh, right, I see. You were bringing it for me. Very sweet of you. Thanks.'

He squatted down on the arm of a chair and poised his finger to jab out the number.

'Hang on, what's the number?'

'I don't know, I don't even know where we're going.' She sounded a bit exasperated.

'Now, now, a little resourcefulness if you please. We know the village, don't we?'

'Corda.'

'Corrrdah!' he repeated, in a way that meant: 'Repeat after me.'

'That's the one,' she said, and left the room.

He looked at the telephone in surprise, the way people do who have been hung up on in films, whether to check for a visible malfunction or as though to say to the machine, you heard that too? Then he jumped off the chair and went over to fetch the book.

He had made the call and was leaning with his elbows on his desk and a pen in his hand when she came back into the room. She went over to him and touched his shoulder.

'Talbot.'

'Mmmm,' he said, 'just there, behind the blade, wonderful . . .'

She withdrew her hand.

'Don't stop.'

Laura stood there with all her hair swept to one side of her head, holding it twisted with her two hands, her head on one side.

'I just came to say—'

'Listen Laura, don't be heavy, come on, you've got to learn I'm going to tease you—'

'Your shirt tail's hanging out.'

He put his pen down and wrapped his arms right round her. She thought if anyone had been standing outside looking in they might have seen his hands coming round full circle onto his own back like someone in the corner of a dance hall doing the old fake-a-kiss routine, till she realised that the hands after all would be her own and she was kissing him back.

21

In days gone by, when lovers' games had been played at Monvanité, and significance had been found in the slightest of oddities, someone had discovered that if you drew a line between the dovecot and the farmhouse where Madame Derrault lived, and then one back to the château again, it formed a perfect right angled triangle. A calculation figured by a meticulous lover, an astrologer's trick of delighting in the inevitable exactitude of some random illustration for someone, somewhere. Albert had a strange, birdlike magnet in his head which had guided him to a perception of the pattern, though he could not have told you what he had understood. For him there was a curious sense of balance and of correctness about the configuration of the buildings, which drew him to the château even though it lay slightly to the west of his natural homeward path. If he had been a prophet, his choice of the telephone box would have, perhaps, provoked serious academic research in American universities in the twenty-first century.

Madame Derrault's new bicycle, with its range of many gears and its special tough-terrain adaptations, could no doubt easily have coped with the direct route. She took the regular road, however, cycling if anything more sedately than usual, as though she were anxious not to scuff a new pair of shoes. Laura and Talbot overtook her on the road, but she did not take her hand off the handlebars to return their wave.

The farm lay to the north of Monvanité, so she left the sun behind her as she went. A hundred miles to the west, the great sea lay and the sun lowered itself gently, gratefully into the water after a long day. She was late tonight. The girl who did the evening shift at the café had been delayed, and then she had had her things to pick up from the château. Ideally she should have waited till tonight to pick the herbs, but she had had other business there this morning and with the sage and thyme providing that plausible little touch of seasoning, her presence had seemed to require no further explanation. Naturally she would return the book the following morning. She was a stickler for rectitude and routine, and it had been lying around unopened for at least a week now, so she doubted Talbot would miss it. She couldn't understand a word of it, of course, but she reckoned that a careful examination would at least give her some clue to what all this business was about. She had her responsibilities as far as the château was concerned and one of those responsibilities was to keep herself informed. The book was in the front basket, propped upright against the white plastic wiring. Behind her, in a similar but smaller receptacle, was the pigs' dinner. She didn't think Elsa and Gilbert had tackled spaghetti before, but the prospect of their first encounter with it held no comic possibilities for her. Pigs were pigs and it all went down the same way. Someone like Ludmilla would have considered it of interest to discuss really which way that was. Should nutritional material on its route down a pig's intestine be deemed to be travelling forwards or backwards? We might consider that Laura's spaghetti was near the end of its journey, that it was a question of dust to dust, or the organic equivalent thereof, whereas for the young pig it was just a beginning, a charging up, a fuelling of the machine in preparation for the great departure into life as a full member of the species *suidae*.

They ate, and in what manner Madame Derrault could not have told you, for by then she was parking her bicycle in the barn and locking the door behind her. She watered her plants, filling the can from a tap on the wall. Her garden was laid out with eighteenth-century-cum-nineteen-fifties angularity, a sort of *Ideal Home* parterre. If a lawn could have been clean shaven without ceasing to be a lawn, she would have favoured such a condition. Potted bedding plants were stationed at regular intervals. Holes had been cut into the lawn with a sharp instrument, but in the end she had held back from implantation. The terracotta pots looked perfectly respectable just sitting on their little pitches, in nature, but not of it. She caught a drip from the lip of the watering can, and returned it to the tool hut.

Unlike Ludmilla, Madame Derrault had no Ruskin in her. None at all. The far-off gleam of the snow-covered peaks was for tourists. The rushing water in the river, the lilt of the wind in an evening cornfield, the feathers of cloud stroking the sky in the west had no more than a meteorological significance for her. Refracted through her personality, nature acquired none of that beauty which is bestowed by love's fancy. And Albert? Did the child in him still bound in Wordsworthian joy o'er the mountains, the deep rivers and the lonely streams? And was the world still apparelled in celestial light? If it was, he gave no sign.

He would already be back. Madame Derrault went inside to make them both something to eat. Then she'd take it through to him and make sure he ate, while they watched a little something on TV. Like some day tripper up from the country, the kitchen was authentic rustic, dressed up to the nines. Formica and aluminium graced the surfaces, but the ancient beams and sheer stone floor won through despite her best efforts. She made steak and chips and a tomato salad and carried it over to Albert's two room cottage on a tray with a picture of the *Mona Lisa* on it. Their private hour together passed off with no variation from the usual pattern. After they had eaten she wiped his mouth gently, patted his hand and turned back to the television, where a number of people were jumping up and down at the prospect of winning a food processor if they could provide three consecutive correct responses to a series of questions, which surely even Albert himself might not have found too taxing.

'Jamaica,' she said.
'Saint Matthew.'
Albert began to snore. *'Tais–toi Albert.'*
He stopped.
'Marilyn Monroe.'
She turned off the television and started stacking up the tray. She would come back in half an hour and see him to bed. That was their routine.

She was crossing the immaculate yard when a car drew up behind her little hedge. A door closed softly and seconds later in tiptoed Norman Davies, carrying the parrot. He was wearing a smart lemon aertex shirt and a rather sheer pair of slacks. All from Marks and Spencer's in Toulouse. You couldn't go wrong with them.

'Bonsoir, Madame D,' he said in a cheery whisper, and shook her hand.

He was just the person she wanted to see, but first things first. Le Touquet was a bit off colour. No doubt someone foolish had been feeding him chips again. Norman lived above the Café du Sport, and had popped in for a quick one on the way up to his flat. It had been immediately clear to him that Le Touquet was under the weather and he'd thought the best thing would be to drive up and put him in Madame Derrault's capable hands. Not that Le Touquet was officially hers. He was a foundling – left on the counter one day while her back was turned. Except in her treatment of Albert, which few people had ever witnessed, she was not a woman noted for her compassion. It had been a fine judgement on someone's part.

They put the parrot in the corner of the kitchen where they could keep an eye on him and Madame Derrault made some coffee. Norman had a large cognac and they settled themselves, at his suggestion, in comfortable chairs outside in the courtyard. Madame Derrault lit a camphor lamp to keep the moths away. She had always got along with Norman. He teased her a little sometimes, and she was generally reproving in her bearing towards him, an arrangement which worked very well. She was capable of swift rebukes which were delivered with utterly democratic impartiality whenever the occasion called for it. Her favours – the odd teaspoonful of geniality, a smile, a moment to talk – enjoyed less indiscriminate distribution and her more willing tolerance of the male sex in general was due not to any weakness in that direction so much as to downright misogyny. The one person she never chided was Talbot. When he forgot arrangements for the key, knocked over the wash basket while reversing his car, left his things all over the house, she just smiled to herself, a wide, full lipped smile and pressed her hip bones thoughtfully with the fleshy part of her palms.

Norman tried to compliment her on running a jolly tight ship up here, but the idiom gained rather a lot in translation and she raised her eyebrows energetically, as though visually taking his temperature. They were extraordinarily thick eyebrows, like well-fed, luxuriant caterpillars, and Norman rather suspected she plucked them – not to make them narrow, but to sharpen the line between them and her high, clear brow. Talbot could have told you she did at fifty paces. He was the kind of man who knew things like that about women. He recognised perfumes and had definite opinions on whether they were suitable for the wearer or not. He would very often pinpoint star signs correctly, even though he didn't believe in astrology. When it came to feminine detail Madame Derrault was not exactly a rococo specimen, but Talbot was a connoisseur.

They talked for a while about the recent death of an actor. He had stepped off the stage while playing the lead role in a farce. Madame Derrault thought he should have stuck to romantic roles.

'*Hé hé*! One of your pinups eh, Madame D? You didn't like him wandering round with his foot in a bucket then?'

'I didn't say that. It isn't a question of what I like or don't like. I said people should know where they fit in. It wasn't his style. That's all I'm saying.'

Norman sighed and looked up contemplatively at the sky. His pudgy hands were folded in his lap.

'No, no, you're quite right of course.' He looked across at her mischievously. 'It was that wife of his of course. Pushed him too far. These young women!'

'She is a young woman of no intelligence.'

'Ah.'

The night had folded in now. Madame Derrault went to see to Albert. She told Norman to fill his glass up while she was gone. It was a real sign of trust – she was an instinctive bottle marker. When she came back he was back in his seat, nursing his glass with cupped hands. Her duties were over for the day. She leaned over her left forearm, which rested in her lap, and smoothed out her stockings with her other hand. Norman found it a touching gesture. In rare moments she looked like a woman in a Degas painting.

'How's things up the road then, Madame D? All running smoothly?'

'*Ça va*. The peach trees had the blight. There will be no fruit there. I told him to spray but he disapproves. I told him there would be blight. You know what he said? "Tant-pis-Madame-D!" Just like that. And now he buys them from the market, where they have been sprayed—'

'—More often than Madame Thatcher's hair!' Norman finished off with a chuckle.

'Exactly.'

Madame Derrault slipped off her shoes and wiggled her toes.

'You keep very fit,' Norman observed, watching her toes and rolling his drink around the glass thoughtfully.

'I work.'

'That's very true, you do too. I expect young Mademoiselle Laura's taken a bit of the load off you though. That must help. You should see if she'd like to give you a hand in the café some time. Be an experience for her. Nice girl,' he said.

He had come across Laura that afternoon, sitting on the threshold of Monvanité. He had taken her for a stranger. Perhaps she was waiting for someone to arrive with a key. They introduced themselves rather formally, and the very formality, the ropes of which they both perfectly understood, put them at ease with one another. She showed him the books Talbot had put out for his shop. When they had loaded them up into the car Laura offered, rather belatedly he thought, to go and fetch Talbot. 'I think he's sleeping,' she said. She said it in such a tiny voice, which was lost on the air as she looked up at a window that might have been Talbot's, that he thought for a moment she must have hurt herself, so he asked if she was all right. She swung round quickly and looked at him as if trying to catch his intonation before it left the muscles of his face, having failed to catch his meaning while she was looking up at the window. Norman rattled his car keys. 'Let him be, it's all right. Say I called.' Laura promised to come down one evening and help Norman do some indexing of his stock. 'It'll make a change for you', as though she had been there for months. She welcomed the idea of Norman's index precisely because it would be a change from the unknown, a glimpse into the hinterland of other people's normal lives.

'I expect Talbot's a bit sweet on her,' said Norman, 'She's got a look . . .'

Madame Derrault put her shoes back on. The special boot Laura had observed on her first day was only for days when her foot was particularly painful. It was also a sign of a bad mood. For a moment Norman thought she might be going to fetch it.

'Very young, of course,' he added hastily. 'Can't quite work out what she's doing here myself. Not sure that she knows either!'

'She is helping with the work on his film. She has nothing to do with the house. I manage the house.'

'Oh absolutely, of course you do. Nobody else could do what you do, Madame D. That's a gift you've got there. No doubt about that. I just wondered though. What work on what film? You ever been able to work that one out? Is he a director? I sort of thought he was a writer, but you don't get the impression he does very much, do you. I mean, I'm sure he does a lot of things, but I was thinking of, you know, bashing away at the old keys and that. Can't quite see it myself. More of a man of action, I'd have said, wouldn't you?'

'It is an adaptation he has taken upon himself.'

Norman was a little startled, thinking she meant it in the Darwinian sense, and then realised she was talking about the film.

'Right, got you.' He paused for a little while, and nodded gently.

'What of?'

'What, what of?'

'What's he adapting? Have I heard of it? What's he going to do with it? I rather thought it was all going to happen here. I quite fancied a little part for myself. We could make some costumes for ourselves, Mrs D. Period, I fancy. A little trip to Cannes for us if it all comes off, eh?'

He tweaked her elbow in a friendly way. 'Don't mind me, I'm just nosy. Can't resist other people's privacy. Like a magnet to me. Still, at least I'm honest about it. Gives them time to clam up if they want. Let's go and have a quick peep at Le Touquet, then I must be off.'

While Norman was washing the glasses, as was his way, she went over to a drawer and took out the book. Her sight was a little weak, and she had that way of looking at the written word at a funny angle which suggests it might be emitting some invisible toxin. She didn't want to go back into the kitchen and present him with it. It would be altogether better if he came into the room and found her looking at it, so he could join her, add his wits to hers. She stood there straight as a post by the mantlepiece, lining up the photographs in their well-kept chrome surrounds. Mother and daughter, fifteen years ago perhaps. Tiny child, herself in a Liberation parade costume, fading now. Single man, a strangely relaxed study for the period, shirt sleeves and baggy trousers. Cigarette.

'That's all done now!' Norman popped his head through from the kitchen, where he was drying his hands fastidiously on a towel. He lifted the cover on the parrot's cage and tilted his head to one side in a question. The bird was asleep.

'At least I think he is. They do sleep with one eye open don't they?' he called over his shoulder.

There was no reply. He dropped the little curtain and came into the room. Madame Derrault was tapping her fingers on the book and looking out through the window. A car approached, slowed down before the house, then sped off again into the night. Slowly she turned back to look at Norman, who was patting his pockets, making sure he had everything.

'I picked this up by mistake,' she said, holding it out to him. 'It was mixed in with my pile of magazines. Of course it's no use to me. It's all in English.'

Norman came over and took it. *'Pierrot Lunaire,'* he read. 'What's that, a circus act? Funny name for a . . . ooooh . . . I seeee . . .'

He gave her a chastising look, then peeped furtively round the room. 'Tut tut, Mrs D. Well done! I say, how thrilling. Let's have a peek shall we? What do you say? Let's see if we can get the gist.' He flicked through, looking at the bits marked by Talbot with a red pen. 'Haven't got my specs with me I'm afraid . . . hmmm, pretty name, Chloe . . . tum tum, blah-di-blah, never looked her way . . . one day, ah-ha! Listen to this Madame D, oh what is it, yes, it says . . . pardon my French . . .'

He struck a pose by the hearth, holding the book up before him like an actor at a first or second reading.

'Ahem!! "Her affliction was bravely born" . . . um . . . *Attendez*

... "Her beauty and her courage lifted it out of the realm of the hideous," I suppose you'd say, "till it shone like some *magnificent jewel* in the panoply" ... that exist? Yes ... "of all her charms," bloody hell, "and he felt it grow, a cancer of remorse in his own flesh." We all know what that means, mon vieux! Where are we – still with me Mrs D? "That afternoon he watched her from the dovecot as she led the horse across the field, talking to it gently, in a language he scarcely understood," tumpty-tum, here we are this bit's got a ring around it, "all nature seemed to open before him, like scent" ... whatsit, sort of ... "exhaled," I s'pose it means, "by the flower of her youth." Phew!! Hot stuff eh! Hope it's not all like that, poor old Talbot won't be able to take the pace. Told you there was a part in it for us though Mrs D. You can be the girl, I'll be the horse!'

He heard her sniff. Now he'd heard Madame Derrault sniff on a number of occasions, and generally it did not indicate that she was about to dissolve in front of you and fetch out her pocket handkerchief.

This was something different though. She seemed to be quite affected. He changed his tack a little. 'Wow. Great stuff! Amazing isn't it, look, Monvanité, 7 June 1938. Makes you feel quite honoured doesn't it? It's certainly got a feel about it that place has. If stones could speak, eh!'

She pointed with a crooked finger at the name. 'How do you pronounce this?'

'Flynn. Tom Flynn. There isn't really anything like it in French, it's a sort of *eee* sound, with your lips stretched.'

'*Fleen*,' she copied, docilely, '*Fleen*.'

'And Chloe. That's quite different. *O-ooo-eee*, two noises really. *O-ooo-eee*.'

'Of course,' she said. 'It is a French name. She is French.'

'You reckon? Well, yes, I suppose she must be, that's why she's talking in that language, you know, the one he can hardly understand. He must be English. Obviously hasn't been reading his Harrap has he?'

'Irish?' she suggested. The French were always happier to think someone was Irish or Scottish, or Welsh, though they knew less about the Welsh. English was always a poor fourth.

He cocked a look at her. 'That's not stupid,' he said. 'It is an

Irish name as a matter of fact. I think you've been doing your homework, Mrs D. A little local history eh? Talbot should be looking into all that, you know. It's important for the flavour of the thing. It's amazing what people remember. You're in a position to hear, of course. You could be very helpful to him, come to think of it.'

'I am very busy. I haven't got the time to stand at my counter talking.'

Norman looked a bit disappointed. 'Well, just little bits of things, here and there, I meant really. It doesn't have to be a full time . . .'

There was a noise from the other room. Le Touquet had woken up and was fluttering petulantly in his cramped little space. Norman went and saw to him, then switched out the light in the kitchen.

'Gosh, what a lot of excitement. Nice to get a bit of an idea, though, isn't it. Doesn't do anyone any harm. As I say, we might be able to put a few ideas his way. Subtly, you know. Point him in the right direction.' He tucked his little scarf in underneath the collar of the tee shirt. 'Well, I'll be off, Madame D. Shall I take that pile of shirts now I'm here? Save you carting them in in the morning. Shall I take Father Bénoit's pile while I'm at it?'

No, certainly not. She and she alone would handle the priest's clothing. She was looking quite herself again, though there was a challenging look about her chins, which probably meant she had to get up early in the morning. He bet she did. She'd have to pop that book back where she found it before Talbot got up. Not that he was the world's earliest riser.

'Lovely evening. See you tomorrow perhaps. Thanks for the brandy.'

She showed him out with a certain impatience, but shook his hand warmly enough as he went. She closed the door after him and went back over to the book and put it back in her bag. She would return it first thing.

Although she was tired, sleep did not come as quickly as usual. Even as dawn broke, for it was June, and the first birds rose from the trees and skimmed quickly down towards the river in the grey light, she lay still and thoughtful in her bed, pondering in her heart all that she had learned.

22

Talbot had been wrong when he said to Laura that the restaurant was very simple – unless by that he meant that you couldn't stroke the wallpaper with the back of your hand or stick your finger into the padded binding of the menu and leave a dimple. It seemed to Laura that it was all very carefully set up, and that nothing, from the colour of the walls to the calligraphy of the handwritten menu, had ended up simple without being sophisticated in origin. She knew about these things, because she recognised a hand like her own at work. Understatement and audacity. *Reculer pour mieux sauter.*

It was called Restaurant Saint Phillipe, and was about a twenty minute drive away from Monvanité. Passing Madame Derrault on the road had set Talbot off. The sight of her seemed to induce in him an unwarranted level of hilarity, one on which Laura couldn't quite join him.

'She's so severe,' she said. 'I can tell you didn't go to a girls' school – mine was stuffed with people like her. We had one woman, in charge of games, though she never seemed to do any running around. She was supposed to have been county table tennis champion or something, but that wasn't any use anyway because we didn't have a table. All she seemed to like doing was taking the register while we were having showers. If you weren't having a shower you had to answer your name and shout out why you weren't. I was a late developer so I never had to do it, except for a having a cold and things, but still . . . Eventually this girl called Monica got a petition up saying it was sexual harassment. A couple of weeks later she left. Miss Widdle, I mean.'

Talbot gave a little thump on the steering wheel for glee. 'I don't believe you!' he cried. 'Widdle! Talk about on a plate.'

Laura put on a very knowing face and spoke across the handbrake into Talbot's ear. 'They said it was a *can of worms*!'

He gulped and jabbed in the cigarette lighter. He handed her his cigarette. 'Do that for me can you, when it's ready.'

They came to a little bridge over the river, which Laura failed to anticipate, so her stomach got left behind for a moment on the peak of the hump. She was watching the cigarette lighter carefully, ready to snatch it out before it got cold. Pop. She lit it and handed it over. He leaned over towards her and kept his hands on the wheel, opening his lips for her to slot it in.

'Thanks. What happened to Monica?'

'She got pregnant when we were in the fifth form and left to have the baby. The deaconess at my father's church went to see her in the hospital when she'd had it and she got really upset because Monica told her it was an immaculate conception and Sister Phyllis, that's her name, said, "Oh no, dear, we all know that's impossible," and Monica said, "You said it sister".'

Talbot pulled sharply on his cigarette. 'Blimey,' he whistled as as he blew out the smoke, 'you must have all been quite something. Any male teachers? I think I might apply.'

'Only my father,' Laura said straightforwardly, possibly stolidly, he thought, and gave her a quick sideways look. 'He came in to do special assemblies.'

Talbot had been going to go on and ask her the details of her school uniform, but after that he didn't feel it was quite the moment, so he just smoked his cigarette and concentrated on the driving. Laura liked the look of his hand on the gear stick. It was quite slender, and very brown. His arms were very relaxed as he drove. He leaned over with the cigarette in the side of his mouth and got a cravat out of the glove box, keeping the car on the road with the finger tips of his other hand. He checked it in the wing mirror.

'That do for you? Have a look in my jacket pocket and make sure I've got my Amex card, will you? It's on the back seat. In my wallet. Don't worry, there isn't a picture of my wife in it. Not that we'll need it, I've got plenty of cash. Just in case though.'

The little familiarities, noticing the lining of his jacket was coming unstitched, wondering what the 'D' was for in his initials on the faded black leather. Suppressing the idea that it might be Derek or Denis. The card was in the wallet. She wriggled back round to face the right way again. 'Yes.' That was one thing settled then. He was paying.

As they came up the drive a man in a white shirt was crossing in front of the house carrying bottles of wine. He waved back at Talbot and disappeared into the house.

'Do you know him?' Laura asked.

Talbot stood on the end of his cigarette and leaned through into the back of the car to get his jacket. 'Seen him once or twice here.' Laura didn't wonder who he had been with on the previous occasions, but was pleased to imagine him having a past in which he had done things independently of her. It was a sort of corroboration of his reality here and now. He was standing with his wallet in his hand, deciding whether he needed his jacket.

'Go on,' said Laura, 'ask me if I think you'll need your jacket.'

'Why? OK . . . Do you think I'll need my jacket, darling?' in a worried little husband voice.

'No,' she said firmly, 'definitely not. Put it back in the car.' He chucked it back in the car and came round to take her arm, laughing.

'Dear oh dear,' he said, 'what have I got myself into?'

They ate outside, so that the light was not really right for talking until near the end of the meal. Through the mussels and the chicken mousse and the sole which, had it been anything else she would have been too full to eat, he told her all about the food and how it had been prepared; about combinations of oil and lemon and garlic and parsley, and about there being really only a few steps to learn and from then on it was all just choreography. She sat there eating silently, protected by a huge white unstained linen napkin which came almost down to her calves while he showered her with illustrations of meals he had eaten in Spain and Mexico, New York and London; how a friend of his had once ordered ostrich at the Dorchester just to test them; how he had eaten vol-au-vents filled with lobster in a hot air balloon over the Masai Mara at dawn; how he had seen someone throw up an oyster deliberately and chomp it down again at a party at college. Look, look, Laura, he was saying, see how richly I have lived, how full I am with living, and how nothing has escaped my interest. And you? Come on, try it, taste the salt on the shores of this white hot tropical island you could never even have dreamed of, this land of epicurean exotica, draw closer now, that's it, and a little closer; and afterwards, ah yes, afterwards, there will be more stories, and more, a never ceasing flow of light entertainment. Come along, let me *endow* you . . .

The man who had carried the wine bottles, the owner, it turned out, lit coach lamps around the terrace. Then he and his wife sat down and drank champagne together, and Talbot, quickly deciding they were celebrating, sent them over a second bottle, pink this time, not of the region. Laura thought the couple looked rather embarrassed as they mimed their thanks. The lady shrugged a little and said something to her husband and he patted her hand, and when Talbot went to fetch some cigarettes from the car the man got up and took the bottle with him into the kitchen. He came back a minute or so later with their food which they ate quietly together, making only the odd comment, drawing each other's attention to something outside themselves.

'Jean-Pierre has ordered scallops for the party on Friday. Ten kilos will suffice, he says.'

'Ah.'

'I had a phone call from Marie. The children are well. Thomas has started to walk.'

'Good, good.'

Talbot came back across the gravel. 'Sorry about that. I couldn't find them. It's all right, I've got some now, chap sells them at the bar.'

He pushed away the remains of his fish and lit his cigarette. When the waiter came to clear away their things he made to remove their glasses. 'Hang on, hang on, let's have some more of that, shall we? Another of those please. You haven't? Oh, well just the Sauvignon then. Half. Okay, thanks,' and he turned back to Laura. 'How are you doing?'

She was actually feeling rather full and tired and the fastening of her shorts, which were baggy down the leg but a bit of a pinch at the waist, was biting into her side. She was thinking of the look on the lady's face and of the way she had not even blinked when Talbot had held Laura's hand all the way through her telling them about the *plat du jour*, which Talbot had dismissed anyway. Laura had got used to people looking at them, but she liked the fact that there was always just that question in the back of their minds as to whether they might not be related, even though she knew Talbot would have found the idea anything but piquant. It made her feel safer. The lady had not seen anything out of the ordinary in a man like Talbot turning up to dinner with a girl like Laura. What *are* girls like me like? Laura wondered, and blushed a little at her fickleness as a mimicking little voice in her head said with Talbot's intonation: *There's no one like you, sweetie.*

It was only a matter of time before he asked her what she was thinking about; in fact she gazed a little over-fixedly at the tablecloth until he did so, so that he accompanied the question with a passing of his hand before her eyes which nearly sent her glass flying. She had willed him to ask her, so that she could say 'Nothing, nothing,' and the slate would have been wiped clean and she would have put a stop once and for all to the little snag of disloyalty which was threatening to let rip in her mind.

He lifted the glass around the candle and lit his cigarette.

'There's something I need to talk to you about.'

What? What? she wanted to say, panicking, and her armpits suddenly felt as though they would gush with sweat, and she put her hands flat on the table, as though it was going to be something dreadful. She must know, though, that it couldn't be about sending her home or finding she really wasn't right for the job because they had already been through how he adored her and rehearsed how this was all a new heaven and a new earth for him over the chicken mousse.

'My wife never brings things up singly,' he began, and Laura thought immediately of the oyster, although that hadn't been Posy, it had been someone 'on my staircase', which had made her think of Christopher Robin at the time.

'I told you about the backers. The people with the money. Well, there's no problem with all that, it's very straightforward.'

Laura folded her napkin triangularly, then the corners into the middle, till before she knew it she was halfway through making a church with a steeple or a bishop's hat, depending how you looked at it.

'However.' He sat sideways to their table with his legs apart and his hands clasped, with just the points of his index fingers touching his front teeth. Thinking. Then he sat up and turned back to her, picking up his cigarette and tapping it aginst the side of the ashtray. She finished the steeple and propped it up in front of her. He moved it aside impatiently.

'The thing is, my name is quite well known in film circles, these things get around.'

He held his hand up as though helping someone to park a car. Stop! Mind that pillar! 'I'm not showing off or anything. It's just part of being in the business.'

'What things?'

'Oh, you know, projects, proposals, ideas, things get tossed about . . .'

A miniature Red Queen, exactly like a tiny chess piece, tickled Laura's ear at the word proposal. She thought it a strange use of the word and made a note.

'Anyway Posy met this man, Hugo somebody, at a party who said he'd heard about Monvanité and how all this had come up, God knows how actually, and she filled him in a bit, you know, as you do, and it turned out he's formed a company that does the kind of thing I used to be involved in, the fly on the wall stuff, the hidden camera and that. I told you about it.'

Laura nodded.

'He and his partner are making independent films for television – apparently they've sold to Australia and are looking at America, so we're talking about a well established, reputable set up. They did a thing on a league football club last season, you might have seen it, I think I read about it somewhere, rings a bell, locker room pre-match drama and so on.'

Laura said no, she hadn't seen it, it had probably been on late at night. Talbot almost interrupted himself to ask her what time she normally went to bed, then thought better of it in case she said ten thirty or something and he'd feel he had to ask if she wasn't feeling tired. She looked as though she might say yes and he very much wanted another drink.

He rushed the ending. 'Anyway, he thinks the whole thing

would make a great programme and I said okay, why don't you come out for a couple of days, I'll fill you in on the story, we'll look into the idea. Great publicity if it comes off. He's coming out on Sunday evening. Not filming, you understand, just to get an idea of the lie of the land, see if there's enough in it. I'd like him to be here for the meeting with the backers – dinner, perhaps. That'll give us a chance to sort things out at lunch. He'll only be here for a few days . . .'

'Here? What, at home?'

'Sweetie!' he exclaimed, taking her hand, 'I'm touched,' and she felt embarrassed, as he meant she should.

'Don't worry, he may not even like the story. They've obviously got some travel budget to use up, it'll just be like having a guest. I expect he'll have a little video camera with him you know, like the one we've got back at the house. Trying out a few ideas. Nothing to worry about.'

'But he's going to eat with us and everything?'

'Darling! You make it sound obscene. Where's the problem? I told you, it'll only be for a couple of days. You'll hardly know he's there. That's the point.'

'How can he be like a guest then?'

'Well, obviously, we'll know he's there, but it'll be as though we didn't.'

'What, sometimes we pass him the peas, sometimes we don't?'

'You'll get the hang of it.'

Laura wanted to say 'Why didn't you ask me?' but she didn't know him well enough, even though he seemed to feel he knew her well enough for almost anything. If he found he didn't, he just did it, which made them better acquainted, and thereby sanctioned whatever it was he had done. She'd worked that one out, although it didn't stop her looking for, and therefore finding time after time, the best in him. *Helas*! as Ludmilla might have said. If she had known to put it all down to charm and sex appeal, to concentrate purely on his attributes and not worry too much about the essence, it would all have been very much less painful and more consistently enjoyable. She would have been able to work out in a trice why one half of her mind was shouting stop and the other yelling, twice as loud, Go! Go!!

'Look,' he said, 'we'll talk about it tomorrow. It really isn't a big deal. If you're not happy you can go and stay with Albert. Let's get the bill.'

Suddenly he seemed terribly impatient.

'But you ordered another half bottle,' she reminded him. 'There's the man coming now.'

'Forget it. They were too slow.'

'Do you think we could have it? I'd really quite like some now.'

'You want some?' He looked at her sharply and smiled, squeezing her hand. He looked as though he were doing a calculation. Perhaps, she thought, he was thinking about the bill. She didn't want to drink any more, but she felt that in cancelling the order, Talbot would be admitting to an earlier instinct towards over-indulgence, whereas if they stuck to it the lapse would go unremarked.

'Okay. And I'll have a Calvados.'

By the time they left, the owners had gone back indoors and the restaurant seemed to have become their house again. Laura would have liked to have been their guest, to have gone in and sat in a comfortable armchair and talked to them about the scallops, perhaps, and their grandson who was beginning to walk. But instead she walked with Talbot back to the car, with his hand on the nape of her neck under the loop of her hair and when he pointed out the stars and one constellation in particular that looked like Madame Derrault and her washing basket and made her laugh, she quite forgot her reservations and was enchanted all over again, as from the start.

23

Posy had rung Ludmilla to say that Hugo would be arriving with a certain amount of equipment, so she was all set for a four-man film crew, lights, boom, make up girl perhaps. It was a bit disappointing that all he had was himself – which she didn't think much of – and a do-it-yourself camera, about the size of a puppy. It came in a sort of snood affair which hung from a shoulder strap.

Hugo had a very broad face and a rather straggly beard which Ludmilla fancied igniting to see if it would connect with his barrel chest and send the whole of him up in smoke. He summed her up as a music hall dame. Get this over with quickly, he thought. He had to film Ludmilla and get back and edit her before he left for the theatre, where he was understudying Lady Hunstanton in an all male production of *A Woman Of No Importance*. He was staying with friends in Windsor overnight, and from there he'd go straight to Heathrow for Toulouse on Sunday afternoon. He popped through the door into her house like a champagne cork.

'Okay! Where are we? In here? Right!'

He whipped off his leather jacket and threw it down on a chair, crossed the room and pulled the curtains.

'No, no,' Ludmilla scolded, 'not like that. You have to pull the cord. There.'

'Great. That's better, okay, plonk youself down somewhere comfortable, that's fine, make yourself at home, I'll just set myself up.'

He was only about five-foot-three, but you could never have got him to stand still for long enough to take his measurements.

• Helen Stevenson

Ludmilla began to fantasise about a human-sized piece of flypaper which she could drop from the ceiling like a banner. She felt compelled to follow him about in circles as though she were stuck in a revolving door. This was due not so much to animal magnetism as to the fact that he looked as though he might very soon break something. It was all going to be terribly quick and she would forget what to say. After a whole hour earlier that morning in front of her mirror with a headband scraping back her hair, pretending to be a starlet! She had even, admittedly a little fancifully, looking back on it, imagined him interviewing her like that, in front of the mirror, as though she had some more important stage to sweep onto – Oh Lord, there was the second bell – last curve of lipstick swooping the underlip, I really have to fly now, perhaps you could contact my agent if you have any further . . .

'Is that what you're wearing, or do you want to go and change?' Ludmilla did a double take.

'I . . . er . . . oh, I really hadn't thought,' she said. 'This will do as well as anything.'

'Okay, let's have a bit of you at the piano, give me something I know. Hey, d'you know that lullaby. Tiny Tears ad, how's it go?'

She sat at her piano with a very straight back and played the first few bars of the Brahms 'Lullaby'.

'Brilliant, that's really clever, just like that off the top of your head. Gosh, I've got to tell you this Ludmilla – can I call you that – I'd really like a drink.'

She gave him a straight vodka, and had one herself. He tipped it back. 'Sod this,' he said. 'I was only practising. How was I? Convincing? Bit over the top perhaps? Have to tone it down a bit for France. Liked the Brahms, though.'

Half an hour later they decided they'd better get on with some work. By this time Ludmilla was in full swing, all guns a-blazing, with the house-on-fire thing between them to boot. He really was a splendid young man – she'd particularly enjoyed the slapstick at the beginning, she told herself.

'Let's just have a laugh and get it over with,' he said. 'You can put a funny voice on if you like. Remember, it's not me you're talking to, it's Talbot Hardy, that is, if I ever work out how this thing . . . ah, there we go, I've got a red light. Moment of truth. Fire away.'

She began by quoting Voltaire's opinion that we owe respect to the living and to the dead only truth. She enjoyed the use of epigrams – for something so chiselled they had a surprisingly elastic quality and could be fitted into a hole of almost any size or shape. Then she handed over the information that was wanting, just as she had to Posy in the train, with the real world skimming by at eye level beyond her touch. For laughs. Abjure the tragic manner! *Quod scripsi scripsi*. All right, but the joke's on you.

Just tell him as you told it to me, Posy had said, so she took a deep breath and stepped lightly over her past, her unwatered sadnesses, as though they had been no more than a patchy row of pallid seedlings. *Pierrot Lunaire* as the cynical satire of True Love, the throw-away jaunt into the world of pastiche, a snigger in the face of Romance. How she had laughed! *Come on Talbot, let's separate fact from fiction here*.

It went on for twelve minutes. Afterwards Hugo got up and drew the curtains, using the cord with its heavy brass weight on the end and the light of day cut back into Ludmilla's music room.

She was a hoot up to the last syllable of recorded time. Even while she showed him to the door she was chuckling and making him promise to be in touch when he got back from France. But when he had gone, taking his videotape with him, her false testimony, the person she had allowed herself, she thought, truly to become, she sat limply at her piano, hanging her head like a very bad pupil, with no courage left in her and the most extraordinary feeling of loss in her heart. Her lips felt as though they were peeling away from her mouth at each side and a grimace of grief stole across her face, as though in the dark watches of the night pain had crept in to call her to amendment. There was no health in her. That was true enough. She sat there like Toad while Badger berated him, hanging her head, though there was no one in the room to see her shame, no Ratty to sit on her legs and demand that she never ride again. Where was the vicar when she needed to be chided? Where was the stern reproving voice, the chastisement before the relief? How shall I know, she wondered, when this grief of mine is real? How

• Helen Stevenson

shall I know it is not just Ludmilla Pike's last enactment, an apt, last-moment and face-saving inversion of what has been my way till now? It was her way not to admit to the rhetorical nature of her exclamations and she cocked an ear wonderingly – waiting for an answer, but answer came there none. She shut the piano lid and wandered out to the kitchen, where Florence, her daily, never-say-die, claimed her assistance with the quick crossword.

24

It took Ludmilla a long time to dress for church the following Sunday. She had gathered that hats were out, but what on earth was in? Would she need to be in kneeling kit? In that case the grey woollen trousers with matching waistcoat would be appropriate. Could she brighten it up with the purple and amber scarf? How about the green button-up-the-front tunic with those thoroughly serviceable beads she had picked up at the nearly new shop? Beads. Bit dodgy perhaps.

In the end it was a relatively sober-looking Ludmilla who shook her brolly in the porch and handed it over to a warden in exchange for the *Book of Common Prayer* and a service sheet. The warden, who was not accustomed to being given unto in quite this way popped it under a table and murmured something about not thinking they'd had the pleasure of welcoming her there before. She informed him that she was an extremely good friend of the vicar's, and despite all her best resolutions to be thoroughly hands-together-eyes-closed could not resist opening her eyes very wide and assuming a slightly louche, if nonchalant, air. She excused herself for dripping all over his prayer books and headed into the church.

Someone was playing the organ execrably. She found an empty pew and squeezed herself in. You had to shut a little door behind you, which Ludmilla thought was an extremely wise precaution. Once settled she took the kneeler off its little peg in front of her and slipped off her booties, which were damp, and more furry than you'd imagine polyester could ever get. There, that was better. If women spent more time looking after their feet . . .

The church was mid-nineteenth-century gothic, black with soot on the outside but pleasantly refurbished with swedish pine pews within. There were flowers on the ledges of the inset windows, chosen and arranged with more style than Ludmilla would have expected. It was really very nice and warm – if only that dreadful noise coming from the organ could be sorted out. The organist was perched aloft to her right and in front, and his lair was equipped with a little mirror so he could see when the choir and the vicar were about to set sail from the vestry, cuing them with something appropriately processional. Ludmilla wriggled herself along a bit, bringing the kneeler with her between her toes and found herself able to catch the organist's eye behind his pebbly looking glasses. She pulled a face. 'Yes, you,' she thought. 'Come along we're all listening, chord of C *minor* in the left hand, yes, there you are, plagal cadence, and so! Back to the tonic. Again!'

The warden slid by, dropping Ludmilla's umbrella into the little brass stand at the end of her pew. 'My goodness,' she thought, 'am I going to need it in here?'

The church was filling up. Children ran about excitedly, huddling up together in their pews, passing messages, and turning round to pull faces at their parents. A West Indian family had just arrived, father and mother holding their son and daughter by the hand. The children were dressed in their very best, the little girl radiant in a pink and white frock, almost skipping for joy in the aisles in her little buckled shoes. She caught sight of Ludmilla sitting there alone rather stiffly in her turquoise raincoat. She lent up and whispered something in her father's ear and he patted her head and glanced Ludmilla's way, smiling. They all took up their seats near the front. Mention my name and you'll get a good seat. The Lord's name be praised, Ludmilla thought, trying to remember how the rest of it went. Oh well, she was quite near the back, no one would notice her much.

The vicar was late in. Obviously giving a team talk to the choir. The organist was getting a little desperate, and had abandoned the prospect of a sixth reprise of 'Jesu Joy of Man's Desiring', much to Ludmilla's relief, and was working his way through the hymn book. She made up a little verse to the tune of 'Lord Thy Word Abideth':

> Keep the tempo steady
> Till the vicar's ready,
> Peering in your mirror,
> Play another filler.
>
> What d'you s'pose he's doing
> While the cud we're chewing?
> Really I don't like to carp,
> But that should be an F-sharp.

She was beginning to think she could really get to like coming to church, when a door opened and in came the vicar, looking not at all his bashful self, but somehow rounder and happier. He beamed at the congregation, bid them welcome, and invited everyone to praise God in singing the first hymn. The organist, fresh from his improvisational exertions and by now developing a certain degree of paranoia about this lady who was pulling terrifying faces at him in his mirror, took a little while to get going, but once he had lurched his way uncertainly through the first line, everyone got to their feet and prepared to sing.

Ludmilla was amazed. How everybody sang! Since the vicar had entered the church a feeling of excitement had spread among the congregation. Pass it on, pass it on! No, it wasn't the collection plate, not yet, but joy, rippling through these oddly assorted troops in their wellies and their twin sets and their quilted coats and jackets and ties and denim trousers and what have you. My word, she thought, I've been underestimating the man. Laura's father – yes, all right, tick for that – but otherwise no special mentions. And yet – had he always been like this? She'd always thought him such a pale creature, an academic in fancy dress, a very minor prebendary from Trollope. (Not that Ludmilla wasn't fond of her Trollope. Why pay £7.99 for some trendy Virago when you can get a nice fat Trollope for £3.50?) It's 'Love', she thought, and wondered whether he found the frequent occurrence of the word in their hymns and prayers a little confusing at this very-special-time.

They were still going strong on 'O God Our Help in Ages Past', and they were singing it with the rampant conviction of a football supporters' club on the way to the Cup Final. She thought perhaps their enthusiasm could be somewhat tempered at moments by a little coaching in respect of dynamic markings and the subtleties of the text. There was an asterisk at verse five. What did that mean – not suitable for children? Oh, I see, optional. 'Time like an ever rolling stream Bears all its sons away; They fly forgotten as a dream Dies at the opening day.'

'That's a bit hard,' she thought. 'No wonder it's optional,' but they rattled through it anyway and Ludmilla girded herself against the fairly immediate prospect of her own flight, forgotten as a dream, by singing a rather unconventional descant. Then they all sat down.

The sermon was short. Jeremy preached on the text, 'I will sing unto the Lord as long as I live: I will praise my God while I have my being'. Ludmilla thought this was a little close to the bone, but admittedly he probably hadn't spotted her, and looking at the other bits of the morning psalm in her prayer book she could only be relieved that he hadn't come up with 'I have mingled my drink with weeping'. The gist of his message seemed to be a sort of Herrick philosophy of hay-making-while-sun-shining, which obviously, in the light of his forthcoming marriage, was much on his mind. (She commented on this to Gertrude later and then had hastily to say, oh no, she hadn't meant that, she'd meant of couse that hay would be made *after* their wedding, goodness me no . . .).

She shook hands in a very jolly fashion when everyone came up and said, 'Peace be with you'; in fact so many people seemed to be coming up at once that she wondered if the vicar had actually said something in code about the lady in the turquoise raincoat being in special need. She replied heartily in her best female bass, 'Good morning!' and they all seemed to move on perfectly pleased with that. The little girl in the pink and white frock pumped her hand with great glee; in fact, instead of leaning over the door to Ludmilla's pew, she calmly undid the little lock that held it fastened and came trotting in, complete with her reading book and a pencil. She sat down happily next to Ludmilla and could not be lured back to her seat by her mother's beseeching gaze. She stuck her little nose in the air as if to say, 'Don't know you!!' Her feet didn't reach the floor, so Ludmilla lent her her kneeler and they made a little tower below pew level.

Everyone else went up for communion, shuffling with that faintly embarrassed air along the aisle carpet, as the organist twiddled confidently through unintentional variations on a theme by Gustav Holst. Now Ludmilla may have been enjoying herself and feeling happy, a lot happier at least than when she had come in. She may have begun to feel her heart a trifle strangely moved. She was comforted by the crowd and felt warm and unexceptional and safe. If God was going to touch her at the last minute though, she thought, He was really holding out for the final whistle. Amen, so be it. So Ludmilla and her little friend, whose name it turned out was Angora, sat joining up the dots on a piece of paper Ludmilla produced from her pocket and were so surprised when the organist wound up his meditative fumble through some of the more obscure areas of the repertoire and burst into a jaunty version of 'Oh Jesus I have promised', that Angora nearly fell off the edge of her seat and lost a shoe. Then she flicked her way through the hymn book to find it for Ludmilla and passed it to her with a modest little shrug while singing away in a pretty, fluty voice into her ear.

Gertrude came up and grabbed her after the service. 'You will come and have lunch with us my dear,' she said, and Ludmilla felt quite dreadful for having called her Eva Braun in her mind, she was such a nice warm lady, and not at all prim or unctious. 'That would be lovely,' she said.

Angora said goodbye and presented Ludmilla with her umbrella, having made sure she was coming back next week. Otherwise, she said, she lived above the newsagent, so Ludmilla could come to her house if she wanted. Ludmilla did not want to tell her there were probably about eight different newsagents in the town centre alone, for fear of damaging the child's sense of uniqueness. Besides she supposed that if she took it into her head to go and have tea with Angora one day she would just jolly well find out which newsagent it was. *Tout est possible.*

Gertrude and Ludmilla let themselves into the park through a gate in the railings which dripped with rusty-smelling droplets of morning rain. A patched up path of tarmac guided them between the borders like some gratuitously complicated board game. Round they went, stepping round puddles and children on tricycles, past grim-looking bedding plants bunched in clusters of hundreds and thousands of flower heads, in designs which might have been created out of tiny blobs of tissue paper glued on card.

Ludmilla wiped a bench with her adequate handkerchief and then wrung it out and hung it over the back of the seat to dry. Gertrude sat slightly twisted towards Ludmilla, managing to look at once tender and sensible.

'I want to tell you,' said Ludmilla, 'about *Pierrot Lunaire*. I want you to understand.' They talked for over an hour speaking in low voices, without fuss, without gesticulation, without reference to surroundings or their present selves. After they had finished, Gertrude said the best thing they could do would be to record a new video and get Laura to substitute it for the old one. They contacted a local photographer who also ran a video service. He came and sat in Ludmilla's music room with the two women that afternoon and they solemnly recorded their interview. The photographer had also recently become involved in video wills, so much more personal than the old scroll of paper, so he did one of those without any fuss at a fifty percent discount for, as he put it, buying in bulk. Jeremy and Gertrude were the witnesses. 'Laura will enjoy this,' Ludmilla remarked. 'It'll be quite like watching *Ask the Family*,' but as she couldn't remember the theme tune she played the music for *Face the Music* instead. Walton's *Façade*. Gertrude patted her on the knee and said that was probably more appropriate anyway, so the photographer obligingly recorded it to go at the end of the film.

25

It was now the third week in June. Hugo had arrived by train from the airport on the Sunday evening and spent the night in the Hotel de la Gare. He was a light sleeper. From his window at dawn he watched the market traders setting up their stalls like circus acts. Each had his little *camion*, which he reversed into position with perfect ease. The street lamps had been turned off ready for day but it was not yet quite light, so the traders looked like performers stealthily disposing themselves and their props about a stage, each finding his appointed position with the minimum of noise, so as not to attract attention on the other side of the curtain. Hugo watched from his high seat on the second floor, and it was almost with shock that he noticed the smell of real vegetables. Across the square, beneath martially pollarded limes, a man was setting up chickens in a cabinet of revolving spits – plump little white bundles, apparently neither fish nor fowl, which by mid-morning, as though by some imperceptible process of incarnation, would assume their familiar form.

A woman was constructing a pyramid of honey jars and stood defensively before her edifice as a long-legged joker came past, bowling a huge cheese between his feet. Across the square a squabble had arisen. The man at the bread stall had placed trays of cakes and *galettes* at one end of the table on the ground and a very small man selling basil next door was contesting the allocation of space. He paced the length of the bread-maker's stall with quick delicate steps, arms half lifted from his side. Then he paced his own, scarcely more than a two step. Triumphantly he swung back round to face the bread-maker who shouted an appeal to no one in particular, laughed, and with the gentlest nudge of his foot, shifted the whole pile of trays back under his own table. A policeman came cycling in to the square at alarming speed, did one cursory circuit then whistled off again. A young man selling plastic clothes pegs and household bits and pieces set up stall with a casual deftness which seemed designed to illustrate the labour saving properties of his wares. A group of women in canvas aprons gathered cooing round a chicken-wire cage of young rabbits, gauging their weights.

But by seven o'clock everything was underway and it was all strangely normal and only a market after all, and Hugo wondered whether they didn't all yearn for the day when the extraordinary would happen, that moment for which they seemed secretly to rehearse, when they would reach into their vegetable crates and out would fly doves, when the flutes and baguettes of bread would trumpet with handkerchiefs and the women would dance and juggle on the tables and the men stand on their hands and weigh out vegetables with their feet. He imagined them carefully transferring the lead weights to the dish, one by one with their toes, then moving carefully back to judge the balance.

He slipped his book and his toothbrush back into his bag, picked up his leather jacket and the video snood and went down to pay. Then he cut his way through the market and made for the Café du Sport which he'd noticed on his way from the station the previous evening. The streets were already hot and busy. Children were running to catch their buses, the estate agent looked him up and down with interest, the *curé* bade him good morning as he slipped by. Hugo found a seat near the window and shoved his bag under the table. '*Un café et un croissant*,' he rehearsed in his head. '*Un croissant et un café*.' Or was it '*une*'? He got his book out. A present from Posy, for a laugh. It was called *Cinema vérité* but it was in English, he had discovered to his relief. He'd been a bit worried for a second that she expected him to be a linguist in addition to all his other talents. She expected an awful lot did Posy. On a card inside, in a flamboyant and inky hand, she had written: 'Don't bother to read this, darling. Only a prop.' Norman, who did not open up shop till the afternoon, was having a little chat with Madame Derrault over by the parrot. He was trying to cheer the bird up.

'The batsman's Holding, the bowler's Willey,' he kept repeating, in the urgent undertone of a *Resistance* leader talking in code. The parrot looked at Madame Derrault with a sullen eye. Madame Derrault turned it back on Norman then went to serve some people at the bar. Hugo sat and stared at Norman who was repeating his phrase with conscientious intonation, so as not to confuse the bird.

Eventually Norman gave up and went over and made himself a cup of coffee. He thought he could probably never leave the village now. He owed Madame Derrault more in cups of coffee than he had at one time owed the Inland Revenue. He also, like Ludmilla, took sugar, but at least that was free.

Hugo found himself watching the old buffer for tricks. You never knew what character parts might come your way. Expat. Cricket type. Clean shaven as an ice rink.

Madame Derrault brought Hugo's coffee and a croissant she had fetched from the boulangerie next door, ten expensive little steps away. She didn't like men with beards, especially not ones with a little tuft like Hugo's. She tended to regard facial hair as a kind of attempt to assume a humanising mask, as though if you pulled it off you could expect to find a farmyard animal underneath.

Hugo had not at first been keen on Posy's plan. She was a great girl and he wasn't the over-sensitive type himself, but he found her curiosity concerning Talbot, his love life, his work in progress and even his financial situation, a bit much. She seemed to be suffering from an obsession with Monvanité which she disguised as a sort of insatiable playfulness, a laugh for a laugh's sake. She was the only grown-up person he knew who still used the phrase 'I dare you . . .' to mean, 'I know this is outrageous, only people like me do things like this, but I wonder if you might be prepared to prove me wrong.' Of course she couldn't say to him 'I dare you to go and spy on my husband and see if he's in love with that nineteen-year-old girl or if he's sleeping with Sally and if he's doing any work, and I wish I hadn't let him go to France because after all it's my place, except, being who I am, I know I would absolutely hate it there.' So instead she had announced it as a game, as if saying it was a game made it one, just by applying the word to it. Most persuasively, she had made it a taunt to his professionalism, teasing that he was afraid he wouldn't get away with it. It had occurred to him that if Talbot didn't find it funny in the end (as Posy had assured him he would) he might himself become the scapegoat, sent off into the desert under a shower of stones. On the whole, though, he was inclined to take Posy's word for Talbot being a good sport. You would have to be to put up with that little firebrand for so long. The bit with Ludmilla had proved he could do it, but he'd only kept that up for a few minutes, because he'd fallen for her and thought she'd enjoy the ruse. He hadn't told Posy about that indiscretion. Complicity was the price he had exacted from Ludmilla for his confession. So here he was now, sitting in a café in France, wondering how he was going to explain to Posy's ex that he didn't understand the first thing about camera angles. He thought he might be able to improvise from what he knew about the stage. He would have to pretend to be widly innovative, like those people who hadn't got the first clue about how to dress and make a virtue out of a bin liner. That would make Talbot feel really old hat, so he probably wouldn't push it. Thank God he only had to stick it out till Thursday when the game would be up. Hugo hadn't a loyalty in the world. He wouldn't have sold his grandmother, not quite, but probably only because he would never be under a moment's illusion that there was a market for grandmothers. He was anybody's man after his own, but only at a good price.

He asked Madame Derrault the way to Monvanité.

'Château Monvanité, *s'il vous plaît?*' as though he expected her to take him on the back of her bicycle, she thought. She gave him exactly the same reply as she had given Laura two weeks before. Hugo was relieved that, although he didn't understand a word of what she said, she was obviously used to answering this question – by a happy chance he had picked on exactly the right person to ask. That was evident from the formulaic ring to her response, as though she had said, 'Yes, Form 22b, in triplicate, by hand to kiosks fourteen, fifteen or sixteen on Tuesdays and Thursdays unless you're on disability, in which case take a seat.' It would have been equally incomprehensible, but gratifying in the same completely useless way. 'Oh,' he said, *'merci beaucoup.'*

Norman had long ears for a home counties accent. He looked over his shoulder and then over Hugo's and murmured, 'Second right out of the village on the road to Soubyrète. Follow the road for 1500 metres and you'll see a sign.'

Hugo thought for a moment that he was being visited by some omniscient dubber. Then he swivelled round to see Norman smiling benignly at his coffee cup, straightening his tie.

'Oh, thanks. Very kind. Er, could you run through that again please?'

Norman picked up his little pile of books and slid round to join Hugo in his little bay. Speaking the language was his party trick. Judging types was Hugo's. They talked rather waggishly of the test score, which Norman hadn't yet heard. He quite enjoyed the position of one who read yesterday's newspaper as though it was hot off the press. It was like being sent pieces of wedding cake.

'Tell you what,' Norman offered. 'I've a chum lives up at the château. English girl by the name of Laura. You know her? Nice girl. I'll give her a bell. She might be able to come and fetch you. Staying long? Come on upstairs and we'll see what's what.'

Hugo followed Norman with a rather exaggeratedly dutiful air up some stairs out of the back of the cafe. As they left the room he caught Madame Derrault's eye. He gave her a mock saucy look, as if to say see now, it didn't pay to be snooty – look what she was missing out on, but for once she was so intrigued she abandoned the outright hostility to which she usually treated strangers and just glared. It was her form of neutrality.

You entered Norman's flat through a heavy sculpted door. He kept the key on a shelf above it, replacing it neatly after use. The door was not high, but neither man had to duck. To Norman, Hugo gave the impression of being much taller than he was, because of the barrel chest and the stockiness.

'This is my little abode. Please come in,' Norman announced rather formally, like the faun in the Narnia stories.

He was in the middle of sorting out the sport section from the shop, and had brought it up to have something to do in the long light evenings. An English lady who had been running a bookshop in the Dordogne had recently died, and Norman had saved a large number of her books from being burned by her late husband's family. Laura had dropped by yesterday afternoon – Talbot was working and cross, she said. She looked tired and upset, and they had gone through the stock together, sorting cricketing memoirs by decades, and mending the spines of rule books for lawn tennis. Talbot was still a little wary of Norman, citing his Catholicism now, grudgingly accepting that his first assessment of the man had been wrong. He was strangely moralistic in areas which did not touch upon his own existence. Hugo tripped over a pile of books as he came round the door. Norman turned at the noise of a scuffle.

'Whoops-a-daisy, all right? That was me, I'm afraid. Left them there last night to take down. I don't know! Forget my head.'

Hugo asked politely if he were a keen sportsman.

He looked a little baffled, then laughed. 'Oh no no no, not me. Never could catch, you know. Cricket I mean. If that's what you mean.'

'Well, generally, I thought, all these books – *The Golfer's Guide to the East Coast* . . .'

'That's not sport, that's travel,' Norman chipped in quickly, and took the book out of Hugo's hands.

Hugo was still bobbing down on the floor by the books. He looked up as Norman wandered off into another room, presumably to phone. The room was open to the rafters, and draped with brocade. Sunlight came through a mansard window. There was no bed. That must be next door. Books, a polished table, all neatly arranged, a little gentleman's lair. Slightly E.M. Forster. Then Hugo put on his hang-on-a-minute face. Over in the far corner was a little group of plaster figurines, each about three feet tall, with writing like headlines on face and limb. Very odd.

Norman popped his head round the door. 'Make yourself at home. Would you like another coffee?'

Hugo turned to look at him, adopting a rather stern expression as if he was going to have to reassess this fellow. His beard was itching. He thought he ought to be getting on.

'Oh, just let me phone, I won't be a tick. No point you slogging all that way unless you have to. If you won't have a drink just take a pew.'

When he came back into the room, Hugo was over by the window, touching the plaster figures.

'What do you think? Charming?'

Hugo asked what they were.

'Why, plaster saints of course. Well, not of course. I mean, yes they are saints, representations, you know, for praying to. It's a little sideline of mine. I told the priest what he'd got in church was a whole load of ticky-tacky – well it *was*, dreadful stuff, not what you want to look at Sunday after Sunday – mass produced in some factory in Lille. Straight out of Woolies – you can imagine.'

Hugo tried.

'I said, tell you what, I know this chap in Brighton. Sculptor chappie, got a real gift – he does animals mostly, you know. But I said, why don't we send him some pictures of old carvings of saints and what not. I had some lovely postcards in a collection someone had made in Bavaria before the war. I said to him, I said, look Barney, knock us up something like this could you – told him what we were about. Six months later these arrive. What colour do you want them painting, he says. You can see where he's written his suggestions. Blue, you see, for her dress; brown there, his sandals and so on. I wrote back. I said, leave them as they are. He said, they're not finished. I said, Oh yes they are. Don't you think? Just white. Sort of alabaster. Course they're not, they're plaster of Paris. But you know what?'

Hugo looked interested, but there was only one thing to be said. 'What?'

'Take this madonna.' He tapped her head fondly. 'Seen it anywhere before?'

'I – er, gosh, I don't know, let's see, well, it does look . . .'

'I'll tell you,' Norman finished, 'you haven't. Why? Because there isn't another one, that's why. She's the one and only, and ever shall be. Only one in the world. By Barney in Brighton.'

He started to leave the room. 'Course we'll break her when the final version comes. That's the way of one-and-onlys. Then he'll break the cast. At least, he better had. That's what we've arranged.'

He came back apologising. 'No one there I'm afraid. They must be out gallivanting. Lovely girl, Laura, you'll like her. Staying long?'

'What are we, Monday? Er, till Saturday, I think.'

'Oh well, probably see you around then. Friend of the boss are you?'

'Sorry?'

'Talbot. Friend of his?' He was going to add 'Nice chap,' but then didn't.

Hugo felt he had not been very cool about the saints.

'Interesting,' he said, taking a step back to look at them. He could afford to linger now that he knew he was going.

'What's your line?' asked Norman quaintly.

'Oh, I'm an – a journalist. A journalist,' he repeated. He wasn't sure whether to spread the heresy would be to strengthen his position or to lay him open to uncomfortable investigations.

Norman looked at him sharply. 'A–ha!' he cooed wonderingly. 'Another one. Are you interested in the area then?'

He explained about the healing waters in the sarcophagus. Hugo listened politely. He was feeling a bit emasculated by Norman, strangely enough. He'd have to get his form sorted out a bit more for his performance at the château. He didn't want to spread too many different versions of his persona around. What he needed to do was recapture a bit of the old routine he'd got going in the first few minutes with Ludmilla.

'Look,' he said brusquely. Whoops, that had been a little too brusque. 'I guess I really ought to be off now. Nice to meet you. Hope it goes well with the statues. Perhaps be seeing you again. Brilliant place you've got here. No, don't bother, I'll find my own way down. Second right you said, fine, sure I'll find it. No trouble. Bye then.' And he was off.

Norman went over and straightened up his pile of books. It had gone quiet in the room, but not because Hugo had left. He'd hardly said anything really. What a lot of coming and going. Funny chap. He looked down out of his bedroom window and saw Hugo crossing the street, with his black jacket slung over his shoulder, walking slowly in the wrong direction and thought he reminded him rather of a bear. No charm. Not very sure of himself. Needed a good shave that was for sure. There were some people like that. You did your best to be friendly and they just sort of exhausted you. 'You've been away too long, Norm,' he said to himself. 'Living in a world of your own.' But he felt none the worse for all that. You had to make your own life.

26

Circling at a hundred metres above Monvanité, a blur of sandy stones below, peaks of grey slate, a dark dab of olive trees to west and north; the solitary cedar, a line of poplars pencilled in. Creamy cornfield, wind broken by bamboo and pampas grass, still in the prenoon sun. Circling lower, the river starts to move, white tips of water over the stones, then falling away to clear pools, where unseen fish eddy in the darkness, shadows cast by near black rocks. The dovecot hidden by its own peak of slate. The little farmhouse to the north, perfect square of green in front. Swinging back over the trees, Monvanité reappears, birds' nests in the broken tiles. Flaking mortar, ivy splayed across the walls, at once luxuriant and meanly clutching. Ground level, by the delicate tree of jasmine, her bicycle, abandoned in haste. A wooden table, bowl of unshelled peas. He sits alone, sleeves rolled. Head slightly bowed, cigarette grinding under his foot into the brittle grass in tufts at his feet. Young, but not in his youth. The gaze drops and levels, becomes his own. Against the sun, her dress is blood coloured. In her arms are trails of ivy and other foliage, against the sun it could be something live. She walks away from him, stirring the grass only lightly with her feet. He reaches for the bowl of peas, splits one. Examining the soft cushion of pod, down to the last spindle of thread. The world in a grain of sand.

'It's a bit corny,' Laura said, pushing the bowl of peas back towards him, having taken her pile.

'I don't think so. What I'm saying is that's how he experiences it! That's how it comes to him – a sort of revelation. You know, not in the vast panorama, the acres of oh-so-impressive scenery, sweeping countryside, violins what have you, but in the tiny pod of peas. Suddenly he's there, suddenly he can *see* nature – and in the same moment he sees her. His love for Chloe, his love for – for God's creation if you like – it's all one and the same thing.'

Laura slit the pod she was holding and scooped the peas into her hand. She began to pick at them.

Talbot jumped up. 'Okay, what do you want?' He ran to the bay tree and knelt before it, head flung back. 'O Chloe,' he groaned, 'O woman made from dust, to dust you shall return, O nature, all women thou, O mother earth take not this woman from me. All mountains and rivers she, immerse me in the flood tide of her young beauty . . .'

'Okay, okay.'

He got to his feet and came back to the table. 'You see,' he said. 'It's not as easy as you think. It's all very well to be dismissive. Come on now, let's hear your version.'

She stood up and shook her skirt into the bowl for the shelled peas. 'I haven't got one for the moment. But I'll let you know. I'm going to put these inside.'

'You've no soul,' he told her ruefully. 'Where's it gone?'

'Sold,' she said primly, and went indoors. His sort of language.

He sat on alone, chewing at a pea pod. He seemed not to notice the sun rising in the sky. He was feeling troubled by his own distraction, an inability to get on with the job in hand. Four days till Posy's financiers arrived, and he hadn't much to show them. He hoped they would fall for the place and the idea. Laura could help there. Perhaps the arrival of this Hugo fellow would get him going.

The two of them had fallen into a rather sticky pattern. Most of the time they were happy. Laura had reinspired him to work on his script and he had rediscovered the magic of *Pierrot Lunaire* which had been dispelled by Ludmilla's visitation. He'd put Ludmilla right behind him now. Laura seemed to have heeded his rebuke and to have made an effort not to bring her up too much. Yesterday he had called her a great black shadow-casting bat, and Laura had only pulled him up to say actually she was a butterfly, a giant black butterfly, so they were able to compromise on that particular image. They had spent

Sunday evening lying out on the grass, listening to the Franck violin sonata with the library windows open. That morning they had driven into the village and shopped for fruit and vegetables in the market. Talbot taught her all the names in French of the things she had never come across in England, so that the words were not translations, but wholly new. They described for each other the limits of their experience without each other, the most frightening. the saddest, the happiest that had been, and compared it all with this, where the moments couldn't be isolated and there were no superlatives or comparatives, but only this summer time, which like the universe could neither be imagined going on for ever nor be supposed to be finite. For what could lie beyond? Talbot told her about time being circular. God, he said, or what we call God (God of our fathers, to you, he said), was like a point in the centre, occupying no space, with no perceivable dimensions, and to whom time was related as points on the circumference of a huge circle around Him. So you see, he explained, though it seems to us that we are covering distance around the circle, in relation to God we are all in one and the same moment. Laura asked if that meant that the first time round for *Pierrot Lunaire* in the thirties was happening in the same moment as they were in now. Er, no, said Talbot, the circle was probably a bit bigger than that. Well, for God anyway, Laura corrected. Sort of, Talbot reckoned, or at least there was an original *Pierrot Lunaire* somewhere, of which they were making more and more perfect copies all the time.

'This is damned near perfection,' he said, as they walked back through the park to the house one day and then struck a Robin Hood pose peeping out from behind the great cedar with a pretend camera in his hands snapping her from all sides. 'But just wait till you see the film!' To himself he thought there would be a darn sight more sex in the movie.

That was where it was sticky between them. Laura was happy the way things were. Talbot had accused her of being hypocritical. She had argued that it would be hypocritical of her to do anything she didn't really want to. She was waiting for the moment when the body took over so completely from the mind that there would be no question of having to still a voice within her, somewhere beyond good and evil. As yet it hadn't happened like that. Talbot was making the most of his frustration, using it as a yardstick for his love for her. It was not altogether a happy state of affairs.

Hugo had been intrigued by Talbot's performance, from a distance. Unable to hear what he was saying, he had at first assumed Talbot was rehearsing a scene from the film. It was a flamboyant performance – not Hugo's style at all. He was of the naturalistic school himself, except that where films were concerned he could well do without the colour. He liked to see things in black and white. Or was Talbot being serious? Posy had hinted he was somehow involved with the girl, Ludmilla Pike's protegée. Poor kid. Then he saw the little exchange in the everyday key and Laura, back turned against Hugo, stand and take her bowl indoors.

He presented himself, unannounced by footsteps, stepping out from the shadow of the house. 'Ah.' Talbot stuck his hand out. 'You must be Hugo.'

'Right first time! Talbot Hardy?'

'Yes. Where've you sprung from? You look as though you could do with a sit down. You should have phoned from the village.'

'I did. You were out. It's quite a walk, I must admit. I say, this *is* a wonderful place. I came the back way, I think. You don't see the house from the road.'

'Just the dovecot.'

He thought Hugo might have blushed for a second.

'Yes, yes, I did see that. Very picturesque.'

Hugo's sweat was patching his black tee shirt and beading his beard. Talbot didn't offer to take his things. He was thinking westerns. Let him sweat, he thought, and began to realise to his surprise how much he resented Hugo's arrival. What was this documentary nonsense anyhow?

'I did happen to catch sight of you just then – a little rehearsal? Glad to see things are getting underway.'

'Oh dear,' sighed Talbot, 'I think you must have mis-eavesdropped. I was just telling Laura I thought we had ants in the bay tree. Still, I hope you didn't hear anything bad about yourself. I always think that's pure superstition, don't you? Or the subconscious, which comes to the same thing. The fear of discovery making you feel everything *is* about you. Terrifying. Why don't you step inside,' he suggested. 'You'll find Laura in the kitchen I should think. Get her to fix you a drink and show you upstairs. I'm just off to the village to fetch some cigarettes.'

Hugo's rather hairy hand slid automatically to his trouser pocket. 'Oh no – don't bother to do that – I've got hundreds. Literally! Have some of mine!' He offered his little packet with hope rekindled in his eyes. Wrong foot, wrong foot. Handsome bugger, Posy didn't warn him. Damn. Talbot looked at the cigarettes with a little frown and allowed himself his first sincere smile. By their brand ye shall know them.

'No thanks. I won't.'

Laura heard his car start up and came to the door as Hugo was about to call.

'Oh,' she said politely, 'you must be Mr Grears.'

'Hugo. My friends call me Huge.'

'Do they? Which way shall we go? Er, why don't you come into the kitchen while I finish – that's quite odd isn't it? Nicknames are usually to make things smaller aren't they? You know, like Timmy, or Tommy. Diminutives. Shall I call you Hugo? Will that be all right?'

She's taking the piss, he thought.

'That'll be fine,' he assured her and was relieved when she offered him something to drink.

'Can you just wait here a minute while I go and check there's a room ready? We're not terribly organised here, I'm afraid. There's a lady who was going to see to it, but I don't know if she's been. Will you be all right? Talbot'll be back in a few minutes. Or me.'

She ran quickly upstairs and along the corridor, past Talbot's room to the end. You went up a little flight of steps and then left. The door was stiff.

It was a room she hadn't seen before, though Talbot had pointed it out. It was large, but on the dark side of the house. There was a sooty fireplace set into one of the exterior walls, blocked with a large screen covered in peeling green and white wallpaper which, as far as she could make out, had once shown a scene of aristocratic shepherdesses going on some kind of mass rally. Then she realised the pattern was just repeated many times over, so in fact the shepherdess was alone. The walls were very faded and patches showed where damp had crept in during the winters. It had obviously been swept, and the bed had been made up, but the smell was of rotting wood and, faintly, mice. She stepped carefully over the boards to open a shutter which had missed its catch and swung back in. The paint was flaked on the woodwork and, in a cobweb strung from the handle, a spider was eating a fly. She threw the cobweb down onto the grass below, rubbing her hand on the bricks of the outside wall to remove the last threads. From here you could see parts of the road to the village and she looked for Talbot's car, wondering why he had disappeared so quickly. Then she closed up and turned back into the room. Despite the presence of the man downstairs, she suddenly had a sense of being alone in the house.

On a table opposite the window was a mirror. She blew on it and rubbed it with the edge of her skirt, tilting it in its frame to catch the light so she could check for streaks. Her face was slightly puckered, unprepared for the reflection. She stepped back, then pulled away the chair and sat down, setting her lips and trying to relax her eyes. Talbot had told her she didn't look people in the eye enough. She practised in the mirror, trying to see into the bottom of her own gaze, discovering you could in fact only do one eye at a time. He had said the place to look was the bridge of the nose, but she felt that rather defeated the purpose, which was to be what Talbot called up-front. There were people who seemed to bear down so close upon you that it was impossible to stand your visual ground – Talbot, on occasions, was one of them. But if you couldn't face up to it, she felt it was more honest to try a sort of restless sweep technique – now eyes, now nose, chin and back up – which, she believed, flattered people into thinking they were so interesting you just couldn't take them all in at once.

Looking into her own eyes she was suddenly aware that it was completely quiet in the room. What if, what if? What if she turned in her chair or closed her eyes and another face came to fill up the mirror, a face from the past, another girl, other eyes? Stiff collar, unmistakeable misshapen hand at her throat, eyebrows sketched faintly into an arch of suspicion or surprise.

And behind her, by the window, the other figure, sulky, bored, ready to leave. Laura was utterly immobile, not a flicker of a hair not the tiniest husk of a breath; there was a pain singing in the top of her head, pain from her concentration, her fear of losing whatever it was that had appeared, the visual equivalent of a low, soft hum, gone now. An expression belonging to someone far older than herself hung on her face. Aghast, she thought, I am aghast. No that wasn't the right word, but it was the one which had occurred to her just then, seeing her face in the mirror. She was slumped in the chair, with the small of her back collapsed into itself and her legs stuck out in front of her, but slightly twisted looking, as though they had not been properly arranged. You could see why people told those suffering from shock to pull themselves together. She felt physically dislocated, in need of being laid to rest like the little puppet dolls in their softly lined shoeboxes. And at once she could make no sense of her presence here, of the room, the house, the time of year, time of day, of the people she knew were near and those that were not. The learning of recipes, of codes of behaviour, of coyness, of being a woman, of Talbot Hardy's love scenes, all seemed to pour away from her: there was a vacuum in her head which would make her faint in a moment. Then it passed, and she was left with a new thing, a kind of lucid seriousness – lucid, but quite glazed – piercing but misdirected.

Hugo had left the kitchen. Talbot's car was back in its place. He had been suspiciously quick. Perhaps he had just wanted to leave Hugo in the lurch. He often did that kind of thing. She needed the keys. Don't ask me why, she thought, don't ask me why. She ran into the garden. There was no one there. She went once round the outside of the house, through the herb garden and back, covering their voices, which were low, with her own fretful footfall. She began to feel she was the last person in a game of sardines, that they were hidden somewhere watching her search, squeezing away from her into some tiny space, pulling in toes and fingers, stifling laughs. Then she remembered her bicycle.

By the time she had reached the road she felt she had lost the mood herself, that she was back on the other side again, with all her yes-buts and on-the-other-hands, all the objections to folly which made her who she was, safely back in place. As she pedalled more thoughtfully now, shifting a little from her seat to ride the hill before the drop down towards the telephone box, she wondered whether it was possible to experience someone else's panic, whether while imagining herself in need of someone, her father, Ludmilla, it was not rather that one of them, perhaps, had needed her. She believed in these things because it seemed unreasonable not to, unwise even, like not believing in God, which was much the same thing. Albert was absent, off on traffic duty. It was funny without him. The kiosk was so obviously designed to contain a human form. Transparent. Two metres high. Just so wide. Albert seemed to serve as a charmingly aberrant illustration of the thought behind its design.

She spoke to her father, who was very well indeed, quite excellent. He wanted to know all about how things were going, how her French was, whether 'they' were treating her well. He was pleased she was happy, but he was afraid he had some rather disturbing news. She wanted to shout tell me, tell me quickly. She didn't want to experience the telling, the being told, only the knowing – it being out, in front of her, as though on a piece of paper, typed.

'I'm afraid Ludmilla is very ill,' he said, 'very ill indeed. It's her heart. She had an attack late last night.' So that was it. Right. She needed to take it away now and look at it in peace and quiet, somewhere where no one could see her. Her father was telling her there was nothing she could do, it wasn't necessarily a question of days yet. He didn't tell her that Ludmilla was not receiving visitors. No phone calls. She was on a drip, wired up, little strings, lifelines running from her arms.

'I should have rung her,' she said. 'I should have known there was something wrong.'

'How could you have known? Now please don't panic Laura, she's in a very nice nursing home, Gableford House, you know the one, they're doing everything they can for her. Don't worry yourself, everything's under control, we'll just have to see how it goes. She's had a good innings you know, dear. She's been very active up to the last. We've – ah – I've seen quite a bit of her. She often talked about you. Perhaps you could write her a nice letter. That would cheer her up, I'm sure.' He gave her the address of the nursing home.

Before she could say whatever it was she would surely have had to have said, he went on, 'Now as I'm talking to you, I know it's difficult for you to find time to phone me, I seem to have been so busy myself these last few weeks. Anyway, I have some news for you. I hope you won't mind, Laura, I'm going to be married again.'

Having never really known her mother, she had always somehow associated her father's unmarried state with his position as a man of the cloth. It seemed a double violation.

'Married? Who to?'

'Well – I have to say – to a very lovely lady. I think you will be very happy when you meet her. I'm sorry if it's a little sudden, dear, I haven't really known her very long, but you know, I think . . .'

'*Who*?'

'Ah, yes, well, her name is Gertrude. Gertrude Herbach. She is from Germany, you know, but has lived here for a long time now – not here, in Hertford, actually, but she is very involved with the Church, you remember the ecumenical gatherings I've been attending for the last year or so, well . . .'

'Shall I come home now then?' Is it *all* finished? she wondered.

'No, no, you stay where you are and enjoy yourself. You've got another few weeks to go haven't you?'

'Yes.' He *wanted* her to stay. All those times she had said, oh no, please don't bother to meet me I'll be fine, no really, I'll see myself home, honestly – he was doing it to her.

'OK Laura?'

She thought it might have been the first time she had heard him say 'OK'. It sounded odd. Perhaps it was the same word in German.

'Yes, I'm fine. I'm just a little bit surprised. Does Ludmilla know?'

'Oh yes, she and Gertrude have become great friends.'

Gertrude and Daddy. Gertrude and Ludmilla.

'I feel a bit Grimm – you know, Brothers Grimm. There's always a German lady marrying your father.'

'You'll find it isn't at all like that. In any case,' he said, rather defensively, 'you're grown up now.'

'Yes I suppose so.' She tried to sound bright. 'I'll . . . say, tell her I look forward very much to meeting her. When I get back.'

'That's marvellous. Well, I'm sure you're very busy. I'll ring you at Mr Hardy's house – shall I? – if there's any more news.'

More news? She thought. What, like the church blows up, or you get made Archbishop of Canterbury? Oh, Ludmilla, of course. If she dies.

'Thank you. Lots of love then. And . . . you know . . . Congratulations, Daddy.' She felt as though he were twenty-one. 'Congratulations.' It was never a natural thing to say – the generic and not the particular term. Like saying 'Commiserations', instead of 'I'm so terribly sorry.'

She was dull at lunch, which annoyed Talbot who wanted her to sparkle in front of Hugo. She could be so immature with her sulks and silences, he thought. She seemed like a child again today. Afterwards she found Hugo wandering through the avenue of trees, looking like a spare part whose order no one had remembered to cancel. She caught him up. Talbot, who did not want her to sparkle in front of Hugo when he wasn't himself present, watched from the bedroom window until they had walked out of sight.

'How are you getting on?' she asked.

'Oh, fine. Just feeling my way in, you know.' She pointed the way down a slope to the left, cutting through the trees. 'How do you like it here?'

She paused and pulled back a branch to reveal some newly formed elderberries.

'Look – another month or so and you'll be able to make cough mixture. I don't really think I think of it like that. Liking it or not. I work here. It's my job.'

Oh yeah. 'What is? Pleasing Talbot?' Pleasuring him, he thought, pleasuring Talbot Hardy.

'Yes.'

'I'll show you the woods,' she offered. 'Then we can do a circle and end up back at the house. It takes about half an hour.'

Hugo was nice, she thought. Fumbly and a bit awkward. He should shave his beard off then he wouldn't get so hot all the time. But if he did it here he'd be the same as Talbot and perhaps that wouldn't be a good thing.

'You don't like him very much, do you?'

'Who, Talbot?' He was taken aback. 'Oh I don't know, I've only just met the man, it wouldn't be fair to say. Why do you ask?' She was so direct it took away all embarrassment. You could only have this kind of conversation off the record. With a child.

'He's not your type. I can tell. You think he's too slick. Sort of loud, even though he's trying to be smooth. That's what you think.'

'No,' he corrected. 'That's what you think.'

'It isn't, it's just I can see you might think that. That's all. Just because I can see somebody might think something doesn't mean I think it myself. Just because I can see other people believe in God doesn't mean I have to believe in Him myself.'

'But I bet you do,' he laughed.

'Yes,' she admitted, 'I was just seeing what it felt like to pretend I didn't for a moment.'

They walked in silence for a while. Hugo had picked up a stick and was touching each of the trees with a brief benedictory movement as they passed. Laura went on ahead a little, so that Hugo couldn't see she was crying and he thought, watching her, that it would have been better if she had dropped behind, because then he would have known not to look back. She should have loosened her hair so it could screen the movement of her hand to her face. He guessed that probably, though she didn't know it herself, she wanted him to know she was crying. He began to walk more slowly, looking to right and left, trying to see where they would come out. She looked like some kind of siren leading him into the wood with her tears and a pretence of having forgotten she was followed. He had been shocked by her looks when he first saw her and had felt that Talbot had no right to this, that if he wanted beauty he should go elsewhere. She had the air of someone who up to that moment has never looked in a mirror. If she was unhappy, could it be because Talbot Hardy was playing her back an image of herself which surprised and frightened her at once? She was waiting for him up ahead.

'Did you have any pets when you were little?' he asked her.

He could have sworn she was surprised he did not ask her something more personal.

'No. We never had room. It was in a town. They would have got run over.'

'I never heard of a hamster in a car crash, but I see what you mean. I can always tell,' he said, 'when people haven't had pets. It's a knack I've got. They're very good for children. They teach you to love without expecting anything in return. Not to give love because you are loved. You always have to start and you always have to keep it up. Then you know after a while, whether you need them or not. Then they die. Particularly,' he added, 'if they are a hamster.'

Laura thought she could tell him now. This was what she had brought him here for. It was too good a link not to be providential. Just ahead there was a clearing where the sun shone in like a spotlight. She stopped there.

'My best friend is dying,' she told him and she sounded like a little girl telling someone her rabbit was touch and go. And she told him about Ludmilla.

'It was because of her I came here,' she said. 'She wanted me to grow up a bit, so she arranged for me to come and work for Talbot. I mean, I was quite grown up . . . I don't mean . . . but I didn't know much about the outside world, she said. You wouldn't really call it the *real* world, would you? You see she was here too when she was young, and she knew about the book Talbot's making a film of. Talbot thought she was Chloe at first, that's the heroine, but then he thought she couldn't have been because she didn't really look the part. I think she was, but I don't know because I haven't read the book. I'm not allowed. Talbot doesn't want me to be affected by it yet. He says I'll be better able to judge the screenplay on its own merits. Ludmilla didn't want me to read it either. It's quite funny. Not being allowed. Like being Catholic all of a sudden.'

Hugo thought he had never heard such a load of nonsense in his life. The girl was caught up in some kind of ridiculous fairy story, with arbitrary dos and don'ts issued by the classic self-interested stand-in patriarchs and matriarchs. She was in a kind of sleep of unreality. He too, was bound by his role, unable to tell her he had met Ludmilla, had made the film which was to be Talbot's nemesis. He had thought her amusing but with a distinctly villainous streak, the kind of person he personally got on with very well, viz. young Posy. He found it very hard to imagine what Ludmilla and Laura found to talk about. He couldn't confide in Laura (although he promised himself he would do before all this was over), because, selfishly, he wanted to see how it all turned out without his exercising some right of *deus ex machina*. The backers were due on Thursday. She couldn't come to much harm in that time. Then, looking at her, she suddenly appeared quite normal again, capable even, and he wondered whether he was not himself getting fanciful, seeing her as a maiden in distress.

'Perhaps I *want* her to be one,' he thought, thinking also that life got very double edged when you began to admit that your own motives were not necessarily always the ones you believed.

'Hugo. You know you're making this film. About Talbot making his and *Pierrot Lunaire*?'

Hugo had almost forgotten. 'Yes,' he said.

'There's something I want you to do for me. I wouldn't ask you – I don't know you – but I think it might be really important. I know that sounds stupid, because probably nothing to do with all this is really important. I know that. But if anything was, it could be this, because Ludmilla's dying.'

She stood with her back to a tree with her hands behind her and he thought that she looked as though she had been voluntarily strapped to it.

'You want to make a film of what's happening here. You can't do that without her. Whatever Talbot says. She knows everything. If you talk to her, you see, she'll tell you, because she'll like you, I know she will. Specially if you say you're a friend of mine. I can't go back you see, she wouldn't want me to see her ill, she wouldn't let me and she wouldn't tell me anyhow, not unless she'd decided to and then I'd already know. She's in a nursing home called Gableford House in Castleford, near Lincoln. You wouldn't have to tell Talbot, though, not until you've done it, because he doesn't like Ludmilla, but I'm sure if you did an interview with her, she'd love it, it would really cheer her up. Then when Talbot saw how good it was, it would help him with the film and everything – and we'd know the *truth*.'

'*And the truth shall set you free?*' he thought.

'Hang on a minute. Have I got this right? You want me to fly back to England, interview this old lady, then come back here in time for the lunch. I have to be here on Thursday. Talbot says it will be interesting to get the money side of things. It seems an awful trek, Laura. I've only just arrived. It seems ridiculous to go such a long way for one interview. She might not even be fit.'

He didn't mind that aspect to it, he didn't need to because he wouldn't have to go. He already had Ludmilla in the can, though he hadn't paid much attention to what she'd said, he'd been too busy getting the thing to work. He thought though that even Laura couldn't be so naïve as to imagine he'd go roaring back to England just to interview Ludmilla Pike when he'd only been here a day. Talbot would think he was crazy, though he'd probably be relieved if he cleared off for a bit. She was about to pop off, of course, there was that. It added a certain urgency to the situation.

'What do you suggest I tell Talbot?'

'Tell him you've got corns and you've got to go and have them seen to in Toulouse.'

'I see,' he thought. 'That's what's behind all this confidence. She really *seriously* doesn't fancy me,' and he smiled.

'I might be able to think of something a bit better than that,' he said. Eventually he agreed. There wasn't much to lose. It was like being sent back to the start in the first minute of grandmother's footsteps. 'What you must promise me, though, and I really mean this, is not to tell *anyone* what I'm going to do. Not your father, not Ludmilla, no one. I want to be able to slip in and out and do my business, full stop. Promise.' This is brilliant, he thought, just being able to say 'promise', and knowing she takes it seriously, and for a moment he wished all the world were like that.

'I'll give you the money back when I've got it. I'll get a grant next year. You can have some of that.'

'You needn't worry about that. That'll be seen to. Tell you what, tell Talbot there's been an urgent phone call. I've had to go to Paris on business. He'll understand that.'

She came and hugged him and he stared rather bleakly over her shoulder. He felt she was too young to touch. I must have a problem, he thought, patting her self-consciously. She's only ten years younger than me.

'I'll drive you to Toulouse. It's only an hour and a half. Talbot'll let me take the car. Come on, let's get your stuff. You mustn't forget your camera. You can leave your bag, you'll be back on Thursday.'

There was a touch of the tea committee about her.

After a while they came back round into view of Monvanité. Laura had withdrawn, become quite demure again now they were out of the trees. She made a show of unsmudging her eyes with a handkerchief from her skirt pocket, just in case he was thinking of changing his mind to reassure him that his decision had been right, for she had been very griefstricken really, though of course she'd tried to hide it. Watch it Laura, Hugo thought, you don't need that kind of trick. Talbot was outside, wrenching angrily at some sort of petrol motor. He wasn't having much success. Hugo thought he'd probably better not offer his help. Best to make a quick getaway. Leave Laura to make his excuses. Yes, he'd be back on Thursday. And he certainly mustn't forget his camera, that would be a real mistake. He just hoped he had Sally Fairfield's telephone number in his book. He was sure she didn't live that far away but he didn't fancy tackling directory enquires.

27

The evening before the day of the lunch had been tetchy and Talbot had tersely told her to go and sleep in her own room. It had been strange waking up in there again, and simpler too. Talbot had got up very early, he said, unable to sleep and his tiredness was a direct reproach to her.

She wasn't wanted in the kitchen. Madame Derrault had come straight from home that morning. She had dropped off the shopping she had done in advance the evening before. Talbot had been filming a reluctant Laura kneading bread on a wooden table outside. Mme Derrault had given them a very curious look as she came past. It was, after all, a fairly ludicrous place to be kneading bread, in the fading light with the mosquitoes swooping through the air. Laura had had to ignore her because of being on the film, which probably put her nose a bit out of joint. On the morning of the day of the lunch Laura had hesitated on the threshold of the kitchen, wondering how best to approach the business of working side by side. Subservience was obviously the order of the day. She asked if she could help. Mme Derrault still affected to find her difficult to understand. She was skinning roasted red peppers with a fiendish look in her eye and Laura could have sworn she saw one of them twitch.

'You?' Mme Derrault seemed to consider her answer on the basis of the services being offered, not of those which might be needed. 'No.' Then she clearly decided Laura would be best out of the way and said that in an hour or so she could pick up some bread from the village.

'Oh,' Laura said, 'I can make bread. I could do that for you.'

Mme Derrault was not going to give up any of her precious

oven or floor space to indulge some sort of things-to-make-and-do urge on the part of Talbot's bit on the side. Or at least that's how it came across to Laura. Talbot had assured her that she was not being singled out for special treatment. It was just that Mme Derrault hated young women. The birdcage had been particularly severely pinned and sealed this morning, a sign that she anticipated a long, hardworking day ahead. There was no way that whatever was in her head was going to fly out today. Laura left Mme Derrault to her work. She hated to be disturbed in her work, she had told Laura, as though she had been a researcher into DNA molecules or a composer. She moved about the château in a way that suggested she was at home there, although she never assumed more than a housekeeperly air. Laura slipped out, not relishing the prospect of scullery service this lunchtime. Her bike was propped up against the wall outside the kitchen window. Mme Derrault's was next to it. What a fine piece of machinery it was too. A very sleek animal. It was, in fact, a sort of racing bike with drop handlebars and a spanner set buckled to the back seat. Talbot had asked Mme Derrault if she was down for the Tour de France this year.

'Not this year,' she had replied crisply, she was too busy.

Ludmilla would have remarked that like most people who complain that others have no sense of humour Talbot usually failed to recognise another's irony.

One thing Laura could do was pick up the post from the Café du Sport. Norman had put a notice on the bookshop door saying that he could be found behind the bar at the café, where he was replacing Mme Derrault for the day. There was probably a set of clean ironed shirts in it for him. Laura and he got on well. She felt he was familiar, that this was not the first one of him she had met. He was a dapper chap of about sixty, with stocky shoulders and weak little eyes. He had been in the diplomatic corps most of his life, but had never risen above Third Consul. He had a very slight trace of a Manchester accent which, in being almost successfully contained, sounded vaguely effeminate. They would say in his obituary that he never married, but this was not actually true. It had been a brief and secret business, and sad at the end. Norman never spoke of it, but he had been wildly, almost tearfully happy for a year, before his tiny Filipino wife died in childbirth. The strapping little Caucasian baby had breached her as though she had been no stronger than an egg and Norman gave him away before he got to know his face. He was pleased to see Laura. He enjoyed her company. He said it was much better than his own, which made Laura feel she possessed a superior model of something, and that she could enhance his life by lending it out to him. He told her things he normally kept to himself. They had had one or two nice little chats about books, which had led to her helping out in the evenings with the sorting. Norman had boasted of and introduced her with pride to his collection of over four hundred recipe books. Alone in bed at night, he told her, he plotted seven course banquets, choosing menus to put before his carefully selected guests. Would Henry James sit happily next to Madame de Sévigny and would she eat snails? He gave almost every appearance of being a happy man.

He gave Laura a glass of lemonade.

'What's afoot, then?'

'Oh, Mme Derrault's in charge, I don't know. I seem to be a bit redundant today. Most days really.'

Norman flicked a fly away with a cloth he was carrying around on his left shoulder as though at any moment he might expect to be picking up a violin.

'That's not what I've heard,' he said slightly mischievously and then, as she looked shocked, squeezed her arm playfully.

'Don't you mind me lovey, I've a tongue in my head when I want. Top up. On me. I insist.' But it was obvious what he had meant.

'You've been in the news,' Norman told her.

Laura thought he said on it and looked up quickly at the television which was playing away to itself above the bar. Norman drew out a little notebook from his blazer pocket and took out a cutting.

'My sister sent me this. Her husband travels up to town every day.'

It was from a London newspaper.

'Ex-TV producer, Talbot Hardy, of *At Home With The Burrowbridges*, is reported to be at home at Château Monvanité, the French property of his wife, Posy Gresham. She has also kindly provided him with reading material – an unpublished novel of the thirties, written in the château itself, about a love affair which took place there involving the author and an unknown girl. Hardy is looking for backing for the film of the book, a *true* story of love and despair which ends in tears over the border in civil war Spain. As none will be more keenly aware than my old friends Sir Peter and Lady Burrowbridge, Hardy has a keen affinity with the truth. His wife dismisses as pure fiction a rumour which has reached me that he is sharing his idyll with a beauteous young teenager of undisclosed identity. With only the facts to go on, though, let's hope Talbot won't be signing up for the Legion before he's done.'

'Has Talbot seen this?' Laura asked.

'I doubt it,' Norman said, 'not if he hasn't shown you. He'll be flattered, I should think.'

'That's what I mean, Norman, please, don't show him. It'd make it worse.'

Norman didn't quite get her drift. 'It's only a harmless bit of gossip, lovey,' he reassured her, 'don't let yourself get upset about that. That's just silly journalist buggers for you.'

'Who told them that though? Why should anyone want to read about that?'

'Search me. Everyone knows everyone in those sort of circles. As I say, you don't want to take a lot of notice.'

Le Touquet was upside down as usual. Laura had an impulse to turf him out of his cage and onto the street. He was staring at her rudely with a kind of almost sexual insolence.

'That's a pretty dress you've got on,' said Norman kindly. 'I like to see a girl in a proper frock.' An expatriate all his life and of a different generation, he was the last person to appreciate any irony in Laura's clothes. The costume effect escaped him, but he thought she looked a picture in red. 'Now stop blushing and finish up your drink. I've got something for you.' It was a book of fashion plates of Parisian models of the 1930s. He had thought it would interest her. So you never could tell.

Laura suddenly realised the time. She had to be back at the château in twenty minutes, when the guests were due. Talbot had told her to put her white dress on. 'And stand against the light. They'll love that.' When Laura realised what he meant she felt a bit sick. 'Who are you trying to kid?' he had laughed when she said she had never realised. She had cut up an old sheet, hoping Mme Derrault wouldn't notice, and tried to improvise a petticoat, but it wasn't finished yet. It was hard to know what to take seriously. The first night, among other things, she had apparently looked like an unravished bride of quietness. That was with it being sort of Greek looking.

'I have to go, Norman,' she said, jumping down off her stool.
'You on your bike?'
'Mme Derrault's, I mean mine, yes.'
'I'll hold on to this then. I'll drop it off when I'm passing in the car. Enjoy yourself.' Laura pulled a face. 'And tell that Talbot to look after you. That's a responsibility he's got on his hands. Isn't it?'

He was talking to the priest who had just come in for his pastis. Laura could just hear herself. 'Oh, Talbot, Norman and Father Bénoit say you're to look after me, I'm a responsibility.' 'What on earth do they know about the subject?' he'd say. 'Anyway, it's me that needs looking after.'

She rushed out to her bike, and Norman followed with a parcel that had arrived by the morning post, chucking it deftly into her basket as she pushed off from the wall. He waved as she disappeared round the corner.

'Nice girl,' he said to the priest, going back into the café.
'Charming,' agreed Father Bénoit, tickling Le Touquet's rump.

A minute or so later Laura rushed back carrying the parcel and several sticks of bread. 'I've got a puncture!' she said, and her tempo changed from quick to slow like a foxtrot, so that a second later she was quite glum. 'I'll never get back for the lunch,' she said hopelessly. 'What on earth shall I do?'

Father Bénoit said he would happily run her up in his car if she could wait five minutes while he finished his drink. He was going up that way anyway. It would be a pleasure to have her company. He had heard her father was a Protestant priest. She drove home with the priest and he told her of his childhood in Le Touquet and how Mme Derrault had been so kind naming the parrot for his fond memories, because he told her the Hotel Splendide had been painted in smart red, grey and black, just like her parrot who up to then had been called Mimi. He smelled pleasantly of aniseed balls and got quite nostalgic having Laura there to talk to.

'It's the pastis talking,' he said.

They both waved at Albert as they sailed past his green sign and Laura thought they might have got a nod back, although they didn't discuss it between them. He dropped her at the back gate, well out of sight of the château. He had wanted to drive up the drive with her; she had pleaded for the back route. There was a bit in *Pierrot Lunaire* with Chloe and the priest in the park, but Laura didn't know that.

28

As she ran up the lane towards the house she passed the Daimler which had dropped off the distinguished visitors, a sleek black insect sluggish under its shiny carapace. It seemed an awfully long way up the path, but then she was late. At least they couldn't see her from the house.

It turned out that Mme Derrault had found the remnants of the sheet she was saving to go under the tablecloth on the floor of Laura's room. Her outrage was beyond expression; the problem had been conveyed to Talbot who would normally have found it amusing but today was a little tense and had sided with Mme Derrault against Laura in her absence. To Laura he might eventually smile and say of course Mme Derrault was a ridiculous old bat and anyway they were Posy's sheets. But for the moment she was on her own and you would have thought from the way Mme Derrault was behaving that it had been some precious relic from the bridal bed of a seventeenth-century Dauphine, waved to the crowd from a morning balcony, when for once a stain was proof of innocence.

Laura kept out of the way of Talbot's guests. He had wanted her to appear first with the vichysoisse. She cut up bread quietly in a corner of the kitchen, meek little vicar's daughter again, legs neatly crossed under her chair. Mme Derrault had everything beautifully under control. There seemed to be no more cooking to be done. She had gone outside to smoke a cigarette. All the stages of the meal were under lids, warming or cooling as required. It was impressive. The cool grey smoke rising above a back view of the basket effect looked somehow Indian, as though there should also have been pipe music. She clearly had a lot on her mind. Male voices could be heard from the library, American, Australian and English. Talbot's own coiled beneath the surface of the babble, a serpentine continuo. It was hot in the kitchen and Laura's head felt as though it were full of mercury. There was a disquieting inertia effect as she tilted it this way and that.

'Laura, I think we're ready to eat if you don't mind.' A public voice, for the benefit of the visitors. More quietly he said, 'You look like a mad woman sitting there with your head swaying. Come on, look sharp, sweetie,' and was gone.

Mme Derrault had placed the tureen on a tray, with a ladle. Laura put the bread in a basket and added that on too. As she bore the tray out of the kitchen, composing her face to assume an aspect of serenity, Mme Derrault stuck her head through the window like a donkey in a stall. Laura thought she must have forgotten something, but she just stared moodily at the tray and nodded, signalling to her that she should pass through to the dining room. She had told Laura she should wear an apron over that dress (and the improvised shoulder fastening had not gone unnoticed either) but that wouldn't have been allowed.

'Ah, just leave that on the table there at the side, could you. Thank you.'

'She speaks English?' A tubby man with hair which had slipped hemispheres and had ended up all on his chin peered at her through dark glasses. He wore a tight white suit and a black tee shirt. (Hugo would have approved, but he wasn't due back till tonight.) On his feet were a pair of thonged sandals. His toenails were the texture of unwashed pebbles. With his gold fillings and all that hair on the bottom half of his face and the bland dark glasses and the baldness on top, you felt you were trying to read something upside down. He was like a wasted eggtimer you wanted to right. This was the Antipodean. He had made a fortune in drugstores in Australia and had recently topped it up with wise investments in the pornographic movie industry. This was what Posy had told Talbot. Talbot had had the videos sent out from London and watched them in the call of duty the night before. He felt that Berthold Quigly didn't quite have the sort of artistic stature he would have liked in a backer but, as Posy told him, he had to take what came along.

Talbot had told Laura not to talk if she could help it. She was there to provide a visual impression. He took Quigly's glass and filled it up. 'Water with that, was it? Er, does she speak English? Oh er, yes, yes she does, in fact.'

A second backer sauntered up to Laura as she was setting the tray down. The former Cambridge don who had written a blockbuster historical novel. He was looking to invest his royalties. In something suitably classy, Talbot had said. His suit was green and restrained and he spoke rather kindly, if loudly.

'Let me give you a hand with that.'

'Thanks,' said Laura, with a fluency which must have struck him as quite remarkable, given Talbot's hesitation, smiled, and left the room.

That was her one lapse. Between courses she pinched one of Mme Derrault's cigarettes and smoked it in the herb garden furiously. Ash dropped onto her dress and burned a hole in the hemline. She stamped angrily on the butt and wiped her eyes on her arm. When she next went in she avoided Talbot's eye. By the time they were onto the sorbets she had recovered herself. Talbot was drinking and reaching to fill up glasses like some sort of frantic octopus. He followed her out of the room. 'Excuse me gentlemen.'

He trapped her in the kitchen. Mme Derrault had disappeared.

'What's up?'

'Nothing. *Rien*, I should say.'

He took a pile of empty plates from her and put them down by the sink. He was wearing light green trousers and a white shirt with a gold flecked cravate. His face was flushed. He tried to kiss her but she pushed him away.

'Get lost Talbot.' He blinked and took a handkerchief from his pocket.

'Look, okay, I know you're cross, but you mustn't take it so seriously. It's all a game, sweetie. A *mise en scène*. Can't you go along with it for an hour or so? Come on, princess, you know I love you.'

'I'm not a princess, I'm a puppet.'

'That's rubbish,' he said. 'You chose to come here. Anyway, this is professional. Nothing personal.'

'Nothing personal. That's what I mean!'

But she let Talbot hold her in his arms for a second or two before they heard Mme Derrault coming downstairs.

'You wipe those eyes poppet,' he said jovially, 'and Mme D and I will take the coffee in. Won't we Mrs D?'

She stared back at them, not responding. Talbot kissed Laura proudly on the forehead and directed her towards the door.

'I'll come and see you in a minute,' he said, 'I have to go back in now.'

He translated for Mme Derrault about the coffee. She followed him back into the library with a look about her that suggested she had turned off the stopcock in her nose against the alcohol fumes and was having difficulty breathing. A few minutes later Laura saw her steaming towards the herb garden where she herself was sitting on the hot stone wall. The slow foot followed as hard as it could on the quickstep of the good one and the rhythm against the hot stones of the path was markedly iambic. Duh-dum, duh-dum. She was breathing hard. It was brittle hot in the herb garden. She squelched a ripe orange medlar underfoot. She had come to fetch mint to flavour a tisane. One of the backers, the tall American in shorts, didn't drink coffee. They both started to speak at once. Laura wanted to talk to her, to apologise. She was a woman, she would surely understand something. Mme Derrault spoke through her.

'*Qu'est-ce que ça veut dire? Eh, vous traduisez!*'

'What?'

'What does it mean, this expression, "Chloe eez dayd"?'

'Chloe eez dayd? Chloe is dead. *Eh bien, Chloe est morte.*'

'Oh, I see,' said Mme Derrault. 'I see. Thank you.'

'They're just discussing the film.'

Mme Derrault looked almost grateful. She sighed heavily. 'That sheet,' she said, '*n'en parlons plus.*'

Next out was Talbot. 'What's going on?' he said, sounding fuddled.

'Nothing, she's just a bit exhausted. I'll go and help her clear up.'

'Good girl,' said Talbot vaguely.

'How's it going. Do they like it?'

'Hard to tell. They read the synopsis before lunch. What

there is. They're going to take the draft scenes away with them. They've had too much to drink now. My fault. They keep changing the subject.'

'The English one seems nice.'

'Yes he's better than the other two. All as rich as Croesus though. Better get back to it. Laura, I'm sorry I upset you. It'll be over soon. We'll get it right.'

'You told them Chloe's dead. What about Ludmilla?'

'All in good time. Step at a time.'

'You've killed her off. She might die.'

He had not been particularly interested when she had reported her conversation with her father – he reckoned Ludmilla was probably just seeking a little attention.

'You're a vicar's daughter,' he reminded her, 'you're not allowed to be superstitious.'

She smiled uncertainly, prepared to drop it for now.

'What time did Hugo say he'd be back?'

'Sixish.'

Laura shifted, about to get up, and Talbot noticed the parcel she had put down at her right hand side. It looked hidden to him. He recognised Ludmilla's handwriting.

Laura had just read the accompanying note: 'You *must* substitute this for Hugo Grears' film of me. This is the real thing. Absolutely essential darling. Life and death.'

Ludmilla had already made a film with Hugo. And if this was the replacement, the revised version, it must have been made at least two or three days ago, before Ludmilla had fallen seriously ill. She realised that Hugo must have just been humouring her, pretending to go back to do what he had already done. She supposed he must have thought the pretence would lend more credibility to his story when he produced the film. Sorry Talbot, Laura asked me to. Felt I owed it to her. It was all quite ridiculous. Who had introduced Ludmilla to Hugo? There was only one person it could have been. Posy. It was all beginning to click. They were trying to expose Talbot in some way, show him up as a fraud. Not the real thing. Cheap copy. Thanks a lot, she thought.

'We're in the garden. I came to fetch the port. Ostensibly.' It was a long word. 'There's a present for you in the dovecot.

Go fetch.' Squeezed her once more. Sometimes she felt like an empty tube of toothpaste. She gave a little, kissed him back quickly, and watched him go back into the house. His back was stiff. The sight of the parcel had angered him.

The entrance to the dovecot was on the west side in the shade. She stopped on the first step of the little circular staircase. She could hardly see where to put her feet. She was listening for the noise of rats. There was nothing. Talbot knew how she felt about the dovecot. Why had he left a present there? It was a kind of test of valour. She didn't want a present, but as he must have planned it before she grew angry with him it couldn't be a bribe. She felt along the wall with her hand. Dried moss crumbled beneath her fingers, leaving tobacco-like strands under her nails. The steps were wooden and a little unsafe. She imagined she was being pursued, a childhood trick when she was too scared to go upstairs alone in an empty house. In her fancy it was Ludmilla, friendly Ludmilla turned fiend, tearing over the field with a big black bag of secrets over her shoulder. Laura could hide in the dovecot. That got her up. In the circular room there was only one window, a lookout slit, which let in more light than you would have suspected looking at it from the outside. She looked around. Ludmilla was already forgotten, it had been a tangential trick of the mind. There was a noise. No rats, not that she could see. A pair of binoculars hung from a nail. She was about to take them down and turn them on the little lunch party sitting a few hundred yards away by the bay tree. Then with a lurch of shock she noticed the bird. It was knowing she had been in the same room with it for half a minute without noticing that made her scream. Then she saw the blood on its wing and that cut her dry. A huge-bellied white dove sagged from a rafter above her head, one wing dreadfully battered, trailing a leg. It was her present. It was as good as dead. Her whole body kicked over inside and she felt faint with disgust, hating herself at the same time. She bolted for the door. It was vital to run at once, while the instinct was upon her. The bodily impulse she had been waiting for in Talbot's bed overcame her in the dovecot, but it was a revulsion, a shrieking away from horror.

She leapt down the stairs two at a time and collided with Sally, who was on her way up.

'Good Lord,' said Sally, 'what's going on here?'

Laura had skidded past her on the heels of her shoes and sprawled inelegantly in the doorway. She propped herself up on her haunches and her legs felt weak and grazed.

'Just a bird,' she said in a high voice. 'Just a bird.'

Sally gave her a funny look and ran lightly up the steps. Laura felt foolish in her dress, on the floor, as though she had been playing childish make-believe in broad daylight. Half a minute later Sally came back down again, wiping her hands on an old rag.

'I had to kill it,' she said flatly. 'It had ripped its neck on a nail.'

She sat down next to Laura. 'I know who you are,' she told her. 'Do you know me?'

Laura shook her head. She felt about five.

'I'm Sally. Talbot's girlfriend. Is he in?'

'No,' Laura managed to say. 'Well, yes, but he's got people for lunch.'

'So you went up to spy on them, did you? That'll teach you. Well I won't disturb him. I only came to put these seedlings in for him. I'll go round the back. Sorry about old Columbine in there.' She stood up and walked away in long strides across the fields, looking, in her slim blue jeans and white shirt, like a head girl off to feed her pony.

Laura sat there for quite a few minutes. Then she steeled herself to go up and look at the bird. It wasn't so dreadful now it was dead. It was the pain that was hideous. She had called it Columbine. Laura promised she would come back and bury it later. She never saw the cocoa-coloured rabbit sitting shyly in the corner. Talbot had even given him a ribbon. Golden rule, Sally could have told her. Never tell a man your dreams.

Twenty minutes later she was back in the garden. Sally had started a bonfire to get rid of some of the old dried weeds. She had said hello to Talbot and his chums, who were all quite far gone in the garden, discussing actresses past and present with a certain lascivious connoisseurship. She had dropped Hugo off in the village where he was whiling the time away till six, when he could turn up at the house. She had been slightly surprised when he had rung, but had duly gone to pick him up from Toulouse, where Laura had dropped him. She told him she thought he was an idiot to have got involved with Posy. Rather to Sally's embarrassment, they had come across Albert in the car park of the local hypermarket the previous afternoon. (Madame Derrault always took him with her when she went to the hypermarket, although he would never go in. She suspected he liked the way they parked in the little white lined box. It appealed to his sense of order.) It wouldn't do for it to get back to Talbot that Hugo had been spotted not fifteen kilometers from Monvanité when he was supposed to be in Paris on business.

Laura went upstairs and changed into her red dress. She was glad the white one had cost nothing because she never wanted to wear it again. Albert could have all the buttons.

She appeared in the garden while they were all laughing at some joke.

'Aren't you sweetie?'

'What?'

'My muse, my inspiration. Chloe reincarnated. My charm.'

'Chloe isn't dead,' she said quietly. Clap your hands, she thought, and she won't die.

'Chloe is dead, long live Chloe,' chortled the Antipodean in the white suit, and winked quickly at her. There was complicity in his open eye. Laura was shocked.

'Let's get back to the hotel and have a swim.'

'We could certainly do with a little dip,' agreed the blockbuster don, making them sound like sheep. His hair had flopped over his brow and was sweating steadily into the lining of his worsted suit. 'Damned hot here, Talbot. Then we'll come back over this evening. Meet your documentary chappie. Good sign, though, this media interest, wouldn't you say?'

'I'll run you back.' Talbot insisted that Laura come with them in the car to their hotel which was a few miles away on the other side of the village in a watermill which had been made over into an exclusive if small-scale leisure complex. It was a hot jumbly journey, and two of the men squabbled noisily about who had put up the money for a hugely successful film which had been on general release the previous year, about the director of a merchant bank with a pet iguana.

'You wait,' said the American, who had had to sit next to Laura who was driving, because his legs were too long to fit in the back. 'They ain't seen nothin' yet. That right Laura?' Albert was on green.

'Yes, probably.'

They dropped them at the hotel. Talbot saw them to the door. He stayed there for four or five minutes talking. They would come back up in the hotel taxi and crunch some numbers, the American said. Then they drove back into the village. Talbot was looking drunk and thunderous.

'Go into the cafe will you, Laura, and get me some cigarettes.'

Norman was full of himself.

'They've done it!' he cried.

'What?'

'The General and Andromache – Yvette's done a test. There'll be plenty to go round. I'm going to have a puppy!'

'That's wonderful, Norman,' Laura smiled. 'I'm really pleased. Packet of Gauloise filter for Talbot please.'

'Won't he be thrilled? He worships that dog. There you go. Oh, I mended your bike. Don't mention it. We like your face, don't we?'

He was talking to Le Touquet. When she got back outside Talbot was in the driving seat.

'Hop in,' he said. 'You and I are going to talk.'

He stopped just beyond the church under a tree, switched off the engine and turned to her.

'What's in that parcel?' he asked.

Laura shrunk away from him. 'What parcel?'

'Oh come on, Laura, I've had just about enough of this. You're in league with that bloody woman aren't you? Stopping me getting at the facts. There's a secret there, and I'm jolly well going to find out what it is. I'm not having you ruining my life. I can do without you. Now go on. Get out.'

Laura shrank away from him and hesitated before reaching for the door handle. He was so drunk she thought he might hit her. He laughed. 'Mustn't do that now, must we, or Uncle Talbot might get home before us and find his parcel. This is my big chance Laura, I'm going to make this film whatever anybody does to try and stop me. You saw those guys. They believe in me.

Ludmilla Pike's got some sneaking little secret and I'm going to get to the bottom of it. Go on, get out. Find your own way home.'

He leaned over and opened her door, shoving her furiously out of the car. Short of a stand-up fight in the street there was nothing she could do. The door slammed behind her and Talbot roared off round the corner. She rushed back to the café and grabbed her bike. Norman came rushing out with his cloth over his shoulder as she pushed off.

'I'll call it Hector!' he shouted. 'For both of them!'

Laura didn't stop to chat. She thought there might be a quick way across the fields. She didn't have a hope of beating Talbot but she might be able to calm him down and persuade him not to destroy Ludmilla's evidence, whatever it was. Laura needed to see it.

It was too late not to know. She found the path across the field and along the riverside to the little wood, where she rammed her bike through the undergrowth and it bucked and reeled against the knotted oak roots bursting through the earth.

She was home in just under half an hour, and never heard the screech of brakes and the smack of metal as Talbot crashed into the rear end of a crane. For once, Albert had got his signal wrong. It was, as Mme Derrault later remarked, uncharacteristically careless of him. He lost his job, but it was worth it.

29

Sally was busy by the roses, spreading ash. Talbot's girlfriend. Fine. She could have him. Laura spared a thought for the roses. Surely she should have waited for the heat to leave the ashes first, with the sun like this and the ground already baked to a crust. It was salt into the wound.

Talbot wasn't back. That was strange – he'd shot off like a pellet when he dumped her in the street. She hoped he'd had a puncture. She left the bicycle in the garden. She hadn't worked out a place to keep it yet and now it wouldn't be necessary. She passed the little table by the bay tree. Madame Derrault had cleared the dirty glasses, but the cloth was spotted with little flecks of carbon which had been lifted and carried through the air from Sally's fire.

She went upstairs. Madame Derrault was moving about down below, wiping and stacking the plates. Back they would go into their appointed piles, restored to original condition and position. She had had no time as she hurtled along through the woodland to work out what would happen when she got back. Talbot would be there. With luck she might salvage Ludmilla's parcel, if he hadn't ransacked her room. She hoped to find a way of punishing him, of making him regret. That was as far as she had got. It had been good to have a drama to run to. Now the house was quite empty, and she was caught off guard. She collected Ludmilla's parcel, which was safe where she had left it, and went off down the corridor and up the little flight of stairs. Hugo's room. Hardly Hugo's room, he had done no more than leave his bags there. He'd taken the camera with him, for authenticity. There was the same undusted feeling in the air. Perhaps a hint of Hugo's aftershave. 'Wow,' Talbot had said, behind his back. 'What's he got to hide?'

The video-tape was in his holdall, next to the instruction manual for the camera. L. Pike, 12 June, a.m. She slipped it out of the case and put in the new one. She held the two Ludmillas in her hands. Same size, same shape. There was nothing to show it was a substitute. Or the real thing, as Ludmilla had said. Then she went to pack her things. Curtsey while you're thinking, it saves time. The Red Queen again.

It was remarkable how matter of fact you could be when it came down to it. All turbulent emotions seemed to be in retrospect or anticipation when distance allowed you to perceive their impact on the heart. But the real thing – ah, that phrase again – grief, elation, bereavement when it came, was sharp and transparent as cut glass. She packed methodically, listening out for Talbot's car. All she was afraid of was of being caught in the act. She didn't want her decision to be corrupted by Talbot. He would point out to her what she was doing, why she was doing it, what would be its consequences, reconnect her to the situation, tie her down with a thousand Lilliputian threads to his world, which she had decided to leave. She could not say she wanted no further part of it. It was a sickly paradise and she had been exposed to the contagion. It was a dramatisation and that the sickness touched only those (not Madame Derrault, not Albert) who were aware of that fact, who were watching themselves, whose eyes were open not to their own nakedness but to their clothing, their costume, their script, and who were ashamed. Love be fed on apples while you may, he had quoted to her, and now she understood. It was all to do with knowledge.

The light was good at this time of day. It had a golden tint, as if each day had its own brief spell of autumn in the late afternoon. Laura's skin still held the warmth of the midday sun, but her shoulders were cold. She laid the blue and orange swimming costume without the belly button out on the bed for future secretaries and went through to Talbot's room to find her book. He had read from it to her at strange hours of the night, choosing passages he remembered, although she had felt that he had not so much remembered the passages as remembered having read them before. *Le Rouge et Le Noir*. One night she had been unable to sleep. He read page after page of the book to her at a frantic pace, as though he wanted the smallest, weakest hours to come and find them there before she slept. She had begun to feel quite giddy and wretched with the sleep pacing up and down inside her head, unable to settle. He had gone downstairs and come back with a cup of something very hot and sweet. 'That will do the trick,' he had said, and she had drunk it all, believing him. Her trust had done the trick and she had lain down and slept. Many months later she drank black coffee with five spoonfuls of sugar after a long walk in the rain on Dartmoor and recognised the taste.

His shirts were tossed onto a pile on the chair by the window. It was a wonderful chair, hand made in 1755, he had told her, English. She had never known a chair be so much more animal than vegetable or mineral. It seemed to be sitting in itself, to be comfortably at rest, with its legs splayed and back gently curved in repose, as though there by right, in front of its own favourite view. Talbot had thought that if it were an Englishman it would be portly and gouty and that the view would be of his own extensive properties. In which case, he had added, he would be vegetable, not animal. It was the only indication she had had that he disapproved of private ownership.

There was his car grinding into the drive. She went back to her room and looked out. The feeling was creeping back and her instinct was to hide. But it wasn't his car. Where was his car? What had happened to it? What had happened to him? As it drew up underneath the cedar she recognised the priest's old Citroen. Benedict, he called it, and she wondered whether she would ever be able to repeat the joke to her father without seizing up against the sadness of the memory. It was the second trip he'd made to the château that day. He ought to think of trying to make it pay. Two men stepped out. Hugo. Talbot. Talbot banged the roof of the car with the flat of his hand and the priest reversed obediently back round the tree and set off down the drive again. They started walking towards the house. Talbot was rubbing his left shoulder and round to the back of his neck. She saw Sally catch his arm and draw him to one side. They walked slowly away, just a few steps, and stopped. Talbot was listening to her, but Laura couldn't see his face.

She went to the top of the staircase and looked down. He came marching through the library doors with a battery of bangs and heavy footfalls and went straight through to the kitchen. No one there. He rushed back into the hallway and collided with Madame Derrault, who was taking the plates back through to the dresser. Smash! The china crashed to the floor, skidding off into corners, plates wheeling playfully in once-in-a-lifetime cartwheels towards inevitable collisions with chair, table and wall, where they chipped and splintered and lay in fragments, one or two spinning with a final rattle before they came to rest. Talbot and Madame Derrault stood clutching one another in the middle of it all, she with her eyes squeezed tight and her head ducked, as though the next thing would be the house falling about their ears. Talbot detached himself and brought his foot down on the last trembling saucer with a crunch.

'*Eh bien*,' sighed Madame Derrault, '*c'est triste.*'

'Too bloody right it's *triste*,' Talbot shouted and sat down heavily on the bottom step.

Madame Derrault looked down sadly at him, and then at the broken pieces of china, as though wondering what she should pick up first. Then she noticed a deep scratch down the side of Talbot's chin, below his ear.

'But – you are wounded!' she exclaimed, and fumbled for a handkerchief in her apron pocket.

'Leave it,' he said. He got to his feet and started to climb the stairs. When he got to the top he saw Laura. He sucked in his breath sharply and she saw there were tears in his eyes when he looked at her. He seemed to set her aside with his eyes, out of mind, where she could do him no harm.

'Clear up this mess can you, sweetie,' he said in a tired voice, 'I'll be down when I've changed.'

30

She avoided Hugo. She wanted to be able to land him in it and she doubted whether, if they came face to face, he'd be able to lie to her for long enough to allow her the opportunity. Together with Madame Derrault she cleared up the broken china. Sally wandered through with a pair of secateurs in her hand and looked askance at the pile Laura was scooping up with the dustpan.

'Dear oh dear,' she said, in her chippy *Homes and Gardens* voice. 'Not your day today, is it?'

Laura felt the split second pass in which she might happily have tipped the whole lot over Sally's head, realising it was not something she could do, because it was not something she would do. They folded the fragments up in newspaper and put them in the bin with the leftover bits from lunch, as though it had been a party with disposable plates.

Talbot came down fresh from the shower in a luxuriant white towelling dressing-gown and handed his clothes to Madame Derrault. They were scrunched up and damp with sweat. He put his hand on Madame Derrault's shoulder.

'Sure you won't change your mind about that washing powder?'

Ah, the man himself again, once more himself; a glide and a rustle of his snowy white down! Laura was in the library, trying to keep out of range of his conciliatory warmth. She was going. She didn't turn round when Talbot came into the room.

'So you met Sally?'

'Yes.'

'She's a bad girl. Acts like she owns the place!' But he didn't sound annoyed with her.

'So do you.'

'*Touché*.'

'I'm *not* touchy, it's you!'

Talbot grinned at her back.

'Aren't you going to ask me what happened to my car?'

'No.'

'Or me?'

She turned round. She supposed he had calculated that it was all right to fritter away all your bonus points for coolness at this stage of the proceedings. That was what made it into a showdown.

'You smashed your car?' she said rather weakly with the lack of intonation characteristic of a theatre prompt.

'That's right. Albert on his lollipop. Don't think he's quite mastered the idea yet. Probably take him a few years. Bloody imbecile.'

She turned back to the window, half impressed by Albert's sense of timing, half agreeing with Talbot that he wasn't fit to assume the responsibility of the lollipop.

'Luckily,' continued Talbot, in a chirpy storytime voice, 'who should be passing but Father Bénoit, on his way to drop Monsieur Hugo at Château Monvanité. All very Camberwick Green. The garage came to fetch the car. Try not to pick at the paintwork please, sweetie.'

She realised she had been chipping away a fleck of paint on the window pane. It was a mistake, a slip of the brush, years ago, but not worth arguing over. Talbot came up behind her.

'You going to turn round and talk to me then?'

She knew she was avoiding the confrontation. But if she left without it she would always wonder what they would have said. She knew what she would say, but that was only half of it. She could state her own position but he would storm in confidently and scribble all over it – corrections, crossings out, suggestions for a better version, and finally 'try again', which she did not want to do.

'I don't know where to start,' she said, staring gloomily out of the window. He stepped outside and looked in at her through the glass, a couple of inches from her face and started to kiss the pane which framed her face with Hollywood passion. Then his hand came round and pushed up the catch which held the window in place, pushing it gently towards her, so that the glass came up to touch her own lips, which she could not stop from smiling and he moved forward so there was only the eighth of an inch of glass between them. Laura started to laugh, then pulled away crossly.

'You're an idiot Talbot,' she said, and thought he must look particularly like one to Hugo, who was shambling up behind him.

'Look,' she hissed to Talbot, 'Hugo.'

Talbot stepped gracefully back from the window and let Hugo go back inside in front of him.

'So, Hugo old chap, what are you up to? Anything exciting going on in your life? You look like a lost sock. A propos of which, we were wondering, have you *got* a girlfriend?'

Hugo looked guilty, wondering if he could carry it off. 'Come on, play up,' he thought, and said nonchalantly, 'Yes, yes I have as a matter of fact. As you ask.'

Laura was looking sharply at him, he thought. Steady on. Change the subject. Talbot offered him a beer and went to fetch it from the kitchen.

'Don't you have anything to ask me?' Hugo said quickly to Laura.

'Not for the minute.'

Talbot came back in with beers all round. Hugo was about to change the subject when Laura said abruptly, 'Talbot, there's something you ought to know. Hugo's going to say I shouldn't tell you, but it's only fair.'

'What's that? Hugo, have a seat will you, grab that chair over there. Meeting of the tea committee. Beer committee.'

'You know I told you Ludmilla was very ill. On Monday. When I spoke to my father.'

'When you spoke to your father. Yes, I remember that.' It had been downhill from then on.

'Laura, hang on a minute . . .' Hugo was looking rattled.

'I won't be a second,' she interrupted, 'I just want to put Talbot in the picture.'

'I should think you do,' Talbot said, leaving off blowing lightly over the top of his beer bottle. 'I'm all ears, sweetie.'

Hugo wondered if he used to call Posy sweetie. He couldn't imagine her going for that, but then with men like Talbot you could never tell. They seemed to get away with things.

Laura sat down at Talbot's desk, so she could see both of them.

'I asked Hugo to go back and interview Ludmilla for the documentary. That's where he's been. At least, that's where he's supposed to have been. Not in Paris. I knew you wouldn't allow it, so I didn't tell you. I'm sorry I hijacked your,' she looked at Hugo, 'resources, but I felt so strongly about it – she's going to die, remember, so I wanted her to have her say. She wouldn't want to leave a mystery. She's the kind of person who would always think the truth, if it was about her personally, was more interesting. Whatever happened. It may not even be very interesting. But there is a story behind it. I wanted Hugo to find out what it was. Okay Hugo? Isn't that where you've been?'

'Oh, yes. Mm.'

Talbot took a big swig of beer and blew a high pitched whistle, keeping his eyes on Hugo. He had his feet hooked over the side of the armchair and the tails of his dressing-gown tucked into his lap. Both of the others were looking at him with a slightly frightened expression. Hugo was beginning to wonder who would win if it came to a punch-up.

'Well well, and there was I quite convinced you were visiting some old holiday romance in Montparnasse on expenses. You are a sneaky bugger aren't you?' He looked at Laura. 'And you. I still don't see why you've decided to rat on poor old Hugo though, Laura. Seems a bit hard on him after all he's done on your behalf. Look at him. You can tell he's had a busy time of it. He looks quite wrecked. You might have given him time to get a couple of beers down. What's he done to annoy you?'

'I just couldn't stand any more lies.'

'Well no, I can see you might be rather tiring yourself out with them my dear, it is slightly difficult to keep track. You should keep a notebook. It's a habit worth acquiring if you're going to be doing a lot of it. Trouble with you, Laura, is you've no experience. You stick with me and I'll show you the ropes. Now

Hugo, tell me about this trip of yours. Successful was it? You should have told me you were going, I think I've got some spare Air Miles somewhere. I suppose you got the flight to Manchester direct?'

'Yes, then the train. It's quite an easy journey really.'

'Jolly good, I'm glad to hear that. Weather nice?'

'Fine, yes.'

'And Miss Pike. Tell us about Miss Pike now. I expect you found her blooming? Large as life?'

'Well, she's a lot better than I expected . . . in fact I think you'll be quite surprised really . . . at home, you know . . .'

'Excellent. You see Laura, you must cut out this alarmist streak. Now Hugo, what about the scoop eh? Or is that none of my business, perhaps, just between you and Laura. Shall I leave the room maybe, give you time for a little tête-a-tête?'

'Talbot, don't be silly, of course it's not a secret from you. I don't understand, Hugo, you mean she's not going to die at all?'

'Well,' Hugo spread his hands helplessly. He wore a fish-like expression and his Adam's apple looked like something live and out of breath. He was not happy. He was finding the whole business of acting in front of an audience oblivious to the conceit rather disturbing.

'Why don't we take a look at it? Talbot – what do you say?'

Talbot shifted slightly. He was concentrating on pushing back the cuticle of his left thumb with the top of the beer bottle. He looked up at Laura.

'What do you reckon? Do we want to see his little film? What do you say Laura? I tell you what I say. I say Hugo, go and pack your bloody bags old chap and take yourself off. Do us all a favour. And don't come back. Stuff your little documentary, I don't know why Posy put you up to it, probably because she's a hysterical cow, perhaps you're – yes? Ah, right, thought so, nice little blush there from Hugo-just-call-me-Huge. And much pleasure may it bring you. I don't think we really need to take a bet do we? Does *anyone* believe there's a film in Hugo's camera? You must think I'm a complete and utter fool Hugo. Now get out.'

Hugo was tempted to give up then, but his loathing of Talbot was swelling by the minute and he wanted the satisfaction of seeing his face when Ludmilla actually came up chortling on the video. That would take him down a peg or two.

'Look Talbot,' he said, trying to be placatory, 'this is really ridiculous. I'll show you the film. Then we'll talk about it. I think it might at least interest you. You can have it afterwards. Do what you want with it.'

'Very nice of you. I'll have my beer back too while you're about it. Okay, off you trot and get it. We'll have a little film show. Perhaps we can get Madame Derrault to walk up and down with a torch. I'm all for authenticity, as you know.'

When Hugo had left the room Laura asked, 'How did you know?'

'What?'

'That he was a fraud. You think he's just a friend of Posy's. A spy. I thought that too. I did ask him to go back, but you can tell he hasn't. He's just pretending.'

'Thanks for the confidence sweetie. I really owe you one. How did I know? You don't have to be Brain of Britain. He's hopeless with a camera. Never made a documentary in his life. There's no plane from Toulouse to Manchester. But to be honest, if I may be so bold when it seems to have gone out of fashion, Sally told me. He's been staying with her. Not only that, Madame Derrault saw Sally and him in the supermarket. Of course one sighting would have been too much like a plot. Confirmation just shows what an oaf Hugo is. Posy seems to have lost her touch in that department. So you see, I have a loyal following. Unfortunately, I happen to be in love with you who are a sneaky little hypocrite. But we'll talk about your role in things later. Dirty linen and all that. Any more questions?'

'I'm not that,' she said, 'but you're entitled to say so. It won't change what I am.'

'You'd be surprised. Public opinion can be very influential.'

'You're not public.'

'No, it was a manner of speaking. The interesting thing to note, of course, is that Ludmilla has been in on the racket too. If Hugo there didn't spend the last few days lapping up her death bed secrets but has nevertheless got a little film to show us, he must have made it some time ago. On Posy's introduction. Which means that Posy and Ludmilla are now chums. Fascinating how it all links up isn't it? Ah, here's Hugo, found what you were looking for?'

'Yes thanks,' Hugo replied with a sort of cheerful terseness.

'You'll find the video recorder underneath the television. You have to switch it on and press play. Not too tricky for a chap in the trade like you. Sally!' he yelled, spotting her sauntering past the window.

She popped her head in.

'Anything I can do?'

'Come and have a look at this. Revelation of the season. The nail in the coffin of *Pierrot Lunaire*. A gothic sensation. The strange and terrible truth of Ludmilla Pike ARCM.'

'How thrilling. I'll just leave my shoes outside here and wash my hands. Don't start without me.'

'Why d'you do that?' Laura was looking at him furiously. He rejected the idea of the pretty-when-you're-angry tack and just shrugged.

'Might as well get some mileage out of it. At this rate it may be the only film about *Pierrot Lunaire* ever made. It's unlikely to find mass distribution if my estimate of old Hugo the Hands here is anything like correct.'

Sally came in and perched on the edge of Talbot's chair. Laura glared at her.

'Come and sit round this side, Laura,' Talbot said. 'You're a distraction there.'

She found a seat. Talbot got up and closed the shutters.

'Like watching the Cup Final. You two met before? Hugo? Sally Fairfield.'

'Hello, Hugo Grears,' said Hugo confidentially, coming over to shake Sally's hand.

'For God's sake Hugo, sit down and shut up,' Sally said impatiently, so he did.

31

Hugo pressed play and handed the remote control over to Talbot without looking at him, as though he were passing him a joint. Talbot was wishing he could remote control Sally off the arm of his chair but she seemed very happy where she was. Laura was sitting wrapped up on the pink *chaise longue*. Talbot pressed pause.

'You can't possibly be comfortable there, Sal,' he told her. 'Have this chair.' He went over to his desk and perched on the edge, as always with his legs well crossed. Sally wondered for whose benefit. He lent over to Laura, passing her the remote control. She took it with a slightly puzzled look.

'Off you go,' he said. 'You're in charge.'

Hugo was sitting uncomfortably on an upright little cane chair by the door. Laura hesitated.

'Which is fast forward again?'

'Fourth row, third button.'

She released the pause.

Ah. Ludmilla's room. The piano, like a sleeping black labrador, keyboard safely closed. The Pissarro reproduction over the fireplace. Sweetie tin for good pupils. Hugo squinted. Hang about! The camera moved. Bit of scene setting.

'Very nice, Hugo,' Talbot commented. 'You should think of moving into weddings.'

Hugo ignored him. He was staring at the screen, waiting for the moment when his own work would appear. He'd done a rough edit before he came out. It wasn't brilliant quality but, following the instructions carefully, he hadn't made too bad a job of it. He didn't recognise any of this, though. What was going on?

Ludmilla appeared. Looking quite well, considering. Lipstick dabbed down to a healthy matt, possibly satin. Still Fuschia Breeze. Cheerful scarf. She smiled at the camera and gave a little wave.

'Hello!' she said.

'Hello!' answered Talbot prettily and waved back. Sally snorted. Laura stopped the film.

'Talbot . . .'

Sally looked modestly into her lap and sneaked a look up at Talbot, who looked a little embarrassed.

'Sorry Laura. Okay, no more messing about. Off you go.'

'Right.'

The machine clicked. A red light pipped on and Ludmilla appeared in shocking colour. Hugo was looking very pale. Ludmilla opened the piano and played a few bars of 'What a Difference a Day Makes'. Then she turned and spoke to the camera.

'This is Sunday afternoon, so Mr Huddlestone really ought to be at home with his family but he's very kindly agreed to come and work with us this afternoon, so I'd like to say a big thank you to him. (SHE MOUTHS TO THE CAMERA.) Thank you Mr Huddlestone. (THE CAMERA BOBS SLIGHTLY.) Now I'd like to introduce to you my friend Gertrude Herbach, shortly to be Mrs Jeremy Cranshawe. I'm saying this right at the end, but I'm going to ask Mr Huddlestone here who's filming us, to put it at the beginning so you know what's coming – as I know what's gone, you see. I hope it's not all a terrible muddle. We won't have time to edit it as we thought, so you'll just have to take us as you find us. Almost live. I think you'll find it's all fairly self-explanatory. Apologies to Hugo.'

She cleared her throat rather delicately with her hand flat against her breast bone. Sally sat forward to get a better look. 'My God, I see what you mean,' she said, and buried her own well-lotioned pair in her lap.

Gertrude never actually appeared. They could see her head from the back as she faced Ludmilla but as Mr Huddlestone only had one camera she had preferred to feature only as a voice.

'I hope it isn't too formal,' Ludmilla went on. Mr Huddlestone had done a lot of weddings. He could make anyone look good.

Ludmilla had wanted warts and all. Her face seemed to be slightly distorted by the lens, as though she were looking in a fairground mirror. Or perhaps, Laura thought, it was that something about her face had changed. It had relaxed into itself. A mixture of defeat and relief. 'We did do a little run-through before, to get warmed up. It takes a little practice. You'll find my technique a little sparse I expect, Laura, a little on the Marlon Brando side, but I wanted to stick to the facts, so don't be surprised if I'm slightly *News at Ten*-ish, it's deliberate. Off we go then. Bye bye.'

'Just a minute, Laura,' Hugo broke in. She stopped the film. 'Let's get this right. That's not my film.'

Talbot was looking at Laura with a querying little grin.

'I know,' she said. 'Ludmilla sent me this one. Sorry. I swapped them. And I cut the tape on yours. She asked me to.'

'*O là là*,' said Sally in a detached voice.

Talbot looked at his watch, and Laura pressed play.

GERTRUDE: (*A soft voice, but deep and rather formal. It is obvious she has notes in front of her*). First of all, I thought it might be helpful to ask a rather basic question. What is *Pierrot Lunaire*?

LUDMILLA: (*Promptly*). It is a cycle of poems by Albert Giraud about a clown who is in love with the moon.

Pause.

It is also a song cycle, a setting of Giraud's poems by Alfred Schoenberg.

She seems to be uncertain whether to continue. Her eyes flick between the interviewer and the viewer. She shifts her shoulders back in her chair and lifts her voice slightly.

Thirdly, it is the title of a novel which I wrote in 1938. The action is set in Château Monvanité, where I wrote it.

Laura looked across at Talbot in astonishment, trying to read surprise in his face, but finding none.

> LUDMILLA: (*Leans across to Gertrude and whispers*). Do you think that was clear?
> GERTRUDE: (*Reassuringly*). Perfect. Let's try some more. Everything all right Mr Huddlestone? (*The cameraman's nod is unrecorded*)
> GERTRUDE: (*Still reading from notes*). Now Ludmilla. The story you wrote. Was it true?

'Ah,' said Talbot.

> LUDMILLA: (*She smiles slightly at the question, nodding almost before Gertrude has begun to ask it. Her reply is ready*). Not true, no; truthful, you could say. (*She reads from a piece of paper on her lap*). The basic pattern of love, betrayal and rejection had been that of my love affair with a woman, Isa Fontaine, the owner of the château and a childhood acquaintance of mine. (*She looks over at Gertrude*). That's the best I can say. (*And at the camera, smiling with some strain*) Still with us Mr H?

Somewhere in the house a door banged. Madame Derrault's footsteps were heard crossing the hallway and starting up the stairs. A wind was rising.

> GERTRUDE: The story itself, however, was fiction?
> LUDMILLA: Ah, no. Stop. No. At least, not what I'd call fiction. The characters were lifted from real life. (*She makes a little gesture with finger and thumb, as though taking two pinches of salt and dropping them into a bowl*). They were both at Monvanité that summer. Tom Flynn and Chloe; just as the book says. As real as you or I. (*She looks fleetingly at the viewer*). He was a leftover guest of Isa's. She worked in the stables. You could say I was the third person. An observer. What fascinated me was that the pattern of their affair followed an almost identical course to my own, like a parable. Isa had returned to London to be married. It was very quiet. We thought the war would start any moment.

Sally, losing concentration, began wondering at what point she could slip out for a bit.

> GERTRUDE: (*She puts her pencil down and looks up from her piece of paper*). I don't know about these things, you may have to put me right, but I always thought it was quite common practice for authors to give emotions, even experiences, which have been their own to their characters? And you are clearly not the first writer to borrow characters from real life. It is a convenience, like supermarket shopping.

Laura had a feeling of being chilled from within. She wished Talbot would open the shutters. She was shivering. Talbot slipped off the desk and came and sat beside her with his arm across the back of the *chaise longue*. Sally looked up from her nails and checked the screen out. Just the voice now, the camera walking round the room. Nice piano. Couple of good chairs.

> LUDMILLA: You must admit I took it rather far. It seemed reasonable at the time. (*She glances at her notes*). A rather useful analogy has occurred to me since. I think we've got time for a little illustration, don't you? If you play two musical notes a fifth apart in the scale you will hear simultaneously another note created by the fusion of the two. It will be an exact reproduction of the first note, but an octave lower. I liked the idea of a replica being produced out of a synthesis.

Talbot got up and went over to the desk to pick up a jersey. He touched Laura's head gently as he moved back and put it round her shoulders. She was sitting with her legs tucked up underneath her, with her elbow on the arm of the *chaise longue*. She reached up and held Talbot's hand there on her head. He came back and sat beside her, keeping her hand on trust. He was wondering how she was taking it. He couldn't say it was only a film.

> GERTRUDE: (*After a pause, in which they both seem to be listening*

out for something). You said to me this morning that you felt the need to confess. Shall we go on to that now?

> *The camera returns rather abruptly to Ludmilla. She seems almost to have forgotten it is there. She talks slowly, with obvious deliberation, not looking at Gertrude, as though determined to omit nothing*

LUDMILLA: Yes. Back to the story. Flynn and Chloe. She was a nice girl, Chloe. A good soul. He treated her so terribly. An arrogant, selfish man, I thought. Attractive to look at. I didn't come across them all that much. We lived in separate parts of the house. Chloe lived on a farm up the road somewhere. (*She looks up at the camera*). I could see what was going on though. When things came to a head I confronted him. Poor Chloe couldn't speak a word of English, and he wouldn't talk to her in French. (That's different in the book of course. I upgraded her.) I laid into him on her behalf. I told him he was a talentless bourgeois. That put the wind up him.

GERTRUDE: Fairly?

LUDMILLA: (*Shrugs*) Maybe. He had written nothing worth reading for years. I hated the stuff he did write, but that's a matter of taste. I don't much go for realism myself. I'm saving it for utopia. Anyway, his thing was as long as Chloe was her normal healthy self, he ignored her. Just another village girl with the moon in her eyes. Then one day there was some sort of scene in the dovecot. I heard voices then a terrible clatter and silence. She fell on the steps. Her limbs were like a puppet's – dangling in all directions. (*It is a moment before she can speak again*). From then on of course he became a model of devotion. But it *was* a model, scaled down, and for demonstration purposes only. He invented what seemed to me to be a sort of fake pastoral idyll, while in fact he was playing with her suffering and his own morbid fascination with it. I suspect he hoped it would lift his writer's block. I argued with him, fought for him for her. She'd put her respectability on the line, as they say now. He wouldn't listen. In the end I told him to go and do his own suffering. In Spain. The Civil War.

GERTRUDE: And he was killed.

The phone began to ring several doors away. No one moved. No footsteps from Madame Derrault. Hugo was nearest the door. He shrugged and went out to answer it, shutting the door behind him. Some geezer speaking French. He hung up. While he was there he tried Posy. He got her answerphone and left a message in almost a whisper. 'Posy, the game's off, sorry about that, Talbot twigged, I told you he would. He's pretty angry, I should leave your phone off the hook for a bit. See you soon.'

He came back into the room. They had been sitting in silence, staring at the frozen screen. Talbot looked up.

'We kept it for you. Anyone I know?'

'Just my office.' He was getting better at it.

Talbot released the pause.

LUDMILLA: Yes, his head was blown off.
GERTRUDE: Oh dear. (*Pauses*). And Chloe?
LUDMILLA: I don't know, she was just a local girl. Quite ordinary, apart from her face. No doubt she had to marry quickly because of the child. I expect someone would have had her. Her limbs recovered, after a fashion. Her heart was quite broken at the time. Not by his death. By his leaving.
GERTRUDE: Ahah. I see. So that is what you feel guilty for?

> *There is a cut in the film. A new frame. Ludmilla's position in the armchair has altered slightly.*

LUDMILLA: No – no, no, I'm fine thank you – no, there's something else. When I sent *Pierrot Lunaire* to a publisher – Isa Fontaine, by the way – I pretended it had been written by Tom Flynn. (*She leans forward towards Gertrude*). I put his name on it. I was at Monvanité when his things were sent on from Spain. I roughed up the manuscript a bit to make it look as though it had been salvaged from the battle front, as it were. A sort of facsimile.
GERTRUDE: Why?
LUDMILLA: (*Leans back in her chair. She seems to be searching for an answer. It is slow to come. She wipes the palms of her hands on*

> *her knees*). Oh, I suppose I just like obfuscation. (*She looks at Gertrude and grins*) Lying. I like to make things complicated. Not a very good reason, I know, but you'd be surprised how strong a force . . . (*She purses her lips, as though she has decided to have another shot at this idea, then changes her mind and continues*) I had already transformed the story, remember, so that it should not appear to be about myself. If I had put my own name at the end obviously the disguise would have been apparent.
>
> GERTRUDE: So that it would no longer have served as a disguise at all?
>
> LUDMILLA: There you are.

Sally stood up. 'I'll be outside,' she said. 'Tell me what happens,' and left the room. She opened her eyes rather wide at Hugo. Head girl again, silently asking someone to report to her after prayers. Hugo followed her out. Talbot reached for the pause.

'Just a moment, Hugo. Before you go. I assume those three clowns at lunchtime are chums of yours?'

Hugo, thinking of Posy and how to save the day, lied and said yes, so that Sally was instructed to ring and tell the three perfectly authentic gentlemen that Mr Hardy had no further interest in their cooperation and declined to discuss any aspect of his future projects with them. The American and the Australian shrugged at one another, bore no rancour and expressed little surprise. Talbot even went up in their estimation for having an artistic temperament. The Englishman from Cambridge took their word for it being all part of the business, but the business went down in his estimation for having little if nothing to do with art. He stayed an extra day to avoid travelling back to England with the other two. Strolling through the village that evening, admiring church and gable, he came across the Café du Sport and decided to rest up a while before ringing for a car back to his hotel. There, quite by chance, he got talking to Norman. A common interest in Christian iconography and pastis provided fertile ground for an acquaintance which was to last many years. Not all that long afterwards, Norman installed Barney in a workshop close to Soubyrète, where, with a generous and most welcome injection of cash, they were able to go into small scale reproduction of the plaster saints. Barney made bronzes for Father Bénoit's church with specially commissioned imperfections built in for Norman.

The screen was still frozen. Talbot's finger hovered over the remote control. 'Are we going to go on with this?'

Laura nodded, looking at Ludmilla, trapped in mid-performance.

'Okay. No more interruptions then. My poor brain.'

He went over and bolted the door.

32

The film resumed. Talbot and Laura watched in silence, completely still, as though it was Ludmilla who had the power to freeze them. Two speechless people on a pink *chaise longue*. It lasted no longer that fifteen minutes.

> GERTRUDE: (*Her face is still hidden. We can see her legs from behind, crossed rather elegantly, and a hand holding a pencil. She gestures little, so that it is difficult to tell that the voice comes from her. The impression is of a disembodied interviewer, almost as though Ludmilla were conversing with someone in her own head.*) Let me put something to you, Ludmilla. It is a little digression, so we can cut it out later—
> LUDMILLA: Keep rolling Mr Huddlestone. Time and a half. Thank you.
> GERTRUDE: From what you have told me – and that's as much as I know – the problem seems to be very simple. You are a woman so you lead a double life. You are at once inside looking out and outside looking in. You perform with an acute awareness that this performance is being watched – and not just by the rest of the world, but also by yourself. Each of us is watching herself being watched. Do you follow me?
> LUDMILLA: I think so.
> GERTRUDE: Take an example – the leading lady in a film. The actress who has played the role attends the first night. She is hidden in a privileged box, out of sight of the audience. As the film plays, she watches herself acting out the role of a woman – a woman who is admired, perhaps, certainly

directed, by men. And of course by other women too. Whatever that woman does on the screen, the character she has portrayed, the woman in disguise, will never have to meet the gaze of the audience. There is an illusion, much stronger than that created on the live stage of a theatre, that she is unaware of the attention of her spectators. This affords her a temporary kind of immunity from censure. Not censure for a bad performance, or a bad character, or even bad legs, but censure for narcissism. Suppose the lights were suddenly to go on in the box where she sits – in a flash the attention of the audience is turned upon her – and, oh dear, she is caught in the act of narcissism, which ill becomes a woman. It is perceived in us as a lack of grace.

LUDMILLA: O wad some Power the giftie gie us, To see oursels as others see us.

GERTRUDE: Quite. Now, where was I?

LUDMILLA: You were, I rather hoped, on the point of offering absolution.

GERTRUDE: Oh no, not that. I am suggesting an explanation. That in adopting another's identity you were doing no more than deflecting the charge of narcissism. Do you think you can admit to that?

> *The camera has been still for some time, resting on Ludmilla's face as she listens. There is a slight feeling that Mr Huddlestone may be napping.*

LUDMILLA: Yes. Although Narcissus was in love with his own true reflection. It was him.

GERTRUDE: We don't know that. But I suppose . . . (*There is a silence. Mr Huddlestone clears his throat. Gertrude looks round in surprise at the camera*). Goodness, we'd quite forgotten you.

> *She and Ludmilla both laugh, as though they have achieved something.*

GERTRUDE: My analogy is not of course completely correct.

LUDMILLA: (*Draws herself back into her chair*). They never are. You think that by drawing your analogy you are defining the original more closely, whereas in fact all you are doing is giving birth to a wayward identical twin.

GERTRUDE: Do you think that Isa, for in the end it is she you have betrayed, guessed that the book was by you? Presumably, subconsciously, you hoped she would guess?

LUDMILLA: Yes. Yes I think I probably did hope that. I gave her a big clue, of course. *Pierrot Lunaire* is written in the form of a journal, with daily entries written over a period of six weeks, apparently by Tom. But at the same time the diary is not that of either Tom or Chloe, but of an invisible observer, a voyeur.

GERTRUDE: The conceit being that Tom, as the unnamed, unconfessed keeper of the journal, was indulging in the same kind of self-disguise, the same faked appearance of objectivity that you yourself, the authentic author, were showing?

Talbot frowned at the screen. 'Sorry?'

LUDMILLA: Yes.
GERTRUDE: Do you think she picked up the clue?
LUDMILLA: I imagine not.
GERTRUDE: But surely, if it hadn't had some special significance for her, why would she have given it to Posy?

'Ah.' Talbot had wondered that.

LUDMILLA: I wondered that of course. When I met her niece she seemed to see it as a hilarious send-up of the sentimental novel. The kind of cynical thing Flynn might just have been capable of writing. When it became obvious to Posy that I had written it she congratulated me on having written a post-feminist satire. She says that Talbot's view of it as a poignant love story proves her point.

GERTRUDE: I see. And to save face you pretended that she was right. That you had written it in a spirit of mockery? And you recorded this admission on your original video?

LUDMILLA: Yes, that's it. It was a spiteful and degrading performance. No other word for it. Degrading. It was only when he played it back to me on my own television that I realised. What I had made myself into over all these years. I don't want to go out like that. I don't want Laura to see that.

> *There is another cut in the film. Ludmilla is suddenly nodding, as though in answer to a question we have not heard.*

GERTRUDE: You want to talk now about Laura and Talbot. So much of the rest is past and gone. I think we tend to overestimate the connection between the past and present. We like to believe analogies are there for some reason other than that it is we who have made them. But people will resist. They will let you dress the stage, but not write their lines. And though you had a hand in their beginning, you will not have a hand in their end. That will be another story. (*This has been a digression. She consults her paper*). When did you first decide that you would play against Talbot, not for him?

LUDMILLA: I have to think about that. Do you think we're going on a bit? I've run out of notes.

GERTRUDE: I think it is useful. We can always cut it down afterwards.

LUDMILLA: Cut me down to size. Snip. Well, let's see how it goes. They can always skip bits. Careful though, fast forward me too much and I'll be six feet under. Well, when I came across the advertisement in the magazine I was naturally intrigued. And surprised. Even looking back on it, it was the one real coincidence without which none of this would have happened. I got in touch. When he told me he wanted to make a film of the book I was excited. Of course I was. I wanted the film to be made. To be made well. I still do. Because however bad my book was – (*She resists an interruption*) – it is still the story of what happened to me, and I would like there to be a record of that. I thought of the Dutch masters, you know: the still life painter bringing together all his funny disparate objects on his table. Then he paints a picture which at once hallows and degrades the original collection of bits and pieces – which, once the painting is complete, will be destroyed. There is no longer any need for it to exist.

GERTRUDE: You mean you would like the book to be destroyed?

LUDMILLA: Well, actually no. To be perfectly honest with you, I'd like it to be a huge bestseller, then all the royalties can go to Laura. I told you analogies were useless.

GERTRUDE: And what about Mr Hardy?

LUDMILLA: I think his reaction was 'get that thing out of my sight'. I contaminated his vision. Someone like me could have had no part in such a story. Of course it was his idea that I was Chloe. Before he met me.

GERTRUDE: Why didn't you tell him straight out that you had written it? For the same reason you had always pretended it was not your work, I suppose.

LUDMILLA: Oh, yes, and more so. He was a very handsome man. Vanity and fear. And I wanted to be able to go on enjoying his appreciation of it. I didn't want him to abandon the film because of what he discovered about its origins. Of course I hadn't met his wife then. I hadn't learned to laugh at it.

GERTRUDE: Let us leave her to one side. And her opinion. It may be valid, but for our purposes it is quite irrelevant. I think you are wrong to imagine that Talbot would have abandoned the film on discovering the 'truth', be it Posy's version, as given in the first video, or your own as you have given it to me. He's going to make his film, his and nobody else's. He's a professional, presumably. Tell him the truth and let him sort it out. Start again if he wants. Pick and choose.

LUDMILLA: And Laura?

GERTRUDE: Yes, now where does Laura come in? That was one of my questions, wasn't it. I've lost track a little, ah yes, why did you send her out there?

LUDMILLA: Partly for the reason I gave her father. I wanted her to have something of the experience I had had there, for however brief a time. It is such a beautiful place. It could only be good for her. And having her there was, I must admit, a way of keeping a foot in the door. You haven't met her yet, of course. Well, you'll be surprised. You'd have to see her to understand. I was wise and experienced. She was beautiful and ready to sit at my feet and learn. I believe we did love one another. So I wanted her there. She has been my envoy.

GERTRUDE: And did you hope he would fall in love with her?

LUDMILLA: Dear oh dear, I hope all this isn't going in. (*Pauses*). Yes. Yes, I did. She's very similar to Chloe in the book – no coincidence, of course. In my portrait of Chloe, which was a sort of tidied up amalgamation of at least two other people, I gave a similar description of my ideal – indeed, how I would have liked to have been. That is obvious enough. I chose Laura because she shared those qualities

GERTRUDE: Did you hope she would fall in love with him?

LUDMILLA: No. Even now I'm only speculating on her silence. Do you know, I somehow thought she would be immune. I have made the mistake of thinking of her as opaque, a reflecting surface. When I began to realise my error, I started to feel afraid for her.

GERTRUDE: Why exactly?

LUDMILLA: I don't know, exactly. In general terms, well, the classic reasons. He's too old, too experienced. He will always lead her. She will be his subject. He will always show her how it is to be done. And not only in their real life relationship. He will have noticed her resemblance to Chloe. Supposing he decided he must therefore make her suffer? I shall be responsible for that.

GERTRUDE: Laura knows nothing of the truth?

LUDMILLA: No. Well she does now. Then-now. (*She peers in the direction of the camera and seems to meditate briefly on the idea*). At the time of speaking she knows less than Talbot. At the time of listening, of course, she knows it all. Heaven knows what will have happened in between. I forbade her to read the book. I was afraid she would recognise the style. I was afraid she would turn against me. I would have had to tell the truth if she had asked me.

GERTRUDE: So you lied by omission – thereby making her more vulnerable still. He can play out *any* story with her.

LUDMILLA: (*Looks searchingly at the camera as though hoping to be able to see through to the other side*). Yes. (*It is as though she can see the pair of them sitting there watching her. Her eyes are sharp but tired*). But I don't think he will. (*Turns back to look at Gertrude*). And yet any other story might have been better, don't you think? (*She looks back at the camera and makes a slow gesture of slitting her own throat*). Cut.

There were no credits, apart from a little ticket with Mr Huddlestone's name and telephone number. The will was in a separate box, in Laura's father's keeping. All that remained when the picture had gone was a very faint, constant buzzing, as though there were a fly in the room.

33

Sally tried the door to the library once, very quietly, then gave up and went home. She gave Hugo a lift to the Hotel de la Gare and drove back rather recklessly to Montmarcy.

Talbot and Laura stayed in the room for some time after the film had finished. It grew dark, inside and out. He stroked Laura's hair gently. She lay on the *chaise longue* with her eyes closed, breathing very softly, the only sound. He watched over her, as though they were on the last stage of a long journey. She should try and get some sleep while he watched the coachman. Back in the old country after an absence of many days and nights, they would not salute it till the morning. Darkness cancelled out his knowledge of the room; at night all cats are black. Time stopped dead in its tracks in the dark, when even the sexton sleeps.

After a while he tiptoed to the door. In the kitchen, Madame Derrault was ironing with long, smooth movements. Ironing sheets. Talbot always told her she needn't bother, but she took pride in them. She would have liked for there to be somewhere she could lay them out flat and unfolded, so that she need never introduce a single crease. Ideally she would have enchanted them so that they could hang horizontally, like magic carpets held aloft on a current of air, in a well sealed room, undulating modestly, for freshness.

'It's a bit late for you isn't it Mrs D?' Talbot said very quietly. 'What about Albert's supper?'

Madame Derrault nodded at the open window. Talbot crossed the room and looked out. There was a full moon in the sky, which had not yet turned quite dark. Madame Derrault said the moon had been up since early evening, when Albert had come to find her, white in a clear blue sky. She guessed he was waiting for Laura. She had given him something to eat. Monsieur Hugo had told her there would be no dinner as planned. *La Blonde* had translated. Even after they had left, Albert had refused to come into the house. He was sitting out there in the garden, half sleeping, nodding away to himself. Talbot told her about the accident. Madame Derrault ran the iron swiftly down a fold, then turned and folded once again. She looked up at Talbot.

'It happens,' she said.

Yes, he said, it had.

'How will he get home?'

'We'll walk together. It's only half an hour.'

'You're tired. Why don't you stay?'

No, no, they would go home.

He said goodnight to her and was about to go back in to sit with Laura when she stepped up close to him and looked him beseechingly in the eye, like a mute woman.

'What?' he asked. 'What is it, Madame Derrault?' She was quite limp tonight, all the starch had gone out of her. Her face was blanched with tiredness and there were shadows about her eyes, where fatigue deflected the electric light.

She handed him the photograph of the man in the shirt sleeves and the half-smoked cigarette. She looked at it with him.

'Where did you find this?'

'I didn't find it. It belongs to me. My mother gave it to me.'

Talbot smiled. 'You,' he said. 'I always thought it was Albert.'

'*Comment*, Albert?'

'I thought he was the child.'

No, no, Albert was not from here. Albert was a stranger to the village. He knew that. She had first met Albert on the road.

'We must talk. Tomorrow. How did you find out?'

Norman had helped her.

'Ahah. Well done.' And he said goodnight once more.

He was not surprised by the note on the table. Laura was to ring home urgently. Tomorrow would do, he thought. It was like waiting just that one night longer to hand a suspect over to the authorities. Ludmilla would be dead a long time.

He opened the library door very gently. Laura had gone outside. She was standing by the bay tree looking at the sky.

It would only be possible to leave by an act of violence, like the crumbling of a jigsaw. Tomorrow morning, early, she could walk free along the road she had first come by, brushing against the nettles and cow parsley again with her bags. Monvanité would be left behind her. And unlike the strange dog, met on the road, who gives chase a little while, then returns forgetful as the dust settles, Monvanité would not even lift its head as she moved out of sight.

Talbot clicked the button one more time, and the tiny red light on the machine died to black. He came out into the garden, where the nightingale alone sang on, like some madwoman on a late night train as it trundled into darkness.

'Though you have had a hand in their beginning,' he thought, 'you will not have a hand in their end.' She had been wrong. It was too soon, perhaps, to start looking for her shadow, but when the wind, dying now, moved in the long grass by the dovecot, her spirit, the memory of her, already seemed to be out there, waiting.

Madame Derrault unplugged the iron, picked up the pile of linen and went to close the window. A woman of fifty or so years. The linen went away inside the deep dark cupboard upstairs in Laura's room. She noticed the neatly packed suitcase, the turned back bed, the empty vase decanted and rinsed, back in place beside the jug and bowl. She closed the shutters carefully and laid out her best pair of sheets on Laura's bed.

As she and Albert made their way along the road back to the farmhouse, the branch of a knotted oak caught her hair, and they had to stop and untangle it from the complicated skein of loops and coils. She let it fall, still thick and heavy like a young girl's, through lack of use. Set free the birds! She had, for a fragment of a second, a sense of having been here before, on this road with her hair loose down her back and the shadow of a man at her side; like the moment when an archaeologist opens up the catacomb to catch a glimpse of how the past has lain unknown, unlit, fragile but complete for all those years until he takes away the stone and lets in the light of day which turns it all to dust.